"I don't know what I ever saw in you," Meryl told him.

He backed her against the wall. "Don't you?"

The warning signs were flashing in his eyes, but she couldn't stop. She wasn't about to let him best her again. "No, I don't know why I let you into my life."

"Then you weren't paying attention."

Irrationally, she leaned in to kiss him first. Only to end the suspense, she told her outraged mind. She felt him stiffen in momentary surprise, and then he scooped her body in against his.

Suddenly she was free of a burden of two years. She understood!

In the midst of the incandescence that was James's kiss, she knew why she'd acted as she had two years before. It was for this, this overpowering hunger, this dark dizzy madness. For this she had stopped thinking, stopped considering the consequences, stopped being wary or reluctant or careful.

Suddenly it all made sense.

Dear Reader,

Merry Christmas! I hope you'll like Intimate Moments' gift to you: six wonderful books, perfect for reading by the lights of the Christmas tree. First up is our Heartbreakers title. Welcome veteran romance writer Sara Orwig to the line with *Hide in Plain Sight*. Hero Jake Delancy is tough—but the power of single mom Rebecca Bolen's love is even stronger!

Terese Ramin is back with *Five Kids, One Christmas*, a book that will put you right in the holiday mood. Then try Suzanne Brockmann's *A Man To Die For*, a suspenseful reply to the question "What would you do for love?" Next up is *Together Again*, the latest in Laura Parker's Rogues' Gallery miniseries. *The Mom Who Came To Stay* brings Nancy Morse back to the line after a too-long absence. This book's title says it all. Finally, welcome Becky Barker to the line as she tells the story of *The Last Real Cowboy*.

Six books, six tales of love to make your holidays bright. Enjoy!

Leslie Wainger
Senior Editor and Editorial Coordinator

Please address questions and book requests to:
Silhouette Reader Service
U.S.: 3010 Walden Ave., P.O. Box 1325, Buffalo, NY 14269
Canadian: P.O. Box 609, Fort Erie, Ont. L2A 5X3

TOGETHER AGAIN

LAURA PARKER

Published by Silhouette Books

America's Publisher of Contemporary Romance

SILHOUETTE BOOKS

ISBN 0-373-07682-7

TOGETHER AGAIN

Copyright © 1995 by Laura Castoro

LAURA PARKER

A Texas native, Laura recently made a "major" reloca-tion. Her office is now on the third floor of a turn-of-the-century colonial house in northern New Jersey, where she lives with her husband and three children. Laura is often told that she must have the best career around. "After all, my hours are my own. I don't have to get up, dress and commute to work. I'm available if my children need me. I can even play hooky when the mood strikes. Best of all, I get to live in my imagination—where anything is possible."

For Brenda Taber; thanks for the conversation.

Chapter 1

It wasn't supposed to happen like this!

Moments earlier Meryl Wallis had been chatting with her escort. Now she was standing alone by the buffet table in the middle of the ballroom floor, watching as the last man she ever wanted to see again came striding toward her.

The party was supposed to be just another stop in the hectic endless procession of breakfasts, luncheons, receptions, cocktail parties, dinners and soirees during the New England Booksellers Association convention, held this year in Hartford, Connecticut.

Its banality evaporated the moment the notorious publishing tycoon James Brant walked in. A man like James didn't sneeze without someone noting it.

How like him, she thought in despair, to force a meeting in public.

Gazes turned speculatively toward her from every direction. Beneath the black lace dress she wore, her skin quilted with goose bumps. She knew it was only her sense of exposure that made those gazes seem hostile. The dissolution of

her business association with James Brant two years earlier
had made front-page news while the breakup of their personal relationship had been in all the gossip columns.

What no onlooker could guess was that this was the very
first time she'd come face-to-face with James since then.
Time should have lessened his impact. It didn't.

As he approached her, she felt the force of his presence
crowd in on her. He looked the same. Big. Solid. Hard-eyed.
His slate gaze impenetrable. Perhaps the silver in his chestnut hair was more prominent—inconsequential to a man
with a face that was a cross between a prize fighter's and a
matinee idol's. He was attractive in the way a burning des-
ert is beautiful, the way a summer thunderstorm is fasci-
nating, the way an ocean is majestic. His attraction lay in the
stark, brutal and destructive possibility of his seductive
force.

Once she had been enthralled by his power and the possibility of her own destruction. But no longer. She wanted
the ground to open and swallow her. She hoped the chan-
delier would fall and knock her senseless or the walls col-
lapse and bury her. She wanted out—anyway, anyhow—of
the next few moments of her life.

Too late. He was standing before her, more real than
anything or anyone else in the room.

"Hello, Meryl." His voice was the same, like low and
distant thunder.

For an instant the room narrowed to the focus of his
stormy gaze, as turbulent as the New England coast in a
gale. Emotional gusts of anger, hurt, frustration and anguish whipped through her. Mesmerized by his pewter-
colored eyes she felt as if she were being lifted up and out of
her own skin. The room receded into the distant hum of
unreality.

He, too, seemed to sense a change. The arrogance suddenly left his expression. The steely barrier in his eyes lowered. There, gazing back at her, was a man who seemed
unexpectedly weary and more human than the James she

had known. He seemed as bereft of joy as she, marooned in the same emotional solitude of past mistakes and regrets.

Without conscious agreement her hand moved toward his sleeve at the urging of her inner self, as if needing to connect and reassure them both that the pain would pass, the wounds would heal. Then she saw his mouth tighten in challenge and the gray of his eyes alter into a flat remote stare.

She snatched back her hand as if he had snarled at her, and the world dropped back into place with a sickening thud. This was the one man in all the world she could truly say she hated.

She looked quickly past him, as if someone else had caught her eye. "Please excuse me."

To her dismay, he stepped in front of her to block her path, forcing her to acknowledge him. "Why haven't you returned my calls?"

Meryl did a rapid mental regrouping. She had deliberately ignored his messages. After two years of silence she couldn't imagine that there was a single thing they had to say to each other. She gave him the sketchiest of glances. "I'm very busy these days."

"Is that it?" Fissures formed along his cheeks too long and deep to be called dimples. "Or did you assume that sooner or later I'd seek you out in person?"

She ignored his implication that she had engineered their meeting. He had always been good at tying logic into pretzels, making it seem that what he wanted was what she wanted. What she wanted now was to get away from him as quickly as possible. Without glancing again at him she said, "Excuse me, I see someone I must speak with."

He put his hand on her arm to forestall her from walking away. "That can wait. This is about business."

The touch of his palm was unexpectedly rough on her bare skin. It made her recall the feel of the drag of his hands against her body when they had made love. It made her remember the shame of her abandonment in his arms and of his brutal treachery. One simple touch and the frightening sense of vulnerability had returned.

Her startled gaze lifted to his face. He looked like a man ready for anything. She seemed to tremble again on the brink of disaster, yet she gritted her teeth and held on doggedly to her poise. She wouldn't—mustn't—give him the satisfaction of a public scene.

Meryl looked down pointedly to where his workmanlike fingers lay folded over her arm. "We couldn't possibly have business to discuss, Mr. Brant. Now kindly release me."

He smiled confidently as his touch fell away. "How do you know we can't do business until you've heard me out?"

Feeling far too exposed, she turned sharply sideways to where Kent Davis, her escort, was hovering just out of earshot. Kent was frowning, waiting for his cue to come rescue her. Despite her desire to escape, she shook her head ever so slightly. She didn't want rescuing. That would be admitting that James Brant had gotten the best of her. And that was never going to happen again.

"Aren't you going to introduce me to the new boyfriend?"

When she turned back she encountered James's sardonic gaze. "Why should I? You know Kent as well as I do. And, like me, he hates your guts."

"Is that the source of his attraction?" He deliberately glanced again at Davis and smirked. "You have my sympathy. I've dealt with him across the negotiation table. He doesn't measure up to your standards."

Meryl recoiled from the intimacy in his voice. Who the hell did he think he was? "My tastes have changed."

"Liar." He leaned near her as if about to impart a confidential word to a very good friend. She backed up a step and felt the buffet table nudge her right thigh just below her hip. He moved until his lips were on a level with her ear. "You're like me, you like your bed partners smart as well as sexy." As he moved away his mocking smile dared her to argue the point.

Meryl angled her body away from him and turned toward the buffet table, feeling like a piece of cheese skewered by a toothpick. "I remember now why I dislike you. You're about as pleasant as a popcorn husk stuck in a tooth."

He touched her again, the merest slip of his forefinger along her bare upper arm. Enraged at his audacity, she looked up into his devastating smile, which was exactly what he wanted. "You always got under my skin, too," he whispered.

The suggestive heat in his gray gaze lasted only a second. Then he was turning his back on her, walking away the way he had approached her, confidently, casually, certain of his victory.

Meryl released a pent-up breath. Her hands were clammy and, beneath her chic cocktail dress, beads of perspiration were slipping down her spine. She felt like a tiny rowboat in the wake of a cabin cruiser, shaken and momentarily disoriented, but still afloat.

"What did Brant want?"

Meryl blinked, for it seemed Kent Davis had magically appeared at her side. "Nothing, really."

"I don't see any claw marks," he said with a scant smile.

"No," Meryl said upon reflection and pushed a hand through her shoulder-length dark hair. She mustn't allow herself to think too much about what they'd said. That would give it too much significance. "I don't bruise so easily anymore."

Kent bent protectively toward her. "I had no idea Brant would be here. I hear he seldom leaves Manhattan these days. He must have suffered greater losses in his legal hassles than even rumor has it. Why else would the great publishing tycoon lower his standards by coming out to the boonies to attend one of these lowly conferences?"

Meryl glanced pointedly toward Brant, who was now in conversation with a statuesque blonde. The woman wore a formfitting dress so short and tight that it looked more like a swimsuit. "Maybe his standards are slipping all around. He once preferred his women to have IQs in the triple digits. His latest doesn't appear to have one much larger than her dress size."

Kent smirked as he followed her glance. "Looks can be deceiving. That's BeeBe Hatcher, head of Hatcher Associates, the fastest-growing advertising agency in town."

The name made no impression. Meryl shrugged and turned away. "Let's get out of here. I need a breath of fresh air."

Across the room, James Brant was accepting, without interest, BeeBe Hatcher's wicked smile.

"Now wasn't that easy?" Beebe said. "By morning, your names will be linked in every gossip and business column that counts. I'll circulate a bit more, making people understand that yours was a conciliatory gesture toward the Wallis family. Next, we'll engineer a more formal meeting between the two of you. Turn on the old Brant charm and we'll be announcing her return to your employ before the first of next month. Bringing a Wallis back into the fold at Walrus Ink is only the first step in what my company is prepared to do to polish your tarnished image. So tell me, what did she say?"

James ignored the possessive hand BeeBe placed on his sleeve. She was the one auditioning for a job, not the other way around. The sooner she understood that, the better. "Why, what was your impression?"

"That you'd better consider carefully each step in your approach." Beebe's gaze narrowed as she watched Meryl leave the room on Kent Davis's arm. "She doesn't appear to have tempered with time."

"No." James said the word softly. Time and experience had not detracted in any way from Meryl Wallis. He shrugged off Beebe's possessive hand. "I just remembered something I need to do. Call me on Monday."

"Wait!" BeeBe called after him.

But James knew how to make an exit. In his time, he'd left many women behind. Only one had ever gotten the last word by walking out on him. Her name was Meryl Wallis.

James sat staring out the windows of Walrus Ink Press's penthouse office suite atop a four-story brick building in the warehouse section of Hartford, Connecticut. The lights were out. The only illumination came from the city reflected back from the midnight sky. He had been staring at the same spot of deep blue emptiness for nearly an hour.

Seeing Meryl had been like taking a swan dive off the Empire State Building. The rush was undeniable, but the ultimate result would probably be disastrous.

The moment their gazes had locked, he'd felt the world drop away beneath him. For a fleeting instant the connection between them had been so fundamental, so potent, that it had blasted them free of all past mistakes, harsh words and recriminations. And then he'd seen it, that flicker of pity in her gaze. Of course. She knew about his reversal of fortune and felt sorry for him. The very idea of pity, especially from her, enraged him.

She must have seen his visceral reaction to it. She had retreated so quickly she would have gotten away if he hadn't physically detained her. When she had looked at him again her hazel gaze had been so remote, like agate stones at the bottom of a mountain stream. She had seemed almost afraid. She would have escaped if he hadn't put out a hand to stop her. That touch, however brief, had redrawn the battle lines between them.

The pull between them wasn't just sexual attraction. The raw need that had leapt up in him, ready to pounce from the ashes of his regret, was the same hunger that had sent him headlong into disaster before.

James slumped farther down in his chair, legs spread, knees at ninety-degree angles. He was staring out these windows because he had deliberately blown their relationship.

They could not have been more different. Meryl Wallis possessed the uncanny gift of making people do what she wanted them to, simply to please her. Her style was quietly graceful. It made itself felt in subtle but effective ways. He had never understood it, but he had learned to accept that it was real.

He, on the other hand, had cut his eyeteeth in the corporate world of tough negotiations and cutthroat business practices. In an earlier life he might have been branded a brigand or outlaw. Plundering companies in takeovers, he'd earned a reputation as a corporate raider, a twentieth-century buccaneer.

These differences were enough to explain why things between them had gone wrong so quickly. She was class. He was brass.

But that was not the real reason.

By the time Meryl Wallis came into his life he had begun to believe his own press: at thirty-five he had been a man with the Midas touch—everything he touched turned to gold without effort or cultivation. He had never paused to consider anything but what he wanted, and what he had wanted was Meryl Wallis.

They'd shared a hot and heavy two-month affair. He hadn't considered the ethics of it. He'd approached the financially troubled Walrus Ink publishing company, offering to be their white knight. Yet the moment he saw Meryl Wallis, the owner, he forgot about everything but finding a way to peel her out of her clothes and follow her into the first bed they could find.

He realized that she was a little shocked by the power of their attraction. The I-can't-catch-my-breath passion between them was new to her. It was new to him, too, but he'd had a lot more experience at protecting himself emotionally. He had thought that as long as he didn't lie, didn't promise too much, nobody would get hurt.

That was his first mistake.

She had wanted to keep their relationship private. He had wanted everyone to know. She was, after all, an incredibly sexy woman. He wasn't accustomed to attaching a lot of importance to compatibility in bed and so assumed she wouldn't.

James sighed. That was his second mistake.

He had been lying to himself even then. He could still recall every single encounter between them. All he had to do was shut his eyes to summon the memory of her flushed body next to his in bed. She had been getting to him in ways he couldn't afford to allow anyone. His libido wasn't the trouble. He had been very much afraid it was a less reliable region: his heart.

"And so I blew things sky-high."

The bitter recrimination echoed eerily in the vast empty darkness. He had told himself that his decision to put Walrus Ink on the auction block only weeks after he had gained a controlling interest was a sound business decision. It would have given him liquid assets at a time when he needed them. If Meryl didn't understand that and felt betrayed by his refusal to honor their verbal agreement that he would hold her company for her, then she didn't belong in business, or in his life.

He didn't blame her for resigning as editor in chief. She had once owned the company, had pride and a temper. Yet he had been certain that when she'd had time to cool off, she'd come back.

His third and last mistake.

He closed his eyes, envisioning Meryl's dark hair waving softly about her face. He had a knack of drawing people to him, but no one had ever gotten dangerously close, until Meryl. So he had driven her off before she could destroy what he'd spent so many years becoming: a son-of-a-bitch.

He wasn't proud of many of the things he'd done. But he knew from bitter experience what happened when honorable men like his father chose love and loyalty over self-interest. He could not afford vulnerabilities. Meryl had been a loss he thought he could afford. But he'd cut an artery when he'd extracted her from his life. Two years later, he was still bleeding.

Their encounter tonight made it clear that she still had the power to move him. In fact, it had made it clear that if he could accomplish only one more thing in his life, then he wanted it to be to find a way to win her back.

James bent forward and pulled open the bottom right drawer of the desk he sat behind. He didn't need light to know what was lying there. His fingers curled unerringly over the cool, smooth surface of a leather date book. It had belonged to Meryl. He'd come across it a few weeks ago, stuck in the back of this drawer. Curious, he'd thumbed through it and found her last entry, dated the day he'd told her he was going to sell Walrus Ink. Next to his name by their dinner date was a heart and the words *The One!*

The silly notation had struck him smack between the eyes with proof of a truth he had only suspected. Meryl Wallis had once been in love with him!

He snapped the book shut. That was history. He had only to look into her eyes tonight to know that what she felt for him could be summed up neatly in the word *hatred*. She hated him. He understood that. Here in the enveloping darkness he could even admit the truth, that he had cheated and betrayed her. The company was only an excuse to drive a wedge between them. James Brant got what James Brant wanted. That's how the world he lived in had worked.

But he had bent the rules of ethical practices too often. Last year life had caught up with him and he'd nearly ended up in prison. He had taken his lumps and bruises and some of them had made him stop and take stock. He hadn't liked a lot of what he had seen. Most of all, he hadn't liked what he'd learned about himself.

Nor were the ironies of life lost on him. The first move the government had made against him was to immediately freeze his assets, preventing him from going through with his plan to sell Walrus Ink. His long legal battles had left him financially crippled. He had a few viable assets. One of them was Walrus Ink. Ironic. He possessed the one thing in the world that Meryl Wallis had wanted and now he needed her help to keep it.

James shut his eyes, a smile easing into his expression. He liked a challenge. He even had a plan. After tonight, he knew that getting Meryl to come to work for him wasn't going to be easy. Regaining her trust was likely to be the biggest, certainly the most important, battle of his life. He might not succeed. Yet, he could barely contain his anticipation for their next encounter.

One thing about him had not changed. He still never took no for an answer.

Chapter 2

Meryl Wallis stared at her hand poised over the phone dial. Her fingers were trembling slightly. Embarrassed, she lowered the receiver back into place.

"I can do this," she muttered under her breath as she swiveled her desk chair around to face forward. One quick phone call. A few incisive questions and she would know what to expect. But it was the thought of calling that number, the number that had once belonged to *her* company, that rattled her.

She had done more difficult things, like walking away from the family business that James Brant had in every way but legally stolen out from under her. She had learned some hard lessons, endured her own private hell away from family and friends—anyone who could have eased her pain— and then gotten on with her life. She had paid a hard price for her gullibility, but thought it was all behind her... and then he had walked into the reception two nights before.

It was bound to happen. The world of children's book publishing was small. Still, she had thought she could avoid him, despite the phone messages he had left at her business the week before.

Yet as she had stared into James Brant's penetrating gray wolflike gaze, she had realized that she had been fooling herself. It was not over between them. Despite the betrayal, the enmity, the grief and pain he had caused her, the air around them had sizzled like downed wires in a thunderstorm. Her feelings had been on hold ever since she turned her back on James Brant. Now they were surging with the current of life. Too bad those feelings were all negative.

Meryl reached for the "worry stone" made of Galway green marble she kept on her desk. It was a gift from Tomaltach O'Connor, the award-winning children's book illustrator with whom she had produced a series of charming books several years ago. Her right thumb found the worn place on the smooth surface. Considering what she'd endured the past two years, it should have been worn through by now. After a moment, she put it back down. There was only one way she was going to get over James Brant and what he had done to her. It was time she fought back.

She knew James well enough to suspect that it was no coincidence that he had shown up at a reception where he wasn't expected. Then, too, there'd been the phone calls. Why, after all this time, had he decided to get in touch with her? Her sister might know the answer to that question.

Meryl picked up the phone and dialed quickly. It rang twice. "Hello, may I speak with Jacqui MacPherson?"

"May I ask who's calling?"

Meryl hesitated only a second. "Her sister."

"Meryl? I thought I recognized your voice," the voice on the other end of the line said with enthusiasm. "This is Carrine Oliver. I was on the front desk when you were here. Now I'm Jacqui's assistant."

"Oh, hello, Carrine. Congratulations on your promotion." Meryl rubbed the worry stone harder with her free hand. "I'd like to chat more, but I'm really in a bit of a hurry. Is it convenient to speak with Jacqui?"

"Actually, she's not— Oh, here she comes. Just give her a minute to go in her office and I'll have her pick up. So nice to hear your voice after all this time, Meryl. We've all missed you. Not a day goes by when your name doesn't come up."

Meryl didn't reply. She didn't want to think now about how much it had cost her emotionally to leave her company, or all the heartache that had followed that first wrenching decision. As it was, bumping into James Brant over the weekend had left her feeling tender in too many places.

"Meryl?" Jacqui's voice sounded strained and urgent when she came on the line. "What's wrong?"

"You needn't make it sound as if you haven't heard from me in years," Meryl said with a chuckle.

"You never call me at work," her sister responded. "Are you certain everything's okay?"

"Of course," Meryl answered quickly, then wondered, conversely, why she hadn't waited to call her sister this evening at home. By doing so now she had given added importance to the questions she was about to ask. She changed her mind. "You wouldn't happen to be free for lunch, would you?"

"Just a sec." She heard pages being flipped. "Amazingly enough, I am free. Where would you like to meet?"

Meryl named a lunch spot near Jacqui's office.

"Fine, but you can't hang up until you at least tell me why you called."

"Can't a girl invite her sister to lunch?"

"When we saw each other last week you didn't say anything about meeting for lunch on Monday. What's up?"

"You know me too well." Not wanting to admit over the phone her real reason for calling, Meryl used another excuse. "I've been thinking about your wedding."

There was a distinct pause on Jacqui's part. "Is that all?"

"Your wedding is your top priority these days, isn't it?"

"I suppose. As a matter of fact, I had been thinking about calling you. A few unexpected wrinkles turned up over the weekend."

"Really?" Meryl felt a little ashamed to be relieved that her sister had problems, but at least they sidetracked Jacqui from probing for her own. "Well, then, we do have a lot to talk about. See you at one."

At first glance strangers would not have guessed the two young women who entered the café together were sisters—half sisters, to be precise. Meryl was tall and a curvaceous size ten while Jacqui was fragile and petite. Meryl's thick dark brunette hair contrasted with Jacqui's pixie blond cut. Those differences were accentuated by the way they dressed. Jacqui wore a layered ensemble in black, which consisted of an ankle-length vest over a very short jumper, leggings and a stretch-lace long-sleeved shirt. Meryl wore a turtleneck blouse, trousers and jacket all in a soft shade of green.

Yet when one looked closer at the two women, from the wide-set almond-shaped eyes the color of tigereye agate to the straight slim noses and generous-lipped mouths, the similarity of facial bone structure was unmistakable.

"How's Cliff doing in Osaka?" Meryl asked when she and Jacqui had ordered.

"He loves it." Jacqui rolled her eyes. "I mean, *loves* it."

Uh-oh! Trouble in paradise? "It must be difficult to plan a wedding with a groom who's seven thousand miles away," Meryl said in an attempt to continue the conversation without directly prying.

Jacqui met her sister's inquiring gaze with a shrug. "He's talking about going back after the wedding."

Meryl's dark brows lifted. "Back to Japan?"

Jacqui nodded. "He's fallen in love with teaching. The electronics firm that hired him to teach English to their employees is thinking about expanding their program nationwide. Cliff would be made head of the language department. The pay is astronomical compared to what he'd earn as an untenured professor on a U.S. college campus. He's so busy, he's saying he won't even be able to break until three days before the wedding.''

Meryl saw distress edge into her sister's expression. ''Is this the new glitch in your wedding plans?''

''Not exactly.'' Jacqui took a deep breath. ''I haven't said anything before now because Cliff and I just came to a decision over the weekend.''

''He wants you to move to Japan after you marry.'' It wasn't a question. Meryl could see the answer in her sister's flushed face.

''How did you guess?'' Jacqui asked sheepishly.

Meryl smiled fondly at her younger sister. ''I couldn't imagine Cliff letting you get away. You guys have been engaged far too long. He just needed to feel as if he could afford a wife.''

Jacqui nodded. ''You're right. The fact that I had a job while his was only temporary was a problem for him, though I told him I didn't mind supporting us for a while. I guess that makes him old-fashioned.''

''It makes him a great guy with a sense of responsibility. Cliff is thinking of your future.''

Jacqui beamed. ''I've always wanted to see the world. A chance to live overseas for a few years sounds perfect. You know how I've always wanted to take a couple of years off and see if I could cut it as an artist.''

''Sounds wonderful. Of course, I'd miss you like anything.''

Jacqui nodded. ''Now what about you? What are you going to do after your wonderful, charming sister leaves town?''

Meryl smiled and reached for her water glass. ''I'm tossing possibilities around.''

''I hope you mean that.'' Jacqui's expression grew serious. ''You need to get out from under the cloud of the past.''

Meryl shifted her gaze to the empty place before her. "I've managed, thank you."

"I can't tell you how much I admire you. You've gotten on with your life despite what you've been through," Jacqui added when Meryl glanced up. "At least you left with your head held high. I'm going to feel like a rat deserting a sinking ship."

Surprise sketched a shallow frown on Meryl's brow. "What sinking ship?"

Jacqui smiled. "I'm not exactly giving away company secrets when I say if things hadn't worked out for Cliff in Japan, I might have been asking you for a job in a few months."

"Why?"

"You must have heard the rumors." Her gaze was serious. "Walrus Ink Press is in trouble, Meryl."

Meryl frowned. "There were plenty of people eager to tell me how Walrus Ink's change of command got off to a shaky start last year, but I thought the fallout had settled. James Brant made his reputation by beating the odds."

Jacqui glanced skyward. "His reputation is half the trouble. You should have heard a phone conversation he had with one of our top authors a few days after you left. He sounded like a sergeant giving orders to a raw recruit. Word got around and authors began scattering like leaves in the wind. Several jumped ship when their contracts ran out. Others are dragging their feet and have set back deadlines again and again."

"Things can't be that bad, Jacqui."

Her sister shrugged. "Things were beginning to sort themselves out before Brant's legal problems. Since his former partners went to prison, we've had another set of problems crop up. Our customer base fear that Brant's financial problems might become their own. Orders are down."

Meryl couldn't shrug off her inclination to defend Walrus Ink or James's efforts. However she felt about him personally, she knew that he gave his best to his business enterprises. "You know the realities of children's publishing. After many boom years the market's fallen off. Libraries—our meat and potatoes buyers—have lost much of their funding for book purchasing. The competition has stacked the shelves with merchandise. Even the big boys are cutting back their lists, trimming staff, restrategizing. Everybody's feeling a little shaky."

Jacqui nodded. "The worst thing is, we don't have any really wonderful books to push. Remember what you used to say in board meetings? We're a tiny boat in a very big ocean. Everything we do has got to count. If we don't bring out a really terrific spring list, it may all be over."

Meryl shrugged, mentally building a wall between herself and her sister's dire predictions. "Not my problem."

"I wish you were back," Jacqui said impulsively. "You would turn it around in six months. Nobody can handle artists and their temperaments like you."

"Thank you, Sister, but I think you're prejudiced."

Jacqui smiled. "Absolutely."

"If you're so certain you know what's wrong, why don't you ask Brant to let you have a crack at compiling the spring list?"

Jacqui shook her head, causing her pale blond bangs to swing like fringe. "To begin with, I don't have your business acumen. Don't deny it. I'm the Parson's School of Design graduate. You're the one with the MBA from Carnegie Institute. Besides, you always had the vision for the company. You could talk to a writer and an illustrator in their own language, make them understand what you wanted each of them to see and then help translate those visions into salable books. It's a gift. I don't have a vision and neither does Brant." She shrugged. "If he doesn't get someone in there soon who does, we're doomed."

Meryl ran her tongue nervously over her lower lip. This was the moment for her to introduce the reason for their lunch. "I ran into James over the weekend."

"Brant?" Jacqui's eyes widened dramatically. "Where?"

Meryl met her sister's astonished expression with perfect calm. "At a children's publishers' reception Saturday night."

"I knew I should have gone to that reception! But Cliff's mom had invited me to dinner and I so seldom have time to play the fiancée and she wanted to discuss the Japanese offer. Man! I can't believe it. Brant never attends those things." Jacqui hunched her shoulders as she leaned forward. "Well? What happened? Did you speak?"

Meryl nodded. "We traded polite barbs."

"Come on. I work for the man. Brant doesn't trade barbs, he launches grenades."

Meryl conceded this with a smile. "Actually, he was on his best behavior. We scarcely singed each other. Besides, he didn't seem in especially good shape. He looked tired, or dissipated," she added in an undertone of disapproval.

But it wasn't just disapproval, Meryl acknowledged as the waiter laid out their plates. She had been disconcerted by James's wearied appearance. He had always seemed invincible, which was both his attraction and his worst trait. Despite everything, she didn't like the idea of seeing him humbled by circumstance. The man she had known wouldn't have even noticed the scars of the battle he'd just fought. What had changed that?

Jacqui reached for her iced tea as the waiter served them, and sized up her sister over the top of her glass as she took a sip. "I hear Brant isn't dating these days," she offered when the waiter had departed.

"He was with Beebe Hatcher last night."

"Hatchet-Job Hatcher?" Jacqui lowered her voice. "And that's what her admirers call her," she added with an impish grin. "You must have heard about the nasty campaign she ran upstate for that state representative last fall. The mudslinging got so out of hand it made the national news. Only, guess what? Hatchet-Job is hotter than ever. Isn't it amazing how bad publicity is good for some businesses?"

"Walrus Ink Press isn't likely to benefit from her methods," Meryl observed thoughtfully.

"You don't think Brant's considering hiring *her?*" Jacqui responded. "Maybe he's just seeing her."

"James never wastes time," Meryl answered. Suddenly another possible reason for James's worn look came to mind. "If he's seeing her regularly, you can be certain he's doing business with her."

Jacqui's expression gentled with sympathy. "So how did it feel to see him again, after all this time?"

"About as good as a kick in the stomach." Meryl smiled briefly. "But I'm much better at taking a punch these days."

"You aren't over him, are you?"

Meryl glanced down at her plate as she speared a piece of grilled salmon. "How do you get over an enemy who's bested you?"

"I meant personally."

Meryl lowered her fork back to her plate, the salmon untouched. "It was always personal. He came in as a white knight, let me think he'd hold the company until I was able to regroup and buy him out. Yet once he'd gained control he was ready to sell his majority shares to someone else."

"But what about his promise to you?"

Meryl's mouth tightened. "He said he didn't make business decisions based on whom he happened to be sleeping with at the moment."

"The bastard!" Jacqui's piquant features turned crimson in anger. "Why didn't you tell me that part before? As if you were sleeping with him to gain his help! If I'd known he'd put it in those terms, I'd have walked out, too."

Meryl shook her head. "It would only have made things worse. Besides, it wasn't your fight because it wasn't really about the business." She glanced across at her sister and said softly, "What happened was my fault because I fell in love with him."

It was a bitter admission. The hardest of her life. "He was right about one thing. I walked into our affair with my eyes open. I knew what he was like." She shrugged, the struggle an old one. "I knew that if I hadn't walked out first he would have eventually."

"Maybe." Jacqui kept whatever other thoughts she might have to herself. "But maybe not. He changed after you left, Meryl."

"What do you mean?"

"I can't quite put it into words because I don't see enough of him to say I really know him. But he's different since the trial. Quieter, less brusque."

"He had the pants scared off him, that's all. He'll be back in form in no time."

"Maybe." Jacqui looked down at her plate. "He's been asking about you recently."

"What?"

Jacqui lifted her gaze. "I wasn't going to tell you. I told him you wouldn't want to hear from him after all this time. I was right, wasn't I?"

Meryl nodded, but she couldn't resist saying, "What did he say to you?"

"Does it matter? I mean, after what you've just told me, could he say anything that would make you come back to Walrus Ink?"

Surprise splashed through Meryl like ice water. "Is that what he has in mind?"

"Honestly, I don't know. He just wanted to know if you were happy, if your business was doing well, if you were seeing someone."

"He asked you that?" The ice water turned instantly into steamy resentment.

"He didn't ask, exactly. I just worked into the conversation that you were seeing Kent Davis." She smiled smugly. "I felt I owed you that."

"I see." Meryl offered her a smile.

"So what will you do, if he calls you, I mean?"

"He won't." Meryl's voice was brisk, matter-of-fact. "We shared a few minutes' unpleasant conversation the other night. We aren't likely to meet again for a long time—if ever."

"Why, if ever?"

Meryl's tension eased a fraction. "I suspect I'm about to be made another very tempting offer."

"Really? By whom?"

"Kent Davis."

"Marriage?" Jacqui squealed.

"No, silly. It's business. I think he's going to ask me to move to New York City and head his juvenile hardcover imprint."

Jacqui gave her a wicked look. "Are you certain that business is all he has in mind?"

"Of course," Meryl responded, though she had her doubts about that, as well. "Kent's been hinting at it for weeks, asking me if I wouldn't like to take on more responsibility again, take charge of something, a new challenge. Other times he's mentioned that his current editor in chief of his children's book division is about to retire and that he's finding it difficult to replace him. He wants someone who's had a career of specializing in children's books."

"That's you."

Meryl smiled. "So it would seem."

"Are you going to take him up on it?"

"I don't know."

"Why wouldn't you?"

"Well, for one, it would mean moving to New York."

"Remember me? I'm the sister who's going to live in Japan."

Meryl nodded. "And, two, I like running my own business and having my own hours."

"Consulting and free-lance editing isn't exactly living in the fast lane, Meryl. You were the life's blood of Walrus Ink. Dad used to say you cut your teeth on the company. You gave that business the first ten years of your adult life."

"That wasn't enough to save it, was it?"

Exasperation colored Jacqui's voice. "No one in the family has ever said a word against you, not even my mother. Honestly. Dad left you the business because he knew you were the one who could run it. But even he wouldn't have been a match for a corporate raider like Brant. We all know who's to blame for what happened. You didn't stand a chance."

Meryl smiled gratefully. "I hope you mean it."

"Just to show you there are no bad feelings, I'll let *you* pick up the tab!"

Meryl made a face. "Fair enough."

"But I hope you're wrong about Brant hiring BeeBe Hatcher. She'd have Walrus Ink doing picture books on mass murderers and terrorist bombers just to be trendy."

"Jacqui, you're awful." But Meryl couldn't keep back a chuckle.

"Now, let's talk about something really significant, like the color of bridesmaids' dresses." Jacqui pulled a piece of fabric from her purse. "Look at this swatch."

"Eggplant, Jacqui?"

Neither sister mentioned Walrus Ink again until they were out on the sidewalk, about to part.

"Oh, look at the time!" Jacqui muttered. "Got to fly. Brant's in-house today."

"Can't you talk to Brant?" Meryl asked suddenly.

Jacqui looked back over her shoulder as if she expected someone to be standing there. Then she looked back at her sister with widened eyes. "Me? Are you joking? The man totally intimidates me, always has. Can't imagine that you two were once, well, you know, so close."

"Neither can I," Meryl murmured. But it wasn't true.

As she turned toward her car, Meryl realized she had been able to think of little else since the weekend except James Brant and how good things had once been between them. Strange how one's emotions didn't listen to one's brain. It was as if there were two distinct personalities inside her: the one who knew better and the one who didn't care.

* * *

"Of course, accepting this job means that you're going to have to get over your scruples about raiding clients from your former company."

Meryl smiled at the visitor who'd dropped by her office unexpectedly. "Sorry. I don't plan to ever get over my scruples."

Kent Davis rose from the chair he had occupied opposite her desk. "That's what I love about you."

He braced both hands, palms flat, on her desk top and leaned across it toward her with a smile. "But let's look at the facts. When was the last time Walrus Ink Press published a new book by Dorthea McAlroy, Kathleen Martin, or used your favorite illustrator, Tomaltach O'Connor? Not in the year plus since you left the company."

"They've taken on new clients," Meryl said in defense of her old firm. "Besides, they won a Newbury and were nominated for a Caldecott this year."

"That was for work done under your guidance, with the stable of writers you found and nurtured. Brant can't get Walrus Ink's top authors to answer his letters, let alone write books for him."

Meryl frowned as she leaned back in her swivel chair. "You're the second person who's said that to me today. It doesn't make me feel any better to know that the company my father founded and that I had planned to dedicate my life to is teetering on destruction."

"Not even if it takes Brant with it?"

Meryl met his blue gaze steadily. "Not even then."

He levered himself away from her desk. "You should be prepared for that very real possibility. Walrus Ink's wholesalers are griping about the lack of new books from its trademark authors. Tomaltach O'Connor practically paid your rent single-handedly, yet rumor has it that O'Connor hasn't spoken to Brant since last fall. When he asked about the new book, O'Connor told him where to go—in Gaelic."

Meryl smiled. "Tomaltach isn't known for his Irish charm."

"Well, he thinks a great deal of you. He has said repeatedly in the Irish press that he refuses to publish with any editor but you."

"How do you know that?"

Kent smiled. "I wasn't going to tell you until you agreed to take the job, but if it will turn the trick I will." He propped a hip on her desk and leaned toward her. "I phoned O'Connor last week, told him there was a good chance you'd be signing on as editor in chief of my children's book division. O'Connor blessed me in Gaelic. Said he had three dozen illustrations just waiting for you."

Meryl frowned. "You shouldn't have done that, Kent. O'Connor still has three books to do on a five-book contract I negotiated with him at Walrus Ink."

"So you can buy out the contract when you take over for me."

Meryl subjected him to a cool, appraising glance. "That wouldn't be ethical unless O'Connor cut his ties with Walrus Ink first."

Kent's expression soured. "That's what I mean about your scruples. You apply them too literally, Meryl. O'Connor has refused to honor his contract with Walrus Ink. Brant can't sue without bringing more bad press upon himself. I think even he knows when he's on the ropes." He smiled at her. "Admit it, you gained a certain satisfaction from his fall from grace last year."

"Brant was exonerated," she reminded him.

"Well, let's just say that those of us who've done business with him suspect he was just smarter than his partners and that's why he didn't get caught. You're not the only one he mauled. If you'll remember, I lost a big one to him several years ago. I admit it, I wouldn't mind getting even with the bas—well, getting even."

"I see. And you thought I might share your passion for revenge."

He gave her a probing look. "I *thought* we'd offer, as you suggested, to buy out O'Connor's contract. He's not the only writer or illustrator you worked with who's loyal to you. If you crook your elegant little finger, they'll come flocking to you."

"Don't you mean to Davis Imprint?"

He smiled. "All right, so it makes good business to have you on my team. Wouldn't you have done the same at Walrus Ink, given the opportunity?"

"Perhaps. No." Meryl shook her head. "I'll have to think about your offer. I don't relish the idea of moving to Manhattan."

"Don't move. Commute."

"I like the idea of commuting even less."

"How do you know until you've tried it? A little apartment in Soho or the Village. Or perhaps you'd prefer the Upper East or West Side. You tell me what you want, I'll see what I can do."

"You're being very nice to me. Why?"

"I want your client list, of course." He leaned over her desk, bringing his face in close to hers. "And I want you. But you know that, too."

Meryl smiled as he bent to kiss her. They had been dating unseriously on and off for several months, whenever their busy schedules permitted. It was not a heavy-duty relationship, so far platonic, and she preferred it that way. She hadn't given too much thought to what Kent might want because she had been up-front about not being ready to fall in love again. When he moved away from her, she wondered what he hoped to gain by courting her.

No, that was not fair. Her experience with Brant had taught her to suspect the worst in everyone. But she mustn't let his memory tarnish this relationship. Belatedly she realized Kent was looking at her with a puzzled expression. "Something wrong?"

"I'm just wondering what's going on behind those green gold eyes of yours. It looks like a struggle is taking place."

"I hope you're not counting too much on my saying yes." Meryl heard the unexpected note of caution in her voice and realized that her body had tensed.

"No pressure, Meryl. I mean it. If you say no, then we simply go on as before. I like you for you. The kiss is not part of a power play to win you for my company."

"Good."

She let him kiss her again because it was easier than resisting. Besides, it was time to find out if they had a future.

"Saved by the bell?" Kent suggested when her phone buzzed a few moments later.

Meryl reached for it automatically, her mind still pleasantly distracted by the impression of Kent's kiss.

"Don't hang up!" said an autocratic voice loud enough to make both Kent and Meryl start. "I want to talk to you. I'll be at your office in ten minutes. Be there."

"Who the hell was that?" Kent asked.

Meryl set the receiver down carefully. "Mr. Brant. It seems he wants an appointment."

Chapter 3

"Why didn't you stay and fight me for it?"

The moment James Brant stepped into her office Meryl realized she had made a very bad mistake. She had been expecting the man she had encountered two nights before, a man who looked as if life had finally begun to exact its revenge.

Yet the man who stood before her didn't look the least bit worn or tired or battered by life. He wore a pearl gray business suit with a darker toned shirt that made him look like a million. Beneath the unruly waves of chestnut hair his craggy face wore its usual expression of patrician arrogance. She recognized his attire for was it was: corporate battle fatigues. He was spoiling for a fight, perhaps had sensed some vulnerability in her two nights before, and had decided to capitalize on it.

He was solidly planted in the middle of her modest office, feet apart, hands in pockets and brow furrowed. Only the strongest refused to roll over and play dead for James Brant.

"Well?" he demanded, shattering the stiff, short silence that had fallen.

Meryl dodged the question. She didn't have the heart for a fight with him. Some other day, she thought wearily. After dealing with Jacqui and then Kent, she was fresh out of challenges. "I don't know what you mean."

"I was talking about Walrus Ink, and you damn well know it."

Meryl folded her hands and rested them on the edge of the desk as his voice thundered over her. He hadn't even said hello. Not even that. Just down and dirty from the first.

She glanced down at her desk. Three feet of burl wood separated her from James Brant. At the moment it seemed a flimsy defense. She lifted her head. "Why should I have had to fight you for *my* company?"

A look a exasperation crossed his face. Slate eyes stared at her between a thicket of red-gold lashes. "You mean because we were lovers." A muscle jumped in his cheek. "I told you then, business and private matters don't mix in my book."

You're a big girl. You came into this with your eyes open. You can't expect me to make business decisions based on in whose bed I just spent the night.

Meryl hunched her shoulders as the memory of his words spoken nearly two years earlier echoed in her mind. "I'm aware that you think I didn't behave well."

"You walked out on what you claimed was the most important thing in your life," he reminded her.

Meryl glanced past his imposing frame toward the door where the sound of footsteps echoed in the hallway beyond. She hoped someone would interrupt them. The footsteps passed on. "Yes, well, there were other considerations."

"What sort of considerations?"

Meryl's gaze drifted to his hands, which he had jerked from his trouser pockets as if he expected he would need them. Long fingers, blunt tipped, corded with tendons and veins. The millionaire had a workman's hands.

If you're going to survive you have to learn to look after yourself. You can't expect me to bail you out. You're on your own.

Meryl looked away and swiveled her chair toward the nearby file cabinet, then pushed shut the top drawer. No need for him to learn who her clients were. "I really don't see the point in our continuing this line of conversation. What happened happened. It was over a long time ago."

"I'm glad you see it that way."

He sounded relieved. She glanced over and saw the confirmation in his eased expression.

"Because," he went on smoothly, "I'm here to do business. I wouldn't want our acrimonious past to keep you from making the right decision now."

Meryl turned back to face him fully. "Are you serious? You've come to offer me business?"

Her disbelieving tone drew his brows together, but he only said, "Yes."

A smile tugged at the corners of her mouth as she rose from her chair. "Then by all means, have a seat, Mr. Brant. And then, please, come to your point."

James didn't take the chair he was offered and he noted with amusement that she didn't reseat herself, either. He had taught her that tactic, suggesting that your business opponent be seated while you remain standing or appropriating a higher perch. His gaze slid admiringly over her sea green suit with slightly fitted jacket. Feminine but wholly businesslike. In heels she was five foot nine. He was taller.

He moved in on her, ignoring the barrier of the desk. "I want you to come to work for me, take over the running of Walrus Ink Press."

He could tell he had surprised her. Her expressive eyes widened a fraction before her neutral expression slipped back into place. He grinned confidently as he came to a halt, one thigh pressing against her desk. "Surprised you, didn't I?"

Meryl gazed at him impassively. "Yes, you did. Now tell me why."

"I want your expertise working for me. You name the salary, the title, whatever. You want to be editor in chief, publisher? It's yours."

As silence fell behind his forceful words, Meryl stared at him. He was offering her a job. He wanted her to become an employee of a company that she had once owned. Her voice lifted on the crest of her anger. "Get out of here!"

He looked faintly amused by the vehemence in her voice, but he didn't back down. "I realize that at first glance my offer has got to seem like a kick in the teeth. That's not my intention. I need you."

Meryl jerked slightly at that final possessive statement, though he hadn't moved so much as an inch closer.

James let out an impatient breath. "Let me put it this way. You know children's publishing inside and out. You know the client list at Walrus Ink. You have built-in loyalties, long associations. We need every edge we can find, make or bluff. You've got special skills. The job's tailor-made for you."

"Why didn't you say any of this two years ago when I was trying to convince my creditors to extend my company's loans?"

"I did." But they both knew he had not said it then with the persuasive conviction he had brought to bear just now. Nor did he miss her emphasis on the phrase "my company." "You know the rules of the game, Meryl. You can't win them all."

"No, not when the white knight I brought in to protect me was willing to sell my company right out from under me."

"Haven't you come to terms with that?" He caught himself. The edge in his voice was backing her against the ropes. He knew her well enough now to know what to expect if he continued. She would go down under his verbal blows before she would admit defeat. He didn't want to best her. He needed her to win this round, the first of many. "I'm offering you work." A sweep of his hand included her small office in a dismissive gesture. "This is just dallying on the sidelines."

"I like dallying," she said confidently. "I don't need to work." At least she had walked away with her personal finances intact. She had thought, at the time, James had been trying to help her when he convinced her not to invest the bulk of her family inheritance in company stock. In retrospect she knew better. His offer to buy and hold the majority shares in Walrus Ink had given him clear ownership, which was what he'd been after all along.

James watched covetously as she paced behind her desk, trying to give her time to cool off. From the moment he had stepped into her office, he had given up trying to remain detached. Every sense was on alert. He followed her distracting silhouette, noting how her pale green turtleneck hugged the curves of her breasts. He heard the faint metallic clink of the gold links of her belt as she moved. His gaze rode the subtle sway of her hips. He admired the fact that she had never bothered to diet off the last ten pounds that seems to obsess every other woman. It gave her figure a subtle voluptuousness. And it proved that she was comfortable in her skin. How rare that was. In his present mood, his own skin seemed too tight.

When she abruptly stopped pacing he quickly said, "I'm not implying you need money." He tried to sound conciliatory. "But you've got to feel a little left out of the day-to-day workings of an industry whose pulse you once had your finger on."

She stopped short and the sudden stillness of her body sent her dark hair swinging forward across her shoulders in a way that made his palms itch to touch. "You're the reason I no longer have that option."

He made a dismissive gesture. "Put personal matters aside, Meryl. Try to view this objectively. Eliminate the personal and you'll have to agree it makes good business sense.''

I don't think with my dick. Don't think with your heart. Bottom line, it's good business. If you can't see that, you don't belong in the business world.

Meryl stiffened as the hurtful memories played on. ''Why did you think I would ever consider helping you?''

He placed his hands on the desk. ''I thought I was pointing out why this would be a good move for you.''

She saw his eyes crinkle in the corners. She had once loved kissing those laugh lines. Now they only fueled her anger. ''I learned many things from you. One of them is that you never do anything for anybody that doesn't benefit you more.''

He awarded her with a deeper smile. ''You remember that, do you?''

Meryl scowled. ''It isn't a point in your favor. What's in this for you?''

''Right.'' He nodded in approval. ''Now you're thinking like a CEO. Bottom line, certain events have thrown what you might call a pall over my reputation.''

Meryl lifted one dark brow. ''You mean the fact that several of your former business associates are serving time in a federal penitentiary for fraud and insider trading? So I'm not the only one wondering why you aren't in there with them.''

His eyes narrowed. Somehow the loss of his smile didn't make things better. It made her aware anew of the depths of danger in the man he seldom allowed to surface. Was he as afraid of that dark streak as she was?

''You have toughened up,'' he said.

''You can't begin to know.'' Meryl held his silver gaze, but she wished her voice hadn't sounded so plaintive.

''Right.'' He slapped the desk top and straightened. ''Having associates in prison hasn't exactly polished my apple with the public. Some wacko out west is even trying to organize a boycott of Walrus Ink books as a protest against what he calls the immoral character of the company. As if *Goldilocks and the Three Bears* would contaminate a child just because we produced it.''

"You don't publish *Goldilocks*," she observed tartly.

He glared at her. "You know what I mean. Anyway, book sales in the west are off slightly because people are beginning to be concerned about appearing insensitive to family-values issues."

Meryl sighed and folded her arms across her chest. She was not unfamiliar with dealing with misguided people who took extreme exception to genuinely harmless things or characters in children's books. But this time it was not her problem. "I can't help you."

James held on doggedly to his temper, reminding himself that she was at least still talking to him. If only she had changed her perfume fragrance since they'd parted he might even have been able to concentrate completely. As it was, the fragrance was, in its own subtle way, weakening his argument. Maybe she shouldn't come back. Maybe he wouldn't be able to keep his hands off her long enough to convince her that he wanted more than just to have her back in his bed.

He eased away from her desk on the pretext of glancing out of the window, but it was to break the lure of her nearness. "If you come back, your spotless record in the industry will shift attention at Walrus Ink away from me. You've much to be proud of. We could go in with a big reissue of your bestsellers and personal favorites, give Walrus Ink a new image. Yours to choose, of course. Do whatever you think will gain us some positive publicity."

"You mean get *you* off the hook."

He stiffened, his expression hardening into lines of combat. "Look, I'm not asking for favors. You're good. I'm willing to pay for the best. I never thought you were anything less than brilliant at the everyday running of Walrus Ink. You just didn't know how to capitalize on your success. I could do that. Under my management Walrus Ink was gaining ground as the fastest-growing small press in the country its first year."

Meryl remained unconvinced. She knew him too well, knew from experience that what lay beneath the masculine gloss, the glamour, the power and persuasion was not a warm human heart but a cold steel pump. "Why are you really here?"

Their gazes met and melded.

James knew she was really asking another, more personal question: Why hadn't he come after her before now? He didn't want to get into that yet. He didn't know how to explain it without hurting both of them. For that, he needed time, time to regain her trust and gauge her feelings. He jumped to the next question. "Ask me why I don't just sell Walrus Ink."

Meryl jerked a nod.

His expression suddenly softened. "Because it's all I have left of you."

Meryl gasped softly. She hadn't expected that. It was a one-two combination that hit below the belt and over the heart. She had not thought that even James Brant had the gall to try to use her old feelings against her. The realization that his tactics hadn't changed gave her new armor. No one, especially not James Brant, would ever hurt her again.

She turned and moved behind her desk where she sat down. "You're slipping, Brant." She looked up slowly, no longer guarding her expression. There was no need. It registered unadulterated dislike. "I've been the seduction route and it's lost its appeal."

"Really?" He shoved his hands in his pockets. "Then why did you run away?"

Meryl glanced down, retreating into that secret place no one else knew about. When she looked up a second later, the glass wall was back in place. "I had an appointment the other night."

"I don't mean Saturday night." His gray gaze tracked her down. "I mean two years ago."

Meryl braced herself. "I walked, not ran, away. There's a difference."

He smirked. "You left the door swinging."

Meryl looked away first. Okay, so he could outstare her. No big deal. "I was in a hurry."

"So much so you didn't stop to clean out your desk."

An alarm went off in Meryl's head as she looked up. She knew there was something of significance in what he was saying, but she couldn't put her finger on it. "So what?"

"So where did you go for three months?"

"It wasn't any of your business, then or now."

"Then why not tell me?"

"Because you want to know." It was a childish thing to say, an admittance that she wanted to keep something from him simply because it would annoy him. It was also a measure of the precious little power she held over him.

He stared a her a moment longer, then shrugged. "Okay, don't tell me. But one day you will."

Not if I can help it! Meryl thought vehemently. Of all the secrets she kept, that was the one she would rather die with. She realized he must have seen the determination in her expression, yet he changed subjects. "For now, tell me how you'd turn Walrus Ink around?"

The change of subject surprised her. The old James would have waded right in on an opponent who had shown such emotional volatility. He'd let her off the hook. But for how long?

"Ask Beebe Hatcher."

A corner of his mouth lifted. So she had noticed that Beebe was with him at the reception and it obviously annoyed her. "I'm asking you."

"You wouldn't like what I'd have to say."

"Try me."

"You asked for it," she said in a tight, annoyed tone. "The public associates your name with criminal activity. That's a self-destructive image for a businessman whose target audience is parents of the under-twelve set."

He nodded. "Right. I had thought of that."

"Of course you had," she retorted with sarcasm.

He glanced at her sharply, but only said, "What else?"

"I'd take *your* name off every piece of paper associated with Walrus Ink. It's like drawing a skull and crossbones on the packaging. Then, once *you'd* disappeared as a presence, I'd start trying to court all the authors *you* managed to insult, annoy or otherwise run off."

"How do you know about that?" He suddenly smiled. "Unless you've been keeping tabs on me."

"It's no secret you've alienated any- and everybody with your egotistical manner. Ask anyone in the business—the reps, booksellers, wholesalers. They'll all tell you the same thing—James Brant is bad news in children's publishing." Meryl refused to meet his gaze, but a smile of triumph hovered on her mouth. "I'm surprised you haven't taken up writing books yourself, since you seem to feel you know more than anyone else about publishing."

James's eyes narrowed. She was enjoying running roughshod over his ego. Perhaps he deserved her scorn, but he was a good businessman. "Walrus Ink's stock is up and our sell-through has never been higher."

"You must be quoting last year's figures," she continued. "Those figures would reflect the last year of my helmsmanship. Talk to me about your figures next autumn and I don't think I'll have to repeat myself."

He nodded, smiling openly now, and she was unwillingly impressed by the genuine warmth in it. It even thawed the wintry gray of his eyes. "You are tough, aren't you?"

She resisted the urge to smile back. She knew she had won only a skirmish, not the war. "I'm learning."

"Glad to hear it." He rose to his feet as if they had concluded some mutual agreement. "At least you're prepared. You're going to have a fight on your hands."

Meryl resisted the urge to rise to her feet at his cue. "I've no intention of working for you."

"You will." He was nodding at her in approval. "You smell a good fight and you want back in the business in the worst way. And I want you back." His voice dropped in register. "On any terms you name."

For a second time in two days, Meryl felt the tidal tug of desire. The sudden alertness in her body unnerved her. He had presence, a rare but instantly recognizable quality. There was this sense of perfect control in the man, from his platinum stare to his superbly fit body. Time had worn a few crags and cut a few valleys in a face that would only improve with age. But it was that physical awareness inside herself that had made her so foolishly glad that the notorious James Brant, bad reputation and all, had come to see her.

Meryl blinked and felt a lurch of panic inside herself. No, it mustn't, couldn't, happen again! She knew better. James used sexual attraction the way a fisherman used a fancy lure, to hook the unsuspecting.

"Thank you, Mr. Brant, but I won't be taking you up on your offer. I've already accepted another." She saw disbelief etch his face. "Kent Davis was here just ahead of you. He offered me the editor in chief position of Davis Imprint."

His expression reshaped into sharp antagonism. "He's trying to buy your affection."

Meryl felt her world drop back onto the solid surface of the earth. "Isn't that accusation a little strange coming from you?"

"I never tried to buy your affection. What we had—"

Meryl shot up out of her chair. "You can go now."

"All right!" He put up both hands surrender. "I didn't mean to bring up a sore subject. I only meant that you and I began on level ground."

"No, we didn't. I thought you were honest. I didn't know you kept a bottom-line score sheet even in your private life. We don't have a past, as far as I'm concerned, so there's no reason for us to consider a future."

"There's Walrus Ink."

"Your problem."

"You'd let it go under, knowing that you might have been able to save it?"

Meryl glared at him. "If it goes under that's your fault not mine. As you know, I would have done nearly anything to save the company my father founded. It was my life, my baby, my—"

"Millstone?" James took a step toward her. "Admit it. Walrus Ink was everything to you because you didn't have anything else. I don't recall there being a man in your life when we met. Office rumor said you didn't even date." He saw her face whiten, but he couldn't stop himself. He couldn't abide the idea that she had truly been wedded to the company he had taken from her. "That company was your refuge from life. By taking it away, I forced you out into the real world."

"You put me out in the cold, Mr. Brant," Meryl replied in an icy voice that trembled with rage. "Now that I'm acclimatized, I'm going to see to it that you're the one who's put out of my life."

She reached for her phone and punched the key that alerted security. "If you ever cross the threshold of these premises again, I'll have you arrested for trespassing."

James's eyes widened as she asked security to send a man up. And then he smiled. "Right. You win this round. But tonight, when you're in your bed alone, ask yourself this question. If anybody else but I owned Walrus Ink and asked for your professional help, would you refuse?"

Meryl didn't need to ask herself that question. They both knew the answer. Of course she would.

James backed toward the door as he heard the elevator chime, no doubt bringing the summoned guard. He knew he was playing hardball with her, but he felt he didn't have time to play fairly, to coax and plead. The expression on her face told him she wasn't likely to reconsider her hostility toward him. The best he could do at this point was convince her that there was real work to be done at Walrus Ink.

He put his hand on the doorknob as heavy footfalls sounded in the hallway. "Just come in for two weeks, as a paid consultant. Look things over. Convince yourself that I'm telling the truth."

"Your truth," she snapped.

"*The* truth. Walrus Ink needs your help."

Meryl drew herself up indignantly as she saw the guard appear behind him. "Get the hell out of my office, Mr. Brant."

It was one of those rare fall sunsets where the colors of the sky matched exactly the crimsons, harvest golds, pumpkins and smudged ochers of the autumn leaves raining softly to the ground outside her cabin door.

Meryl rested one hand high on the doorframe as she gazed out at the late-afternoon sky. She had left her office early, as soon as she was certain James Brant had vacated the premises. She needed to get away and, when such was the case, she came here to the woods, to the rustic cabin that had once been a hunting lodge. Now the cabin walls sported artists' sketches of book covers, chintz pillows of every shape and color and the greater part of her collection of antique and first-edition children's books. No matter how difficult the day, she had always been able to find peace here among her things and the stillness of nature beyond her doorstep.

The leaves made no sound as they sailed past. Yet she heard whispering. Or perhaps the whispering was all inside her head. Meryl closed her eyes to listen.

One day all this will be yours, Meryl.

I know, Dad.

It's a privilege as well as a responsibility to run a business like Walrus Ink. It's not for everybody.

It's for me, Dad. I can't imagine ever wanting anything else.

So you say now. But if you should one day find that it's not for you, you must walk away and not look back.

Meryl sighed as the whispers inside her head retreated. She had walked away from Walrus Ink, but not because she had grown tired of the responsibility. She had turned her back on it because she had been tricked into giving up control. Had she done the right thing? Or had she let her pride get in the way? If she had stayed, could she have convinced James to hold off on the sale until she had marshaled new investors to back her? After all, he had never sold the company.

Had she been bested or had she failed? That question had tormented her for months before she'd successfully buried it. Now one conversation with James had brought it howling back to her consciousness.

She had come to only one conclusion about what had occurred. After thirty years of rational behavior, she had fallen hard for the absolutely wrong man.

She should have suspected it couldn't last. The hot and heavy fever that had burned between them had been too much like madness to be real. For two torrid months she, a woman who had never lost her head over a man, couldn't think of anything but the next time she would see, touch and be loved by James Brant.

Meryl absently rubbed her hands up and down her sweater-clad arms. Even now she couldn't think of him without recalling the intensity of their physical relationship. It was as if he had imprinted her with his touch, with his taste, with his loving, so that no man would ever again measure up. She had given him everything, more than he would ever know, and he had taken everything she had, including her pride, her trust and her love. So she had walked away and not looked back... until now.

Once she had reined in her temper enough to think rationally, she'd thought of little else on the drive up here but their conversation. He said he needed her insider's expertise to woo back customers and smooth the ruffled feathers of artistic egos. He had dared ask her to swallow her pride and become an employee in a company where she had once been owner. How could he expect her to do that?

If anybody else but I owned Walrus Ink and asked for your professional help, would you refuse?

She couldn't get out of her head the thought that she might be able to save a company that James Brant couldn't. The fact that he had admitted as much quite boggled her mind. Once he'd been a power player without peers or true partners. He was not a team player. But perhaps the rumors Jacqui and Kent had repeated were true. Maybe James's bad press and recent financial loses were threatening to ruin him. He said he needed her. Against her will, that thought moved her.

He also said he wasn't willing to sell the company even though he could. She didn't believe that.

She suspected his reasoning was more practical and calculated. No doubt he wanted to get Walrus Ink on its feet in order to make it a more lucrative prize for prospective buyers.

He would sell when he could get a premium price for it.

He was right, drat the man! She was itching to get back into the thick of things. She had a dozen ideas that her work as a consultant would not allow her to bring to fruition. She had begun making notes the moment she arrived. They lay scattered on the table behind her. Walrus Ink was ripe for some radical rethinking and small enough to quickly absorb those innovations. With a little capital and a lot of hard work, some of her ideas might be readied by spring.

As she turned away from the door, a plan begin to form. James would sell Walrus Ink—of course he would sell when the time was right. So then what was there to stop her from buying it from him?

Her pulse leapt as she reached for her purse and withdrew her bank ledger and calculator. Thanks to James's stratagem in convincing her not to invest her personal finances in Walrus Ink, and thereby keep him from becoming the major shareholder, she hadn't lost a penny in the takeover. The nest egg her father had left her with had grown slowly but steadily.

She looked up several columns of figures and punched the numbers into her calculator. A smile appeared on her face when the sum appeared. She didn't have enough to buy the company outright. And, knowing James, he wouldn't sell it to her at any price. But there were ways to prevent him from finding out who the true buyer was. His tactics had taught her as much. If she were already in place within the company and had made herself indispensable before she approached them, then investors might not stint at backing her. Kent Davis, alone, might bankroll her.

She sat down and began to play with other numbers. She knew from memory the basic costs of running the company that had once been hers. She drew charts and made calculations until, when she finally looked up, the lovely sunset was long gone and an umber blanket of darkness had fallen.

She rose and, pulling her cardigan sweater tightly about her to ward off the chill, went to close the door. When she turned back to the room, she stretched her arms high over her head, pulling every vertebra into alignment. She was tired, but she didn't feel the least bit weary. The work had been worth the effort. She now knew that, with strategic planning and a lot of nerve, she just might pull it off.

As she straightened her notes she speculated on how James would react when she told him she had changed her mind about working for him. She could imagine his smug smile, the certainty in his gaze that once more she had found him irresistible.

Her hands stilled on her papers as she slumped back in her chair. How would she resist that smile and the compelling man who wielded it? She hadn't forgotten how he made her feel by just looking at her. His gaze was more personal than most touches. At least this time she knew what she was up against.

A smile of determination suddenly lit her face. "I'm going to best you at your own game, James Brant!"

Chapter 4

Meryl walked toward her former office not knowing what feelings would assail her when she stepped inside its doors. She was determined to reveal none of them to the man who accompanied her. It was bad enough he had witnessed the emotional welcome offered by many of her former employees who still worked at Walrus Ink. From printers to copyboys, they had been enthusiastically happy to see her while she had barely escaped with her composure intact.

She had played a game of nerves for three days until James had contacted her again. The call had come from Manhattan. She'd heard him out and then said only one word in response: yes.

A tiny smile tugged at her mouth as she recalled the short, stunned silence that had followed her response. She had surprised him. But he had made up for it by greeting her at the front desk this morning. After he had made a point of saying he wouldn't be returning to Hartford until the beginning of the week, she had decided to get a jump on things by coming in today. Yet there he was, standing by the receptionist's desk when she stepped off the elevator. The incident was a useful reminder to expect the unexpected from him.

As she reached for the knobs of the double doors, James reached past her. "Allow me," he said, brushing her shoulder with his.

Meryl backed away from his touch, however unintentional it had been. He didn't seem to notice, but sensations hit her with the force of a meteor impact. She could feel the confidence radiating from him. She tried to block the sensations but, as always, she couldn't ignore his presence. The breath she inhaled contained the faint but undeniable scent of the man. Once his superior height had made her feel sheltered. Now she felt oppressed by his shadow. She felt suddenly trapped as a dozen tiny details assaulted her.

His mood was visible in the relaxed lines of his face. She couldn't remember him ever being so openly at ease. The man she had known had been a restless force, kinetic energy in search of grounding. Yet today the tendons in his neck lay flat and unflexed beneath his skin where his pulse beat in easy rhythm. He smelled of soap and sunshine-warmed skin. She remembered that he never wore cologne because the alcohol content irritated his skin. He didn't need to, the subtle chemistry of his body was attraction enough.

It annoyed her that she was so in tune with his moods. Better to ignore it, she decided. He might be gloating now, but she would have the last laugh.

"After you," he said formally and pushed the doors apart.

She was prepared for glass-and-chrome furnishings or the hard, angular edginess of the modern design that he preferred but that made her ill at ease. She had even dressed in a very tailored suit and swept her hair up in a French twist in order to better fit in with the expected decor. To her amazement and delight the room beyond hadn't been substantially altered since she was CEO.

The walls were still the same warm shade of fresh-churned cream and the carpet remained the shade of new green leaves overlaid with a variety of floral rugs. There were no sharp angles or minimalist spaces here. Mahogany bookcases, elaborately framed illustration art from published books and period furnishings belied the feeling that serious production work was carried on here. Gone was her silver tea service from which she had regularly served afternoon tea to whatever staff or visitors she was meeting with. Yet the bright rose-and-cream floral chintz that she had hand-picked in London still covered the sofa, as did the blue satin-ribbon stripe on the Queen Anne chairs. Sheer muslin drapes diffused the light from floor-to-ceiling windows and shielded the view of the warehouse district.

There was a second desk now in the room, massive and dark, as if an oak tree had suddenly spouted from the grass green carpet. Yet the sense of coziness remained. The feeling of privacy, a little kingdom where thoughts and dreams and imagination would feel welcome; it all remained.

For a moment Meryl shut her eyes, overwhelmed by the bittersweet familiarity of it all. Then she remembered she had an audience. Without voicing her surprise, she turned to stare at him.

"You look surprised," he said as he closed the doors and leaned against them. "I thought you'd be pleased."

Doubt crept into Meryl's expression. "You once ridiculed my office decor, said it looked more like a Victorian garden room than the offices of a successful publisher."

"It did. It does." A smile crinkled the corners of his smoky gray eyes as he surveyed her closely. "But I've modified my ideas about what constitutes the trappings of success.

"I didn't feel qualified to replace your antique book collection, nor your display of dolls," he continued as he moved away from the doors toward her. "However, I did persuade O'Connor to loan us this." He waved a hand toward the corner of the room to her right.

Meryl turned, her eyes widening in astonishment as she recognized the fanciful illustration hanging on the far wall. "Timon the Ash Can Cat!" she cried as she hurried over to the painting.

It was an acrylic and watercolor of a large scruffy orange-and-white tabby with a torn ear from which a gold earring hung. He was dressed in a battered blue trench coat, knit cap and unlaced high-top sneakers.

"It's even better than I remembered." Meryl cast a sidelong glance of gratitude at James until she remembered that this was a game of warfare, no matter how polite, and he was the enemy.

"I tried for years to persuade Tomaltach to sell the entire collection of illustrations from the series to me," she said when she turned back to the painting. "However did you talk him into parting with even one?"

"I bribed him," James replied. "I remembered how much you admired and wanted it."

Meryl arched a brow. "What made you think I'd ever step foot inside this office again and see it?"

One side of his mouth lifted. "You're here, aren't you?"

She'd walked right into that one. Still his smug zinger rankled. "That door still swings both ways."

He raised a brow. "Thinking of running out already? Job too big? Or are you just unable to get past your feelings for me?"

Meryl's breath lodged somewhere in the middle of her chest. "I have no feelings for you," she managed to get out in little more than a whisper.

His brows lifted in mocking surprise. "Sure you do. You hate my guts. I can handle that. Can you?"

Meryl found her breath. He thought that all she felt toward him was simple anger. He hadn't analyzed it into its components of rage, shame, hurt, anguish, betrayal, regret, failure, loss and bitterness. How little he understood her.

Needing to defend her infatuation with the character of Timon she said, "I don't expect you to be familiar with the series aside from the fact that it's our bestseller. Timon is not just an alley cat, he's a homeless cat."

James's lips twitched. "So I've been told."

To hammer home her point that he was not in touch with his company's philosophy toward publishing she said, "Tomaltach O'Connor's genius lies in his ability to incorporate the delicacy of Beatrix Potter's gentle creatures with a more gritty reality that modern children find irresistible. His emphatic renderings of Timon are really what have made the Ash Can series a success."

"I don't imagine the author would appreciate your assessment."

Meryl turned with a challenge in her eyes. "What makes you say that?"

"I've read them," he replied. "Don't look so surprised. Despite what you think, I didn't slither out from under a rock fully grown. I have family with nieces and nephews. I bought each of them a set of *Timon the Ash Can Cat* for Christmas. Naturally, I had to read them to the youngest ones."

"I see." He had managed to surprise her yet again. "The last thing I would ever have imagined was that you were good with children."

He frowned at her. "I earned every nasty accusation that's been leveled at me as a businessman," he said heavily. "That doesn't preempt me from having a heart. I like children."

A sudden pain near her own heart made Meryl look away. She didn't believe him, couldn't afford to believe that there was any gentleness beneath his steely exterior. He was just making nice, trying to soften her up. She had to keep remembering he was a master at manipulation.

She glanced up at him to deliver a little bombshell of her own. "Actually, I am the author of the Ash Can series."

"I know." James grinned at her jerk of surprise. "You forget who signs the checks these days."

"The royalty checks don't go to me," Meryl said in annoyance. At every turn he seemed to stay one step ahead of her.

"I realize you've gone out of your way to keep your authorship a secret, but the homeless shelter organizations who benefit from the sales of *Timon* wanted to honor the author so, naturally, I had to find out who the author was."

Meryl felt a tremor of alarm. "You told them?"

"No."

She frowned suspecting that he was lying, or keeping the information to himself for another reason. "Why not?"

"Because I didn't think you wanted them to know."

"Is that the only reason?" She couldn't mask her skepticism.

He shrugged. "What other reason could there be?"

"I don't know. Give me a few minutes to think about it."

He scowled. "You're welcome."

Meryl turned once more to the canvas. She supposed she was being ungracious, but she had been bitten too many times to cut him any slack. Even if it made for a few embarrassing moments now and in the future, she couldn't afford to let her guard down again.

"I hope you'll continue to keep silent on the subject of my authorship. I didn't write the books for notoriety. I wanted to fund a worthwhile organization without the usual fanfare that goes with a prominent person giving money to the less fortunate. I sent the manuscript to all the illustrators we had worked with. Once Tomaltach's sketches came in, I didn't bother to look at the rest. He had captured in paint what my words could not."

"I can appreciate your altruistic motives, but you must see that it's hard to think of a good reason why I should pass up a chance for a little positive press. Kids and their parents would eat up the idea that those books fund homeless shelters like the kind Timon lives in."

Meryl stiffened. She knew it! "What do you want from me not to use that?"

James could tell by the stiff tilt of her lips and the way her hand had unconsciously clenched on her purse strap that she expected him to propose nothing less than blackmail. "I want you, as one of Walrus Ink's authors, to write another book for the series, something we can have on the shelves by May 1."

"That's impossible!" Meryl snapped and then realized her heated reply was more than the matter required.

She reached up to smooth a stray hair from her eyes as she took a calming breath. The strands sliding through her fingers seemed to vibrate with electricity, as if they were grounding wires for the emotional current streaming between them. If he touched her she knew there'd be sparks.

"Tomaltach requires months to create the illustrations once the script is finished," she said more calmly. "He likes to live with the words until they become pictures."

"Then he'll have to stop indulging himself for this one," James retorted.

The blind audacity of that statement left Meryl blinking. "You really have no idea how a creative personality works, do you?"

"Why don't you tell me," he responded in challenge as he slid his hands into his trouser pockets.

"Creativity requires the right mood and inspiration."

"Moods can be manipulated and inspiration can be manufactured."

Meryl's eyes narrowed as she encountered the smoky warmth of his gaze. Is that what he had done while they were together, manufactured the mood and manipulated her emotions to achieve what he desired from her? She slammed a mental door on that thought. They were discussing business. Why couldn't she keep her mind on that? "In other words, you think creativity can be forced."

He nodded slowly. "If you coddle people they'll spend their time inventing endless excuses. That wastes your time.

Some of the most creative people I ever dealt with did their best work under the crunch of deadlines and drop-dead dates."

Meryl folded her arms under her bosom. "And how many artists at Walrus Ink do you have a good working relationship with, Mr. Brant?"

His heavy brows lowered until he scowled at her. Not for the first time he reminded her of a prizefighter. If she had been facing him in the ring his pugnacious expression would have had her dancing backward in alarm. "I've been busy with other concerns. That's why I've hired you, to work your magic."

Meryl considered repeating her sister's opinion of the handling of writers, but decided against it. He would probably regard Jacqui's words as a form of disloyalty. "Fine. Then I suggest you make yourself scarce for the next two weeks while I assess and try to repair relations with your artistic community. Oh, and I won't use the phrase 'drop-dead date' with any of your writers and illustrators. Walrus Ink was once a place where civility could be maintained during business hours."

"Point taken."

He was still scowling. She knew he hadn't expected her to keep her temper and remain civil under his scathing assessment of her style of doing business. Truth to tell, she was rather surprised and pleased that she had. Everything depended upon her retaining her poise. He was suspicious by nature and she couldn't afford to rouse his suspicions if her plan was to succeed.

She summoned a scant smile. "Now that we understand each other, I can do the job you hired me to do."

"Good." She saw the lines of tension ease around his eyes. "Then I'll leave you to get to it. I have business to attend to myself."

She turned to watch him cross the room, expecting him to head for the door. She didn't even frown when he moved instead toward the massive desk that stood in the corner on the other side of the entry. She suspected that was his desk and that he had left something there he wanted. She only began to frown when he dropped into the chair behind the desk, flipped up the lid of his laptop computer and punched what she assumed was the on button.

After several heartbeats he picked the computer up and settled it in his lap, then he lifted and swung his legs up so that his feet were propped on the desk top.

"What are you doing?" she demanded as she strode over to him.

James looked up at her tone. "Settling down to work."

She shook her head vigorously, freeing a length of rich red-brown hair from her twist. "You can't work here."

"Oh, no?" He looked deliberately around his surroundings. "This is my desk. My chair. My computer." When his gaze again met hers there was the maddening glitter of amusement in it. "Where else would I work?"

She drummed her unpolished nails against his desk top. "Then you can't mean for me to work in here."

"I can and I do." He leaned back in the oversize leather chair as he continued to look at her. "I want you close at hand. We've lots of things to go through if we're going to hit the ground running."

She shook her head, her voice emphatic. "I won't do it. I demand my own office space."

He made a sound halfway between a chuckle and a grunt. "I don't intend to wear out the hallway carpeting looking for you."

"Then phone or fax me."

As she met his implacable gray gaze with one of golden green hostility, James realized he had at last hit an impasse. Backing down was not in his vocabulary. Compromise was the best he could come up with. "I'm not usually here. We'll only be sharing office space when I'm in town."

Meryl was certain there was a trap in that statement. "How often are you in town?"

He shrugged, clearly annoyed that she was pursuing the subject. "Let me ask you something. How do you intend to catch up on things without my help?"

"You're paying me to manage on my own."

"No doubt, but it'll take longer without me, and time is the one commodity neither of us can afford to waste."

He was making sense, but she didn't trust it. "If that's your answer, then you'd better find yourself another consultant. I won't be spied on by the person I've been hired to help."

His congenial expression flattened out. If she had thought it was possible she would have said he looked offended. "Is it so hard for us to share the same space for a few hours a day?"

You bet it is! she wanted to shout. Breathing the same air hour after hour, aware of his every movement, of every word and sigh, it would be impossible. The subtle murmur that had been humming between them ever since they entered the room suddenly rose in volume until all she could hear and think of was the dangerous melody of tension between them. She couldn't handle this pressure on a daily basis.

"Very well." She heard her own words in shock. Her mind had just said no. Where had that yes come from?

He was smiling at her. "I thought you'd see reason in the arrangement. Now if you'll excuse me, Meryl, I have things to do."

"Ms. Wallis."

He paused in midkeystroke to glance again at her. "Ms. Wallis," she repeated. "If you don't want rumors to start circulating about this arrangement, we should keep things formal."

She didn't know how he did it, made his eyes darken and dim, then flash like lightning between storm clouds. "Would it bother you if rumors started circulating about us?"

She shoved all her loneliness into the breach torn in her defenses by his appeal. "It would work against what I've been hired to do, which is improve your credibility with the publishing community. Why handicap me?''

She watched him consider that statement word by word. "Very well, *Ms*. Wallis.''

It was five o'clock before Meryl looked up from her desk to check the time. Pencil in hand, she reached up to massage her brow as she wondered where the time had gone. Through the fretwork of her fingers she surreptitiously regarded her office partner, who was deep in quiet conversation on the phone.

His feet were still propped up on his desk and his computer was once more in his lap. He had shed his jacket, and his pearl gray shirt was drawn taut against his torso. Long lean legs, long lean torso, he was stretched out for the appreciation of her feminine eye. But she didn't want to appreciate his male attributes. She wanted him out of sight and out of mind.

Because she had arrived late in the morning, she had worked right through lunch. She hadn't even allowed James to send out for a sandwich for her when he did. Having expected to have the day to herself, she had packed a breakfast bar in her purse and consumed it during one of the coffee breaks she had allowed herself.

She glanced down again at the work before her. She had been poring over royalty statements and reading the minutes of months of editorial meetings, trying to get a feel for the direction the staff had been pursuing. Most often the staff seemed to have spent their time debating and second-guessing what they thought their boss might want. Afraid to go out on a limb, they had stagnated.

She didn't look up a few minutes later when the chair across the room creaked. She didn't respond to the gentle whisper of her name. She didn't want to acknowledge, let alone talk to, James Brant any more than she absolutely had to. She had to abandon her see-nothing-hear-nothing tactic when his shadow crossed her desk.

"Let's go have a drink to celebrate our new association."

Meryl kept her head down. "It doesn't seem an event worth celebrating."

From her peripheral vision she saw him bend down until his face was almost on a level with her own. Forced to look up, she encountered his mocking gaze. "Once you thought anytime we were together was worth celebrating."

James knew he was pushing, but he couldn't stop himself. She had ignored him all day, giving him no more notice than if he were a block of wood sitting in the corner. Now she waited so long to reply he thought she might not say anything at all.

Finally she shook her head slowly. "Once I believed in the tooth fairy. We all grow up."

Encouraged, he straightened up. He had a hide as thick as a rhino's when he was going after what he wanted. "Then consider the drink a business obligation. You can demonstrate to me your technique in dealing socially with business clients."

She gave him a narrow-eyed stare. "Very well."

A grin eased into his face. "I've got business with my chief printer downstairs. I'll come back by for you in half an hour."

"I'd rather meet you somewhere." She paused for emphasis. "After seven."

He looked annoyed. "You're going to work that late your first day?"

She tapped her pencil against her lips. "Is that a problem?"

"No. Fine. Seven." He seemed to regroup, his speech picking up speed. "I know a great little place tucked—"

"Seven at Charlie's," she injected smoothly. "It's down the block, at the riverfront. Frequented mostly by cops and dockworkers." She glanced pointedly at his expensive suit. "If it's too rough for you..."

"No, fine." But she saw the lines of doubt furrow his brow and knew he was wondering what she was up to. He could soon find out.

At precisely 7:01 p.m., Meryl stepped into the smoky clapboard-walled structure called Charlie's. A horseshoe-shaped bar dominated the room. Along either wall red upholstered booths offered a modicum of privacy from the general boisterousness of the Friday evening crowd. She supposed the decor hadn't changed much in fifty years, except for the fifty-four-inch projection-screen TV that took up a good portion of the back wall. The football teams looked nearly life-size from the doorway. The sounds of the stadium crowd blended and blurred with the chatter of the customers and the country-and-western tune blaring from the jukebox.

Finally she saw James. He was sitting at the bar and, in his executive dress, he looked like someone who had accidently wandered in from the street. Charlie's had a special kind of clientele and James Brant definitely wasn't it. Her smile drew into a grin as she approached him.

"Sorry, I forgot to mention the bar doesn't have a ban against cigarettes. Smoke doesn't bother you, does it?" she asked sweetly.

His expression said he didn't believe she cared one bit whether smoke bothered him, but he only said, "Saved you a seat." He pulled out the wooden stool he had tucked under the bar.

Meryl sat down and waved at the bartender who waved back.

"Friend of yours?" James asked.

"Uh-huh." Meryl looked around the room.

"Come here often?" James persisted.

"Haven't been here in a while," she offered, avoiding eye contact as she surveyed the room a second time. Suddenly her gaze swung toward him. "It is rather seedy. I'll understand if you want to leave."

"Not until we've had our drink." Nothing less than dynamite was going to budge him from her side.

"Whiskey, neat," she said to the bartender who greeted her familiarly.

"Beer, whatever's on tap," James said when the bartender cocked a brow in his direction. "I thought you were a wine drinker," he added to Meryl.

Meryl didn't answer, merely scanned the crowd for the one person she had hoped to find here tonight. Finally she saw him standing in the back with a pool cue in hand, watching a tight end zigzag his way through a wall of linebackers projected on the TV screen.

She turned back to the bar as a full shot glass was set down before her. She waited until James picked up his beer, then she picked up her drink, clicked it casually against his mug and said, "To business." Then she raised it to her lips and emptied the contents into her mouth in one long swallow. When she was done, she breathed and blinked and lowered her empty glass back onto the counter with a distinct clink.

She turned to James. Through the whiskey fumes that seemed to have risen before her eyes, she saw that he was staring at her with his mouth slightly ajar, his beer untouched. "Good night, Mr. Brant."

He reached out to halt her. "Wait a minute. What about our friendly chat?"

She glanced down at her glass. "You said *a* drink. I've had mine. Will you pay or should I?"

"I'll get it!" James snarled as she reached for her purse.

She smiled, but it didn't reach her eyes. "Have a nice weekend, Mr. Brant. I intend to."

He watched her walk away, not toward the door, but toward the back of the room. As she passed down the length of the bar with back straight and heels clinking purposefully, her hips swayed just enough to attract the glance of every man she passed. Feeling that she might need his protection, James decided to wait. Obviously she was going to the ladies' room. Not that she appeared to need his help. Men looked, but not one of them tried to stop her or even engage her in conversation. They seem to guess what he knew, that she was blisteringly angry and in no mood to be nice.

Then she did a totally unexpected thing. She walked up to one of the off-duty cops who'd shed his uniform but not the stance that was a dead giveaway even to a civilian. He saw the man greet her with a big hug and a sloppy kiss that landed just above her mouth by her nose, then shout to the bartender for another round of beer.

James's gut did a flip-flop. What was this? She'd left his company for that of another man? His eyes narrowed on the man who appeared to be about thirty, in enviably good shape and with all-American good looks. He saw the man's hand stray familiarly over the swell of Meryl's hip before returning to her waist. The Meryl he had known had always objected when he touched her familiarly in public. Was this for his benefit? He couldn't tell, but he knew what it was doing to his temper. His face felt as hot as if he'd stepped into a furnace.

Several other men greeted her before the first man used his pool cue to point down the length of the room to where James sat. James stiffened, though he was familiar with the feeling of being the object of interest as other heads turned his way. He couldn't hear what the man said, but Meryl's response drew the kind of male laughter that made every other man in earshot feel very territorial.

Not about to be run off, James settled in and watched until he had finished his beer and then the second one he ordered. An hour later he knew he couldn't risk drinking a third when he had to drive, but the bartender was glaring at him. This was no posh club where the exorbitant cost of the drinks paid for an evening's seat. Obviously if he was finished buying, then he was expected to leave.

Reluctantly he moved toward the door, but not without a last backward glance at Meryl, who was deeply engrossed in a game of pool. She had taken off her severely tailored suit, exposing her long-sleeved turtleneck that clung seductively to every line and full swell of her torso. The cops certainly were enjoying the sight. When she bent forward to make a shot, several of them leaned back to better their view of her backside.

James felt something deep inside him coil and writhe in ugly threat. He was jealous! Flat-out, bug-eyed jealous. And there wasn't a thing he could do about it now if he ever hoped to win her trust.

He had never suspected she knew how to play pool, or drank her whiskey neat, or had ever before been in a bar like this, let alone knew a portion of the clientele. There were obviously many things he didn't know about her. But her actions hadn't put him off; she'd only intrigued him. And perhaps that's what she intended.

A little past eight-thirty Meryl reached for her suit jacket. "Sorry, guys, I've got to go."

"Hey, it's early," complained her pool partner, Ned Miller. "Besides, we're winning."

"Sorry, but I'm beat," she replied as he moved to hold her jacket for her. "Thanks for the beer and the company. I'll be back in touch."

"Anytime," Ned answered. "You know where to find me. Here, I'll walk you out. This isn't the best neighborhood."

As his fellow officers chuckled and razzed him with comments like "Remember the little wife!" they headed for the exit.

Meryl stepped through the exit out into the much cooler dark night. As she half turned to speak again to Ned, a long dark shadow detached itself from the nearby gloom, making her gasp.

Ned whipped around, but the figure stepped into the red neon glow of the beer sign in the bar window, revealing himself.

"James!" Meryl voiced in genuine surprise. "What are you doing out here?"

Ignoring her companion, James sent her a penetrating glance. "Waiting for you. I didn't see your car when I left. Thought you might need a ride."

"I came by cab," Meryl replied. "Ned was going to hail one for me."

James glanced, just barely, at Ned. "I'll take her home."

Ned turned to Meryl. "That okay with you?"

"Yes. Thanks, Ned." Meryl leaned in to kiss his cheek. "As I said, I'll be in touch soon."

Ned nodded, but gave James another long, searching glance before he turned and went back inside.

"My car's over here." James pointed midway down the block.

"You didn't have to wait," Meryl said as she fell into step beside him. The street was dark and empty except for the neon spot of brilliance and muffled sounds of the bar from which they were rapidly retreating. The only clear sounds were their footsteps, her heels echoing one and a half times for each of his longer strides.

"How well do you know that guy?" James finally said.

Meryl smiled in the dark. "Ned? Quite well."

James made a noise that sounded suspiciously like a growl. "Does Davis know about Ned?"

"I don't think so. After all, it doesn't concern him."

"I wonder if Davis would agree."

Meryl glanced at him as she hunched her shoulders against the buffeting crisp breeze. "Are you going to tell me the real reason why you waited?"

James glared at her. "No." His gaze raked down her to where she was hugging her arms to her body. "You're cold." It wasn't a question. In fact, it sounded like an accusation.

"No, really, I'm..." Meryl gave up protesting as he paused to shrug out of his suit jacket.

Moments later he swung it around her shoulders. "Thanks," she said when his hands smoothed out the shoulders and slid down her arms.

Alarm skittered along her nerve endings as he suddenly pulled her in against him. "What do you think you're doing?" she questioned nervously as her cheek collided with his shirtfront, heated by the man beneath.

"You're shivering because you worked up a sweat in there." His harsh, accusatory voice came from somewhere above her head. "Now you're out in the cold without a coat. Any child would know better than that."

She was certain any child would, but that didn't make intimate contact with him preferable. That was because the raw heat surging through her wasn't all his.

"It didn't seem that cold," she said in a choked voice as his palms began rubbing slowly up and down her back.

She wouldn't exactly say they moved with caressing intent, but that didn't stop her body from reacting to him as if this were the most sensual of massages. Where his fingers passed, they left little tingling impressions on her skin that seemed directly connected to her spinal column. That warmth, in turn, seemed to radiate out in all directions in delicious, warming eddies. He was right. She had been cold. Now she was radiantly alive to his touch. His touch?

Stiffening, she pulled abruptly away from him. "Thank you. I'm fine now."

"Liar." She looked up straight into his pale eyes, which despite the darkness, glowed faintly.

"Why didn't you introduce me to your friend, Ned?" Again the gnarling accusation that she had done something wrong.

Meryl shrugged and had to grab the lapels to keep his coat from sliding off her slender shoulders. "It didn't seem important."

He reached up and touched her cheek. The touch accomplished what he wanted it to to. She looked up again. This time he could see her eyes. She had been avoiding that, denying him entry into her inner self. She had more evasion maneuvers than a spy ship, yet he had to find a way to get to her.

"Anything to do with you is important to me." He said each word slowly, weighing them with his rough rumble.

Meryl felt his words roll over her like distant thunder and resonate bone deep. He was staring at her, trying to tell her something she didn't want to hear, yet couldn't ignore. "Why?"

"Think about it." He turned and indicated that she was to walk on.

The drive was accomplished in near silence, the only exchange of words when she gave him directions to her new apartment.

She had cleaned house in more ways than one after they broke up. She had gotten rid of every reminder of him, everything about him. It was irrational, when anybody could tell him where she lived, but she had even changed her location. More to the point she had bought a new bed. He would never know that because he would never again be allowed inside her door. Of that much she was certain. Just being in James Brant's vicinity dredged up reminders of how far beyond control she had once been where he was concerned. His sophisticated form of machismo had once leveled all resistance. But she was older, wiser. She would never lose control to that degree with any man again. Never.

So why was she sitting beside him, enveloped in his clothing, her body only inches from his in the tight confines of his sports car? Why was she so vividly aware of the aura of sensuality cocooning them? Was it because he, like she, was remembering how they had once driven home nightly to her home in near silence?

For the two months it lasted, the anticipation of the erotic hours they would share had made them both uncharacteristically shy. It had been as if they both understood that a touch or word spoken too soon would take the edge off the delirium toward which they were hurtling. James was a man who didn't waste words or actions. Yet he knew how to savor the moment.

Meryl glanced at his profile, rough cut and slightly battered but exuding raw power. There were so many things about him she didn't know. Had he really broken his nose? When? How? She did know his rough hands were a result of his hobby. He refinished antique furniture. He said his Manhattan apartment was full of hand-finished pieces other people had thrown away as unsalvageable. She didn't know how good he was. She had never seen his apartment, not even once.

What had occurred between them had been a reckless wild time, out of sync with reality. Maybe he wasn't as much to blame as the cosmos. Perhaps their meeting had been a random collision in the universe. Maybe James Brant had been her very own natural disaster, a bolt out of the blue that had blasted her heart.

Meryl shifted uncomfortably as the lighted front of her apartment building came into view, aware of the anticipation swelling in her chest. But it wasn't desire. It was the expectation that she might be forced into an altercation with the man beside her. She wouldn't, couldn't, let him into her life again. And that meant her home was off-limits.

He exited his car smoothly and came around to help her out even though she had already opened the door on her own.

Meryl swung his coat from her shoulders and handed it to him without quite looking at him. "Thank you, so much." She hurried her speech, not wanting to prolong the parting. "I'll call New York in a few days, whenever I have something to report."

"That won't be necessary."

Meryl's wary gaze lifted to his face. He seemed angry, yet she could tell his enmity was not directed at her. "I'm not going anywhere, Meryl." He paused, his silver-bright eyes lasering in on her face. "Not until we've straightened out this mess."

Meryl turned and walked quickly away, half-surprised when he didn't follow her. And yet the expression on his face had said he wouldn't. That expression—could she trust it? Could she even believe what she'd seen? Her last fleeting image of him contained an expression she had never seen on his face. It was one of regret.

Chapter 5

The building was eerily quiet on Saturday. The presses didn't run seven days a week unless they were up against a deadline. She had come in today in the hope of sneaking a peek at Walrus Ink's current profit and loss statements. That kind of information would prove invaluable as she planned her takeover. As she rode the elevator from the ground floor to the offices above, Meryl wondered if she was really going to be able to pull off her plan. Things hadn't gotten off to a very good start. If Walrus Ink hadn't maintained twenty-four-hour security that included a guard, then she would be on her way home instead of upstairs.

She hadn't thought to ask for keys or a security pass the day before. But then she hadn't planned on coming in on Saturday until she woke up and realized she hadn't accomplished nearly as much as she had wanted to the day before. If she was going to succeed in engineering a plot to buy back Walrus Ink she would need to know a lot more about the company's present operations. Why twiddle her thumbs at home, she decided, when she could be putting these off-hours to use? Luckily, the guard had been willing to make a quick call to obtain authorization to give her entry.

Eager to begin, she pushed past the opening elevator door, balancing a stack of old records pulled from her personal files, her briefcase, a thermos of coffee and a white bakery bag with two jelly doughnuts inside. As she slipped past the doors the strap of her purse slung over her shoulder snagged, jerking her to a halt. She saved the records, briefcase and thermos that swayed dangerously, but her bakery bag slid off the top of the pile and onto the floor. As she edged gingerly the rest of the way out of the elevator, her right foot stepped into something soft and squishy.

"So much for jelly doughnuts." Meryl sighed as she lifted her foot from the squashed bag. She didn't need them, anyway. But she had been looking forward to the treat.

She wasn't especially surprised to find one of the French doors leading to her office was open. Cleaning services sometimes forgot to shut them. She was all the way inside the room before she noticed that there was someone else in the room. James Brant occupied the deep contours of the leather chair behind his desk.

He didn't look up at once, which gave her plenty of time to register details. He wore a nubby open-weave navy blue sweater. The rolled-back sleeves revealed forearms ropy with muscle and rivers of veins shadowed by traces of dark hair. One denim-clad leg was crossed over the other at an angle. A sheaf of papers rested in the triangle of his lap. His body had a deeply relaxed looseness to it, a sign that he'd been in the same position for a long time. Perched on the last half inch of his nose was a pair of small wire-rim reading glasses. He looked less like a prizefighter today and more like a scholar, perhaps a professor of the pugilistic arts.

Finally he looked up, unsurprised by her presence, and smiled. "Don't I rate a hello?"

"What are you doing here?" Meryl knew that this was the wrong reply. After all, it was his office, his company. But he had so startled her guilty conscience that it seemed as if she'd been discovered flagrante delicto in intrigue.

If he noted the hostility in her tone he didn't show it. He merely shrugged. "What does it look like?"

Meryl gripped the edges of her bundles until her fingers cramped as she reminded herself that, so far, she'd done nothing wrong. "Sorry, it's just that you startled me. The guard didn't say there were other people in the building."

"Who did you think he called?"

"I don't know. Someone else." Some business spy she was!

"Hadn't you better put that load down before you drop it?"

Meryl debated only a moment before turning to walk over to her desk. If she left now it would look suspicious. He was likely to think that she was afraid of him or up to no good, both of which happened to be true.

She bent her knees to slide the stack onto the top of the elegant curve-legged Louis Quatorze-styled desk as the image of her squashed bakery bag came to mind. She had been looking forward to kicking off her sneakers and putting her feet up on her old desk while she enjoyed the illusion that, for a few precious hours, Walrus Ink belonged once more to her.

"What brings you in on Saturday? I don't think I said anything about paying for overtime."

Indignation straightened Meryl's posture as she turned to face him. "I wasn't expecting compensation from you for what I came to do." Quite the contrary.

She heard his sucked-in breath, but he merely said, "Is that coffee?"

Meryl clutched her thermos a little tighter. "Yes, I thought it would save me from having to crank up the office pot."

A rueful smile softened his expression. "I gave the office pot a crack, but there must be some secret to it. The result looks and tastes like asphalt. Would you mind sharing?"

"I suppose not," she replied reluctantly. She had lost her doughnuts and now she was going to have to share her coffee.

Ordinarily that wouldn't have bothered her. But everything James did raised her hackles. "You still take sugar?"

He nodded and made a move to rise. "I'll get it."

"That's all right." Meryl hurriedly moved toward the door ahead of him. "I need napkins and a stirrer myself. I'll be right back."

She saw the scowl on his face as she escaped into the hallway and knew what he was thinking. She had never been a coffee fetcher in her life, nor had she ever asked a subordinate to fetch for her. But she had grabbed at the excuse to get away from him, in order to recompose herself.

She scooped up the ruined doughnut bag as she passed the elevator and carried it with her down the hallway to the small room that served as a combination lunchroom and snack bar. One wall was lined with snack and soft-drink machines. On the other were cabinets for dishes above countertop space, along with a hot plate, microwave and full-size refrigerator. She dropped her bag in the trash receptacle near the door. As she reached for packets of sugar and napkins, she spied the coffee machine in the far corner. The aroma drew her over to it.

She picked up the carafe and stared at it. It seemed to be the right rich color and it certainly smelled good. On impulse she reached for a paper cup and poured two tablespoons' worth into it. Her eyes widened and then narrowed as she took a sip. The coffee tasted fine, wonderful, in fact.

"He lied!" she announced to the empty room. Why? Was it to force her into compromise? Was he trying to reinforce his position as her boss?

Reluctantly another possibility superimposed itself on her more dire thoughts. Maybe he had just been flirting.

That idea upset her more than the other two. With a man like James there was no such thing as a harmless flirtation. He didn't waste words, act on impulse or make random gestures. Had she misunderstood the real reason he wanted her to come to work for him? What, exactly, did he have in mind?

Meryl tossed the rest of her coffee in the sink and ran the water to rinse away the telltale stain. Thanks to a small lie she was on to him. Whatever he thought he was up to, she would counter it.

As she walked back, she considered packing up and leaving, but she hadn't finished checking on inventory, regional sales, the customer list or a half-dozen other smaller details that would help her draw up the prospectus she would need to interest prospective investors. But now that she had caught him lying to her, she felt less guilty about her own subterfuge. She would stay and fight fire with fire.

A grin appeared on her face as she passed back through the office doors. He was right—she had always loved a good fair fight. Now she was going to try her hand at fighting as dirty as he.

James regarded her surreptitiously as she entered, wondering why he had bothered to tell a lie that was so easily exposed. When he spotted her smile every muscle in his body tensed. He deserved her scorn and contempt. He deserved to squirm in embarrassment, but, in fact, what his body was doing was thumping with unexpected desire. He half wanted a confrontation, any excuse to blow off a little of the frustrated desire that made his skin feel too tight whenever she was around.

As she passed him without pause, he took her in from the top of her pinned-up hair with dark wisps framing her face to her long baggy red sweater down to her legs encased in black leggings. Those long shapely legs gave him pause. Visions of her sprawled naked, flushed and inviting in sheets they had just rumpled with their fiercely tender lovemaking sent steamy tendrils of desire to wrap around his mind.

Each time, after they had made love, she would wrap one of those luscious long legs about his hips and hold on for dear life, as if she had thought he would suddenly disappear.

Sometimes he had half wished he could disappear. He had known he was in trouble, falling in love when he couldn't afford the luxury. But he'd been selfish enough to take what was being offered and kid himself that he was causing no damage to either of them.

James set aside his reading glasses, the better to see her. His silver gaze openly tracked her passage across the room with a naked longing he was glad her turned back shielded from her. It was time he faced up to reality. He had hoped her attraction would have lessened. No, that was a lie. He had hoped her attraction would remain the same as before—hot, familiar, manageable. He hadn't counted on her uniquely feminine allure knocking him to his knees.

The need coursing through him now was feral. He felt the ancient pulse of life—thick as his blood—telling him that he was male, that by right of the laws of nature what he wanted was his if he could master it. The urgent hunger was primitive, the instinct to possess and protect something he had never experienced with anyone but Meryl, something unique to his very nature. If he had never thought so before, he understood now that the civilizing influence on behavior was sometimes paper-thin.

As Meryl reached out and began to unscrew the top of the thermos standing on her desk, her baggy sweater draped away from her and the gentle swing of her braless breasts snared his interest. When had she begun going about without a bra? The slightly uptight woman he had known had never even wanted to wear anything too revealing.

Velvet-wrapped steel, that's how he thought of her. No flash but all class. Yet he knew her secrets. When she was aroused by passion tiny golden daggers shot through the green sea of her irises.

There'd been gold in those green depths last night.

He leaned back in his chair, drawing a slightly easier breath. Just maybe he wasn't the only one caught up in this web of desire spinning about them. Just maybe it was going to be as difficult for her to occupy the same space as him day after day. Damn, he hoped so!

Meryl took her time pouring coffee in the two mugs she'd brought back with her. Finally she picked up one, along with two packets of sugar and the stirrer, and carried them across to James's desk. "Here you go." She plunked the mug down a little hard and a few drops splashed over the edge. She didn't apologize.

"Thanks." James reached for the mug and took a sip. Smiling broadly, he lowered the rim. "Perfect."

Meryl gave him a jaundiced look as she extended her hand with the sugar packets.

For a second she didn't recognize the strange darkening that stole over his face. Then the color bloomed deep and rosy on the ridges of his cheeks. He was blushing!

For the next two hours, Meryl worked very hard at concentrating on the folders she had left on her desk the day before. But, unlike yesterday, every move James made drew her attention. He was a rocker, the springs of his chair making a faint but constant rhythmic creaking. He also liked to murmur comments to himself. After a while she turned on the radio, hoping the soothing violins of the classical piece playing would mask his distractions. It didn't work. He began to hum along, driving her wild because his pitch wasn't particularly good. She clamped down on her annoyance, but the moment the piece ended she changed the channel. Marvin Gaye came on singing "Sexual Healing." She passed on. After a few more tries at finding a suitable selection of music he wouldn't hum along with, she flipped it off.

So much for her hope of delving into Walrus Ink's current profit and loss statements. With James on guard duty, however innocent his intentions, she was stuck poring over columns listing the shippings, reserves, and returns of last year's titles, things every editor had access to. Without looking up, she reached for one of her personal folders that contained similar listings from an earlier year.

"What are those files for?"

The sound of James's deep voice so close by made her fumble the folder she had just picked up. Several pages slipped free and sailed to the floor. She looked up in accusation because, despite his constant distracting behavior, she hadn't heard him rise and approach her. "They're my personal records."

She bent to scoop up the sheets but he moved quickly and beat her to two of them. She saw his gaze scan them before he handed them back. With a sinking feeling she recognized them as profit and loss statements from her own files. He didn't say a word. He didn't need to. The expression on his face said it all. He was now suspicious.

Meryl shoved the papers back into her file with shaking hands, knowing she was going to have to try to bluff. "I thought it would be instructive to compare the last two years of Walrus Ink's sales figures—books shipped, percentages returned—with those from previous years, when I ran things."

"You dropped old profit and loss sheets."

Damn him, he didn't miss a thing! She didn't dare look him in the eye as she improvised on her lie. "Yes, well, I assumed you would allow me to see the profit and loss sheets for the current year." Meryl looked around as if expecting to find them already lying on her desk. "Where are they?"

"I didn't hire you as an accountant." Annoyance whipped through his words. "I hired you as a creative consultant. You're to focus on the editorial end of the business."

Meryl looked up. She had nothing to lose now. "I need to know what your financial situation is before I can make reasonable decisions about editorial direction. Otherwise I might offer wholly impractical suggestions."

He shoved his hands into his jeans pockets. "Come up with the ideas. I'll let you know if they are impractical."

"Of course." Meryl let her pique show through otherwise she knew she would look even guiltier. "You're the boss."

He flinched or maybe he just shrugged quickly. "I came over to ask if you'd like to go out and get some lunch. I didn't have breakfast. Did you?"

"Yes," she lied. "A huge one actually, cereal, juice, toast coffee, the works. Couldn't eat a thing." Roused by the image she'd conjured, her stomach issued a quite audible growl.

She saw James smirk. "In that case," he said, "why don't you come downstairs with me as I go out. I want to show you our newest acquisition. It's a computerized press and quite impressive."

"Desktop publishing?" she queried.

"Much better than that. With the software packages we've installed, we can animate practically any illustration. It will save the artist's time if we can a generate a good approximation of their original drawings for future books. We may soon be able to make the hop from books to limited video animation without a hitch."

"Sounds really expensive," Meryl countered, wondering how she was going to explain the need for so outrageous an investment of capital to investors, let alone cover those expenses her first year back in operation.

"I picked it up cheap from a special-effects studio that was upgrading. What's a major investment for an outfit like ours is mere chicken feed for them. They stay on the cutting edge of visual technology whereas we don't have to."

"Even so, that sounds a little grand for Walrus Ink."

James opened the heavy metal cage of the freight elevator, allowing her to step in first. "Frankly, the first time I entered Walrus Ink's premises, I was skeptical of a publishing company whose offices were on the top floor while the actual printing processes took place on the floors beneath."

He pulled the doors shut and punched the down button. As the elevator lurched into motion he said over the noise of the grinding gears, "This hands-on approach to publishing seemed quaint, archaic and inefficient. Subsequent experience with the business proved me to be in error."

He gave her one of those long, thoughtful looks she had been encountering for two nerve-racking days. "In fact, experience has proved wrong just about every conclusion I had drawn about Walrus Ink's management style and its owner."

She didn't quite believe him, but she wasn't as angry as she'd have been even a few days ago. She could even be flip about her own skepticism. "That and a dollar will buy you a cup of coffee."

"You're losing something." He raised a hand and briefly touched her shoulder.

Meryl jumped as his callused fingertip met her bare skin. Glancing down she realized why. The neckline of her over-size sweater had slipped off her shoulder to reveal the soft turn of one shoulder and, through the deep V neckline, the upper mount of one breast.

Annoyed, Meryl reached out to hike the bulky sweater back up on her shoulder. She had intended to wear a T-shirt underneath, but she couldn't find the right one and her strapless bra was in the dirty clothes bin. Since she hadn't intended to run into anyone, it hadn't seemed to matter that she was naked beneath the sweater. Until now, until James Brant realized it, too.

For a second his pewter eyes flared, the silver liquefied by the sudden surfacing of hot currents. Growing as still as prey in sight of a predator, she remembered how those eyes would darken and tarnish with desire as they fell together into bed, or onto a sofa, on anywhere else they could find a suitable accommodating surface to cushion their passion.

Just as quickly, the emotional blaze in his gaze died and he turned away to open the cage. Without either of them realizing it, the elevator had come to a halt on the main floor.

His about-face disconcerted her. James had never backed away from a suggestive moment in their entire association.

Actually, he had provoked most of them. If he had been any other man she might have thought he was being considerate of her feelings by turning away. But James Brant had never known an uncertain moment in his life. She was the only one struggling for composure.

James kept his back to her as he opened the metal doors, not wanting her to see the sexually aggressive creature lurking behind his human gaze. She would panic, run out and never return. And he wouldn't blame her. Just at the moment he was a little uncertain of his control. His hands actually shook as he lifted the grating.

He swung around suddenly. "I forgot I have an appointment at noon and I'm going to be late." He glanced at his watch after the fact and hoped she wouldn't notice. "Right, late," he echoed, glad to see it was a little after twelve. "We'll do this another time." He didn't wait for her to agree, but turned and began threading his way through the maze of printing presses and other machinery toward the service entrance.

Meryl watched him go with a quizzical expression on her face. She had no idea why he had bolted, but she knew that he had.

"You actually spent the entire morning alone in the office with him?" Jacqui's eyes were round as an owl's as she reached over with her chopsticks to snag another shrimp from the platter by Meryl's elbow.

"I thought you'd sooner panhandle than set foot inside Walrus Ink again."

Meryl responded with a warm smile for her other dinner companion. "That's a bit of an exaggeration, Kent."

"If I'm exaggerating it's not by much," Kent Davis countered.

Meryl could tell by the stress lines forming about his eyes and mouth that she had sprung unpleasant news on him. Which is exactly why she'd invited Jacqui to join them for dinner when Kent had called late in the day to say he was coming in from New York to see her. Kent wouldn't reveal his feelings in front of someone else. She'd have a chance to explain what must seem at first glance, her bizarre decision to work for a man she hated. Or rather once hated, Meryl amended in her thoughts and then wondered when that change had taken place.

She didn't trust James, maybe still feared him little, but the hate had subsided. Which was healthier, she assured herself. Hate implied an emotional attachment and she didn't want to feel attached to James in any way. That was much too dangerous to her emotional life.

"Don't stop now," Kent prompted. "When did this occur?"

"It happened Thursday," Meryl said and then realized she felt ridiculous trying to make her sudden association with James sound normal "Actually, it happened so quickly that I had to jump first and consider the ramifications later."

"I wish you'd have discussed the move with me before you agreed to consult for Brant." Kent clicked his chopsticks against his plate in a display of annoyance. "I thought you were considering coming to work for me."

"I was," Meryl acknowledged, feeling equally guilty and awkward about having placed him on the spot, "but that was before I saw an opportunity to perhaps be self-employed again."

"I don't understand." Jacqui's gaze darted back and forth between the pair. "You mean, you think you're going to be working full-time at Walrus Ink?"

Meryl offered her audience of two a coy smile. "Who knows? I might even be running things again before it's all over."

"You've got a plan!" Kent's voice was full of wonder and admiration. "I want in."

Meryl chuckled. "No questions asked?"

Kent shook his head, stress lines collapsing into smile lines. "Absolutely none. If you've found a way to blast Walrus Ink free of Brant's clutches you've got my unconditional support."

"Ah, but will I have your unconditional *financial* support?"

"You're serious!" Jacqui's mouth formed for a scream, but it never emerged. "I knew you must be up to something. You couldn't be coming back to work for Brant just to renew old ties." She leaned forward eagerly. "So spill, Sis, what are you up to?"

"Patience, sibling. I don't have it all worked out exactly. But Brant told me he's considering selling Walrus Ink and that he's already had offers."

"One of them was from me," Kent inserted.

Meryl interrupted her train of thought to stare at him. "Why didn't you tell me? When was that?"

"It was weeks ago and it came to nothing." Kent avoided her gaze, but she couldn't miss the angry tightening of his mouth. "I was embarrassed to say anything, but you may as well know that no matter how desperate he becomes Brant won't sell to just anyone. He declined my offer just to show his contempt."

Meryl filed this bit of information away. She was going to have to be even more subtle than she'd first surmised. Brant must not connect her offer to Kent or Kent's money.

"You've never said what caused the bad blood between you."

Kent's brown eyes shuttered over. "It doesn't matter. The feud has taken on a life of its own."

"It must be a woman," Jacqui offered from her corner as she fished up a snow pea from the lobster sauce. "When men hold a grievance and neither will talk about it, it's usually because it's over a woman."

"Did that insight come out of one of your fortune cookies?" Kent asked with a little laugh.

Meryl smiled affectionately at her sister who had piled a small stack of broken fortune cookies near her plate. Jacqui had a few little quirks. One of them was her insistence on ordering fortune cookies first and then opening them until she found a fortune she liked. Then and only then would she order, feeling that eating a meal would insure the outcome of the fortune she'd chosen for herself.

"You may scoff, but you didn't see the one I kept." Jacqui reached down and plucked her choice from her vest pocket. "It says right here, 'The softest things in the world overcome the hardest.' I've never met a man harder than James Brant while Meryl is all soft-spoken words and elegant femininity. I say this time he's met his match!"

"Thanks for the vote of confidence, but I'm far from certain that I will succeed. James may change his mind any day and decide to get rid of the company before I'm ready to act. He does have other business to oversee, after all."

"True enough," Kent murmured. "I'd wondered why he'd chosen to stay here in Hartford all week."

Meryl evaded his speculative glance. "He said he needed to catch up on Walrus Ink business. I assume he'll soon tire of Hartford and return to Manhattan."

"Maybe." Meryl looked up to find Kent watching her with uncomfortable acuity. "I'm going to have to be away awhile myself. The west-coast sales force is holding its semiannual meeting in San Diego next week. After that, I'm off to Tokyo for a week."

"That long?"

He smiled at Meryl's distressed tone. "It's nice to know I'll be missed."

"Of course you will," Meryl responded, but selfishly she'd been thinking more about how she had been counting on his day-by-day advice rather than more personal considerations.

"So are you guys officially an item, or what?" Jacqui asked in all innocence.

Meryl glared at her tactless sister. "Jacqui sometimes suffers from foot-in-mouth disease. Sorry, Kent."

"Actually, I like her way of thinking. It's refreshingly straightforward." His eyes shimmered with amusement. "So are we officially an item, or not?"

Meryl stuck a piece of Mongolian beef in her mouth to keep from having to respond.

After dinner they separated, Jacqui heading home while Meryl drove Kent back to his hotel. She didn't demur when he asked her in. In fact, she had wanted to be alone with him to discuss her business strategy with him. But by the time they reached his room, she felt handicapped by his wounded pride. It wasn't there in his expression or even in his manner. From his navy blue blazer to his tasseled loafers, Kent was the kind of man who remained polite in all but extremely provoked circumstances. After her stormy affair with James, she had found Kent's manner more suited to her personality.

He had gallantly paid for dinner, insisted on buying her a cognac in the hotel bar before they moved upstairs, all the while keeping their conversation light, amusing and off business. It didn't work. With every passing minute Meryl felt more guilty and more like a cheat. By the time she stepped into his hotel suite she was as nervous as a cat in strange surroundings.

Kent flipped on the entry hall light, but didn't bother to light any of the lamps as they crossed into the sitting area. Meryl sat down on one of the upholstered chairs rather than the sofa. Was it a conscious decision to keep apart from him? she wondered. He checked his stride toward the sofa and came back to sit on the chair beside hers.

He reached out for her hand as he sat down, lacing his longer fingers through hers. "Okay. Let's talk, Meryl."

She squeezed his fingers affectionately. "I'm sorry, Kent. I should have phoned and told you what I was doing, or going to try to do."

"I've been putting off for nearly a month the two second-best candidates for the job I offered you," he said mildly.

Guilt flicked her. She wished she could see his face better.

"Do you mind?" she asked as she turned to reach for the nearest lamp to turn it on. The illumination dramatically altered her perception of the space they occupied as a deep cocooning cavern. The elegant and expensively appointed room seemed to require equal formality from its occupants.

She slipped her fingers free of his and then, on second thought, reached out to lay her hand on his arm. "You're right. I haven't handled this professionally." She took a deep breath. "I haven't been fair to you personally, either."

Kent's mouth bowed upward at the corners. It would have passed for a smile if not for the accusation and hurt in his brown eyes. "It's over, isn't it, Meryl?"

She drew her hand back and hunched her shoulders as she cupped her elbows in her hands. "I didn't think it had really begun." She lifted a brow at him. "Did you?"

"Oh, yes," he said softly. "I most definitely thought it had begun."

She hurt for him even though she knew it wasn't entirely her fault that he'd fallen for her when she couldn't quite get past a very affectionate liking for him. So she said nothing.

He leaned back after a few seconds, perfectly in control of the awkward moment. "I've been patient, trying to read your mixed signals and not push when you seemed to need space. But I thought I was making progress, Meryl. I thought *we* were making progress."

His gentle words took the starch out of her defense. She nodded. "You're right. I have been sending mixed signals because I've been confused. I don't know what I want right

now, but it's not a serious relationship, even with a wonderful man like you." She accepted the weight of his
wounded gaze as her punishment for hurting a very decent
man. "There're too many other unsettled aspects of my
life."

Suddenly she knew she had to move away or she might
offer him the kind of comfort that would only further en-
tangle them. She rose to her feet and began pacing. "Even
I know a good thing when I see it. But I've felt—oh, I guess
you'd call it disconnected—ever since I lost Walrus Ink."

She paused to look back at him, willing him to understand what she wasn't certain she could adequately explain.
"Dad left the company to me with no strings attached. He
even said he thought I might sell one day, and I might have.
But I was cheated out of it, and that's entirely different."

He frowned at her. "You want revenge."

Meryl sighed. "Said like that, it sounds so cold and
heartless. I want restitution, justice, something like that,
yes."

"And you think sitting in James Brant's offices while
waging war behind the front lines is the way to go about it."

How irrational her motives seemed when phrased like
that. "It sounds devious, doesn't it?"

He chuckled and spread an arm out along the back the
chair she had just occupied. "It *is* devious. But answer this
question for me, Meryl. If you get Walrus Ink back and if
James Brant slinks away to lick the wounds you want to in-
flict, how will you feel about us then?"

Embarrassed for them both, Meryl said, "How can I answer a question with so many ifs in it?"

"I think you just did." His expression was so sadly tender
that she wanted to cry.

Of course she had, if unwittingly, Meryl realized with a
fresh stab of conscience. She hadn't rushed in to assure Kent
that she cared for him, that she had deep personal feelings
for him and that she wanted things to work out. She had
dodged the question because she didn't want to face the an-

swer. She moved over to stand before him. "You must think I'm terrible."

"I think you're smart and beautiful and sexy but stuck in neutral." He looked up steadily at her. "Is that Brant's fault, too?"

She could have lied. "Not entirely."

"Then you'd better decide what you're really after over there at Walrus Ink."

Meryl tensed. "What's that supposed to mean?"

"Nothing really." He was studying her now, as if she were a new slide slipped under his microscope. "Despite appearances, you haven't gotten on with your life. Six months into our friendship and never once have we found ourselves in bed." The laugh lines overlay but did not erase the hurt in his expression. "Something's holding you back. If Brant sold Walrus Ink tomorrow all your plans would be over. What would you do then?"

"I don't know."

"Take my advice, Meryl, work out in your mind exactly what you hope to accomplish before you set foot back into that office on Monday. For your own sake, you should know what you're really after."

"It's not Brant!" Meryl said, taking offense at the very idea. Yet her cheeks warmed and her stomach did a somersault. She wasn't after Brant. She wasn't!

"I didn't say it was, Meryl. Then again..." Kent took his time coming to his feet. "And to prove what a good sport I am, I still intend to back you one hundred percent. Whatever you need—money, resources, contacts—you have my word I'll help you. You see, I want Brant brought to his knees as much as you do."

His generosity took her breath away. "Why?"

He smiled a little forlornly. "Ask your little sister. I think she may be right, after all."

Chapter 6

"What on earth is that?"

The noise of the rowdy crowd could be heard four floors above ground level in Walrus Ink's offices.

"Some of Mr. Brant's admirers," Sam Carey offered with a belly laugh. "Helluva way to start the work week."

Meryl had come in via the back entrance near the parking lot and so missed seeing the crowd gathered outside the main doors of Walrus Ink. But there was no denying their audible presence. She stepped over to the front window and pressed her head against the glass to gaze down. What she saw were the heads of about a dozen people. They were carrying signs and chanting. The words weren't clear, but the intent was—they weren't happy and Walrus Ink was their target.

Meryl looked back at the nervous faces of the editorial and sales staff who had left their offices and cubicles to gather at the window and discuss the goings-on below. "Has anybody gone down to see what they want?"

"They want Brant's head on a pike," Sam offered sanguinely.

Meryl smiled at the seniormost member of the staff. Sam was an institution at Walrus Ink. With Sam's help, her father had started this press on a shoestring. What Mark Wallis had been to Walrus Ink's editorial direction, Sam Carey still was to production. There wasn't a piece of equipment on the printer floor he didn't know how to run and repair. Any cover concept the art department could dream up he could make a reality. That gave him privileges that he didn't stint on using.

"The group is protesting Mr. Brant's position as head of children's publishing house," Carrine Oliver said. "They say after his recent, er, trouble, he's not a fit owner for a company that publishes children's books."

"They don't want to line his pockets, so they are calling for a boycott of all our books until he sells the company," Sam added without reluctance. "In other words, we don't eat if Brant stays with us."

"We've been getting letters for months," Corrine concurred, "but nothing like this!"

"What kinds of letters?" Meryl demanded, incensed that Walrus Ink was under attack.

"Oh, the usual. Vague threats, ugly language, accusations that a criminal has control of the press." Corrine blushed as if she were responsible for the ridiculous claims. "I wouldn't worry about it. The police don't seem concerned."

"The police have been informed?" Meryl questioned, growing more uneasy by the moment.

"They have and they're on their way." The gravel tone of James Brant's voice turned every employee's attention toward the elevators. James stepped into the room with a smiling tall blond woman by his side. "So we're going to let Hartford's finest take care of their business while we go on with ours."

The staff dispersed without a ripple of protest. Only Meryl remained as James crossed the room toward her with the woman she recognized as Beebe Hatcher in tow.

She told herself her uneasiness was caused by the demonstration going on below. Yet she had spent a sleepless night trying to answer the question Kent had put to her. What was she really after at Walrus Ink? How much of it had to do with the attraction of the man who came striding toward her with a purposeful frown on his brutally handsome face? She no longer hated him. While it had been easy to maintain hostility to his memory, it was much harder to do the same with the flesh and blood man. Maybe it was impossible. That thought had kept her tossing and turning under her feather comforter.

"Hello, Meryl." He sounded at ease, but his gaze was definitely that of a preoccupied man. "I'd like you meet Beebe Hatcher of Hatcher Associates. She's going to make a presentation on marketing strategy in the editorial staff meeting this morning."

"I see," Meryl said smoothly. "Welcome, Ms. Hatcher." She extended her hand to the woman in a thigh-high kelly green suit and met the woman's surprisingly firm grip.

"Glad to have you on board, Meryl," Beebe replied, then glanced at James with a smug smile. "I suspected any offer from James would be difficult to resist."

Meryl felt her smile freeze on her face. What was that crack supposed to mean? A glance at James didn't clarify it. He looked annoyed, no controlling his fury. What had upset him? Even as she finished her thought she heard the faint wail of police sirens and saw the corners of his mouth tighten. Of course. He was focused on the demonstration going on below. This was a complication he didn't need.

"Why don't you see if things are set up to your liking, Beebe," James said as he turned her by the arm. "I must check my voice mail."

"Sure thing." Beebe sent a vague smile in Meryl's direction as she patted James's arm familiarly. "See you soon."

As Beebe hurried away James stepped over to the front windows to look out. Meryl followed and looked down. The police had arrived. The moment she was certain everyone was out of earshot, she said quietly, "Why didn't you tell me that there was going to be a strategy meeting this morning?"

James turned his head to glower at her, but kept his voice level. "You ran out on me Friday night before I had the chance."

It sounded like such a plausible explanation that she almost bought it. But not quite. "You had plenty of time to mention it as you drove me home. Or even on Saturday."

He looked away from her. "I had other things on my mind by then."

Considering where her own thoughts had been most of the weekend, Meryl decided she didn't want to touch that one. She turned to the window. The police were talking to a man with the bullhorn, apparently the leader. "How long has this been going on?"

"It's our first demonstration. Oh, hell, here comes the press."

Meryl followed his gaze up the block to where a mobile TV van was being parked. She looked back at him and noticed that his expression was now as rigid as granite. "Maybe you'd better tell me what's going on?"

Not looking at her, he shoved a hand through his thick chestnut hair, making the few strands of silver shimmer as it threaded through his large fingers. It was an uncharacteristic gesture for him, betraying as it did a certain agitation. "It's not your problem."

He turned abruptly from the window and strode away. Halfway across the room he looked back at her. "Are you coming?"

She didn't like anything about the past two minutes in his company, but she especially didn't like his high-handed tone. "If it's a command, of course."

She saw a flash of silver as his eyes widened. He looked as if he wanted to throttle her, or someone. Then his shoulders relaxed a fraction. "It's a request, Meryl. Please come."

"Very well. Just let me get my portfolio."

She headed in the opposite direction from him, toward her office. Things were moving too quickly. She wasn't prepared for a strategy meeting, had no suggestions to offer as yet. Besides, she didn't want her hand forced until absolutely the last minute. Well, she would have to wing it. Come to think of it, all she had to do was listen. She was a consultant, after all. She would wait to be consulted.

By the time Meryl arrived at the conference room Beebe Hatcher had taken center stage at one end of the boardroom table.

Gathered around the table were the key people at Walrus Ink, which included Jacqui as head of the art department, her assistant, Carrine, Sam, his second in command from production and the two editors James had hired after she left. She had met them all briefly on Friday and offered each a nod and smile as she settled into the only empty seat, next to James. Restless energy peeled off him in waves. Or was it the exhilaration of her own adrenaline kicking in?

"Now that we're all here, I'll begin." Beebe Hatcher gave Meryl a tight little smile and flipped on the overhead projector. The picture that came up on the screen behind her was that of a fat, aging battle-scarred walrus sleeping peacefully on its side in the sand. It was a mean caricature of the Walrus Ink logo of a smiling, youthful animal.

She drew out a collapsible wand and pointed to the pitiful animal. "To be blunt, Walrus Ink has become very much like this beached brute. You are lax, unfocused. Your methods are outdated. You lack the high concept mentality of contemporary taste. You make no statement. You have no vision."

"I thought we were a publishing company, not a religious sect," Sam muttered.

Beebe studiously ignored him. "I'm here to help you find that vision, solidify your concept. Drop-kick you into the twenty-first century where family values go hand in hand with a leaner, tighter, more combative organization. To rally people at Walrus Ink—"

The sound of snickering over her poor choice of words, considering what was going on outside, threw her only momentarily off stride.

"To grab the attention of your market," she amended, "this company needs a single clear vision that the man on the street can identify with. This is it, people."

She punched a button and another slide appeared. It was a picture of Timon the Ash Can Cat, except that it had been altered to give the character new flashy clothes. The alteration also omitted his earring. Instead of a knit cap, he sported a military buzz cut. "We're going to use Timon as the new Walrus Ink mascot," she proclaimed triumphantly.

Meryl heard the buzz of interest in the room with alarm, but Beebe was on a roll that couldn't be interrupted.

"There's more, of course. Once you get the public's attention, the trick is to hold on to it. With that in mind, I've forged ahead." The next slide to come up contained a collage of various merchandise imprinted with many of the day's most popular cartoon characters.

"I've already developed tentative relations with a toy company who's interested in a franchise deal using Timon. We'll build slowly, starting at the grass-roots level. Begin with a limited line of toys. Perhaps a giveaway to whet the consumer's appetite. If we get a positive response from that we'll be positioned to move quickly, to branch out into caps, cups, T-shirts. From there it'll be a natural progression to videos, a TV series and who knows."

"No. Absolutely not." Meryl stood. "Walrus Ink publishes books. Children are drawn to the Ash Can series because it hasn't been commercialized. Besides, this is a nonprofit venture. The revenue from these books go to a cause.''

"That is a problem," Beebe admitted, "but I've thought of a way around that." She glanced at James as if for support.

"Several celebrities have managed to go commercial with products that also benefit causes without losing their entertainment credibility. The books can continue to fund the homeless shelters, though you might want to rethink your charity in light of recent public opinion, which has turned slightly unfavorable toward such handout places."

"Heaven forbid we should be thought untrendy," Meryl said, more angry than she could believe possible. She turned her disbelieving gaze on James. "This is your great plan, to bring in a hotshot ad exec who'll rim-shot Walrus Ink's literary reputation into the garbage can?"

"Now, Meryl." Beebe smiled as if she were dealing with an enfeebled elderly relative. "I can see how change might unsettle some people, but why don't we just ask the author and illustrator what they think of the idea? There's money to be made all around," she added with an expansive smile that included the entire room. "Who wouldn't want to be rich, right?"

Meryl chuckled. "If you think I'm a hard sell, you have yet to meet Tomaltach O'Connor."

"Really?" Beebe's smile remained confidently in place. "Difficult people are my specialty."

"You won't get a chance to handle Tomaltach. He won't make any allowances for the fact you're a pro or a woman."

"We'll see." Beebe turned her attention to James and, to Meryl's way of thinking, it seemed she practically purred. "Would you like me to contact Mr. O'Connor today?"

"Why don't you start with the author?" James replied, every line of his body arranged in ease as he sat back in his chair.

"Fine. Just give me her phone number."

James shook his head. "Sorry, can't help you. Sylar Lillaw prefers to remain anonymous."

Beebe glanced back to Meryl. "Is this a joke or what?"

"The author is spotlight shy," Jacqui suddenly offered, hoping to deflect an argument.

"Then we'll have to coax her out," Beebe replied, clearly undaunted by the challenge. "The promise of money, or glory—an award perhaps. We'll play to her pride. I bet she'd love to do commercial spots for her creation. Everybody has buttons just waiting to be pushed."

"Sounds like something you'd embroider on a cynic's pillow," Sam offered from his corner and gained the muffled laughter of the rest of the editorial staff.

"I think that if a person wants to remain anonymous, then that person has a right to remain anonymous," Jacqui said with great feeling.

Beebe's head angled toward her. "I don't suppose you could be the author?"

Jacqui looked as if she'd been struck in the chest. "Me? I can't spell mud. I'm strictly a paint-box child."

"Still," Beebe continued as she angled her entire body around to face Jacqui, "that would explain the wish for anonymity. An in-house author, or maybe no author at all!"

She all but pounced on Jacqui, bending over her as the younger woman sat in stricken silence. "This began as an editorial pipe dream, didn't it? You collectively came up with the idea and decided for publicity purposes to put it out under a pseudonym. Am I right?"

"Have you read the books?"

Beebe looked back down the length of the table at James. "I beg your pardon?"

"If you had," James replied, his hooded eyes bright beacons in his emotionless face, "you'd know Timon is the vision of a single, gifted mind."

Meryl held her breath, waiting for his gaze to shift in her direction and give it all away. Instead he leaned forward and flipped open the next of Hatcher Associates' presentation folders on the table before him. "Since we're *not* going into the gimme cap business, let's see what else you have to offer."

Meryl saw the expression that James missed. For a second Beebe's features hardened with anger and insult. The woman was furious. She didn't get vetoed very often, Meryl thought. But then again, Beebe had probably not worked for anybody like James Brant before. She suspected that, even in the worlds of politics and business, James's smooth brand of self-assured autocratic direction was a rarity.

"About the logo," Beebe said after a short but tense silence.

"No dead walruses," James stated without looking up. "See if you can't liven him up a bit." He glanced up with the first smile of the day. "I rather like the old fellow. His fatherly image should play well with your family-values people."

Meryl didn't know whether to laugh out loud or kick him under the table. She did neither. She did a studied examination of her lap until she saw James's hand reach out surreptitiously to touch her thigh. It lasted just long enough for her to note the pressure, but too quickly for her to take real offense. Yet she did.

She felt the blood roar into her ears and heat her cheeks. He had saved her a public unmasking, but she no longer felt safe. She was very much afraid that, one way or another, his protection was going to cost her a lot more than she was willing to pay.

For the next half hour, she sat like a block of wood while the rest of the table debated the issues of packaging, marketing strategies and finally the spring list.

"Meryl has promised to rouse our reclusive author to do another book for the Ash Can series," James said after listening to everyone else. He closed his notes, indicating that, whatever anyone else had in mind, the meeting was at an end. "It will be our lead title for the spring list."

"You know this Sylar Lillaw?" Beebe questioned as she came down the room to intercept Meryl.

"As much as anyone," Meryl replied, not wanting to deal with Beebe in close contact.

"So you won't mind giving me her phone number and address."

"Yes," Meryl said succinctly. "I would."

It was confirmed. Beebe Hatcher didn't take no for an answer very well. She snapped her notepad shut. "What's the big secret? Is she sick or a criminal or something?"

Meryl looked at her in disbelief. "Don't you have a walrus you need to revive?" She scooted pass Beebe before another round could be exchanged, knowing full well she would sooner or later lose.

James had gained the door ahead of her and Meryl followed him out into the hallway. "I want to talk to you."

He nodded. "Walk with me down to the copy room. I want to check on a fax I'm expecting."

Meryl paced along beside him, holding her tongue until they had entered the roomful of copiers and faxes at the end of the hall. For the first time she noticed how tired he looked, as if he'd had a tough weekend, or maybe just a strenuous one—with Beebe Hatcher.

She chopped off her thoughts, but her nervous system had moved on without it, conjuring up images of a woman locked in James's muscular arms, a thin silk chemise all that protected her delicate skin from the rasping touch of his hands. Her gaze began to glaze. The most amazing thing was that the woman she conjured up in James's steamy embrace wasn't Beebe but herself!

The young man who ran the machines smiled as they entered. "That fax you expected is just coming in now, Mr. Brant."

James nodded. "I'll wait for it. You must have other things to do."

Even if the young man didn't have something else to do, his boss's tone made it clear he should pretend that he did.

"I'll be back in a few minutes," he said as he headed toward the door.

The second the door closed, James rounded on Meryl, but he was smiling. "Go ahead. Let me have it."

"Why did you do that?" Meryl asked, holding on for dear life to her temper. Her own daydreams had so chastened her that she was prepared to be reasonable, provided that he gave reasonable answers.

He grinned, looking as if he'd won the daily double. "Because I knew you could handle Hatcher and I was right."

"Handle her? Is that what you wanted?" The buckles on Meryl's anger creaked. "Why, then, didn't you at least warn me?"

James leaned a hip against the nearest copier, hugely enjoying the opportunity to be alone with her. "Because I didn't know what Beebe would come up with, but I knew you'd deflate anything that wasn't suitable for Walrus Ink's image."

Every word he spoke seemed designed to provoke her to great heights of fury. "If you needed a guard dog to keep Beebe away from you, you should have hired one!" The idea hadn't even been in her mind before those words popped out. But now that they had, the suggestion suddenly became fact in Meryl's mind. "I won't be used to keep your current playmate in line."

Something flickered in his expression and was gone. "What's that supposed to mean?"

"It means that I know you're seeing her." From somewhere inside, the voice of a jealous harridan rose out of her. "What you just did, pitting a former lover against the current one, was a sadistic thing to do. I thought you'd reached your sleaze potential years ago. It seems I'm wrong. I quit!"

He beat her to the door because he was closer. He held it closed against her ineffectual tugs to open it because he was bigger.

Finally he backed her to arm's length with a hand flattened against her breastbone. "Jesus, Meryl! How do you get things so screwed up?"

"Me?" She returned in equal fury. "How else am I to view what occurred?"

He leaned back against the door and plowed a hand into his hair. For a second he closed his eyes trying, she knew, to master the anger that contorted his mouth and hardened his jaw. He was very angry and she was suddenly quite afraid of that anger.

But when his eyes opened again, Meryl felt only the full impact of the emotional storm in his pewter gaze in the pit of her stomach. "Meryl, Meryl," he murmured softly.

Meryl held her breath, resisting the drag of the rough caress he made of her name. He wasn't just handsome or arrogant, she thought despairingly as she hung helplessly suspended by those magnetic eyes. He was charismatic. Suddenly she wanted to fling herself against him and beg his forgiveness. She'd said awful, terrible, vitriolic things. But she couldn't even unclench her teeth for fear that she would begin to cry.

"I didn't pit you against Beebe. You chose to jump in." Lord, how reasonable he sounded. Maybe she was a little mad. "You didn't wait to hear anybody else's opinion, did you? Did I direct one word to you? Did anybody ask you to defend the company? No. You took it upon yourself. And it worked out well. Beebe had a few of the younger staff going there for a moment. You came in as the voice of reason to remind us all why we're here. It was good for morale to hear a seasoned voice of authority take on a slick opportunist."

He moved away from the door, but he didn't exactly approach her. "You earned your salary today, Meryl. You did a damned fine job. Now if you want to quit, you go ahead. But for day one, you're A on target."

He moved past her toward the fax machine, which had beeped to signal the end of a transmission. "As for who I'm seeing and not seeing, it's none of your business, just as Ned the cop is none of mine. Now unless you've got something constructive to offer, I have things to do."

"Ned Miller's an author," she offered to his back.

He turned back to her before he reached the fax machine. "I thought he was a cop."

She shrugged. "The two aren't incompatible. I went to see him on Friday because I've been helping him pull his book together on a free-lance basis." She saw him soften, but only a fraction. "I had an idea that his book might be suitable for our young-adult line."

"We don't have a young-adult line."

"We might consider starting one, a nonfiction young-adult line. Ned's book is about living smart. It's full of advice for young people on the street and the many more who are often on their own even if they're living in families. It's about how to negotiate the streets, how to avoid gangs while dealing with them, how to recognize pimps, come-ons from pedophiles, lots of tough subjects but valuable advice. His book covers the sort of things many mothers and fathers aren't equipped to talk knowledgeably about simply because they haven't had any experience with them. I thought his book might give us a new direction to think about."

"Another issues-oriented book because you want to save the world." He nodded. "It's a possibility, more so if he can serve our needs, as well. Can he talk? I mean, is he up to the talk-show circuit? How does he come across?"

"He's a natural," Meryl assured him, pleased that she hadn't met an argument. "He's young, good-looking, talks tough and straight, but not down, to people. He works with the city youth programs in his off-hours."

"Sounds like a regular Boy Scout."

Meryl stiffened. "I happen to admire men who put their principles into action."

He went very still. "As opposed to me who puts his vices into practice."

She bit her inner lip. She hadn't actually been after that particular comparison. "Maybe I jumped the gun a few minutes ago. I have a habit of saying what's on my mind."

He watched her with a deep but unreadable expression. "It's one of the things I've always admired about you."

Meryl felt as if he had passed a warm hand over her skin. "I didn't think you ever found much to admire in me." She ignored the suggestive lift of his brows. "You never liked my manners, my way of doing business, my taste in furnishings, my informality or my way of dressing."

"Other than that you were perfect," he finished as she faltered.

A silly smile bloomed on her mouth. He was handling her. So why wasn't she furious? Maybe because he was looking at her, really looking at her, as he hadn't since that last night before their terrible fight.

He took a step toward her, his hand rising to her cheek. "I can't make up for everything, Meryl." His fingers brushed lightly cross the fullest part of her cheek. "I won't lie to you and say that I can. But this is now. And we're here. And I'm glad."

She stood still as he suddenly dipped his head and initiated a kiss, too astonished to retreat or struggle. She didn't want him to kiss her, did she? How could she respond to the heat seeping through her lips from his? Why did she sigh from pleasure at the taste of him, so familiar and so long missed? She couldn't really be reaching for him, touching his face with its fine stubble, leaning into him when she had promised herself never to get this close to him ever again.

But the lovely melting warmth invading her body was so welcome to the frozen dry places in her soul that she thought, *Just a little longer, please, just a little longer.*

The anguish that rose up in her when he leaned away caused her mouth to tremble. She closed her eyes as his hand fell from her cheek. She didn't open them at once, afraid of what she would see in his face and what he might see reflected in hers.

Finally the sound of the door opening snapped her back to reality. She opened her eyes to see James slipping out of the room.

"Now what have you done, Meryl Wallis?" she whispered in wonder. "What have you done?"

When the door opened again she braced herself, but it was only the young man who worked here. She smiled at him and said, "I don't think I caught your name before. I'm Meryl Wallis."

"John," he replied and shook her hand. "But, of course I recognized you."

"Really?"

"Your picture hangs in the outer office as the second owner and CEO."

"Right, I'd forgotten." Meryl smiled again. "Well, I must get back to work myself."

"Wait. Mr. Brant forgot this," John said and held up the fax. "I don't supposed you'd...?"

"Of course." Meryl reached for the fax and then slipped out of the door. She and James shared an office. What could be easier than delivering a fax?

She hadn't meant to read it. But human nature got the better of her. Once she scanned the first three lines, nothing short of spontaneous combustion of the pages would have kept her from reading the rest.

Chapter 7

Meryl burst into the office, waving the fax sheets in her hand. "Would you like to explain this?"

After the fact, she saw the plainclothes and uniformed policemen standing before James' desk. "Oh, excuse me." She began backing out.

"No, come in, Meryl." James stood and beckoned her with a hand. "I was just being briefed on the disturbance below and the reasons behind it. You might find this enlightening."

Meryl shut the door and came forward, curiosity easily outpacing her embarrassment. "I'm sorry, gentlemen, I didn't mean to interrupt."

"Sergeant Rock, Officer Phillips," James said smoothly, "I'd like you to meet Meryl Wallis. She's the former owner of Walrus Ink and she's recently joined us as our creative consultant."

Meryl shook hands and smiled. "You must find this all rather absurd."

"In what way, ma'am?" asked Sergeant Rock mildly.

"Why, dealing with disgruntled readers. It's not as if they're protesting poverty, gun control or some other more passionate issue."

"The issue at hand seems passionate enough to the protesters," he responded without emotion. He glanced at James. "When, exactly, did you start working at Walrus Ink, Ms. Wallis?"

"Last Friday," Meryl answered. "Why?"

"How would you characterize your working relationship with Mr. Brant?"

Meryl frowned at his interrogating tone. "Fine. If you think—"

"I see you've done your homework," James interrupted. "But you're barking up the wrong tree, Sergeant. Even if Ms. Wallis had ever thought about getting back at me personally, she would never put Walrus Ink in jeopardy in order to do it."

As James's attention moved to her Meryl wondered what he was thinking behind that metallic gaze. "Our previous association was based on mutual interests. So is our present collaboration. She's not responsible for the threats or the demonstration."

"What threats?" Something had just gone past her like a homer into right field. "Ja—Mr. Brant, have you been threatened?"

Sergeant Rock's voice remained monotoned. "Isn't Ms. Wallis aware of what has transpired?"

James shook his head. "I didn't think it was necessary to inform my staff, until today."

"I'm glad you're reconsidering your position," Officer Phillips said, speaking for the first time. "It could save trouble later."

"This may be just another oddball protest, but you never know what sort of element these events will attract," Sergeant Rock added with a dead-level look at Meryl.

"I don't understand." Meryl took a step toward Sergeant Rock. "What exactly is going on?"

"I've received a few threats in the form of letters and calls," James answered. His voice was matter-of-fact, but his eyes were strangely bright. "Some of our readers are protesting my presence as publisher."

"You mean you were serious when you said there was a crackpot out there trying to start a boycott of Walrus Ink's books?"

"When did Mr. Brant tell you that?" the sergeant asked.

"Last week." Meryl glanced at the policemen before her gaze went back to James. "How serious is this?"

"Serious enough to convince the sergeant that we should beef up security here."

"For yourself, as well, Mr. Brant." Sergeant Rock spoke as if it were the most natural thing in the world for a businessman to need protection. "It's just a precaution. According to our experts the letters you turned over to us don't have the hysterical edge that most serious threat mail carries. Still, I wouldn't go out driving alone or for a solitary walk for the next few days."

"I'm not going to hire a bodyguard." The expression on his face precluded an argument. "Not only would I feel foolish, but it's likely to backfire in the press. Children's Publisher Hires Baby-sitter. That kind of razzing I can live without."

"Who cares what it sounds like?" Meryl objected. "If you're in danger—"

"I'm not." James moved quickly from behind the desk. "If that's all, gentlemen, I do have a company to run."

"We'll want to talk with your employees," Sergeant Rock said. As James ushered the policemen toward the door, the detective glanced back over his shoulder at Meryl. "Including Ms. Wallis."

"Fine. But I'd appreciate it if you wouldn't spook my staff. I'm certain this will blow over in a few days. If not, we'll deal with it then." James shook both men's hands and then closed the door firmly behind them.

"You're in trouble and you don't want to admit it," Meryl said forcefully as he came toward her.

A funny, whimsical expression lifted his features as he returned to his desk. "I'm always in trouble. I live for trouble." He sat down. "So why don't you retrench and start again. By your tone of voice when you entered, you were going to read me the riot act—again."

Meryl glanced down at the fax she still held. The edges on one side were crumpled from where her hand had clutched them too tightly. Three distinct emotions were warring within her: latent desire dredged up by his unexpected kiss, dismay over the sergeant's revelation that someone had threatened James with bodily harm and resentment over his most recent dishonesty. The last seemed the safest topic. "All right." She marched over and dropped the sheets on James's desk. "Explain this."

James picked it up and read the few lines. "It seems fairly straightforward."

"Not to me. Tomaltach O'Connor is a proud man. He doesn't beg." She pointed to the top sheet. "This is practically a groveling plea."

She was suddenly so furious she could taste the anger as a metallic flavor in her mouth. Because she could not direct her frustration at the true cause of her anxiety, she chose to vent through this substitute. "What exactly did you say to him to give him the impression that I'm angry with him? And how in heaven's name, if he believed you, did you get him to send that?" She pointed to the illustration of Timon hanging on the wall.

James grinned. "I told you. I bribed him."

"Maybe you'd better explain that."

"Gladly. I'm quite proud of the negotiation." He leaned back and stacked his hands behind his head like a man lounging at the beach. "When O'Connor learned that you were coming in as a consultant he demanded that you be sent at once to Ireland to see him."

"You didn't tell me you've spoken with O'Connor since I returned."

"That's because we spoke beforehand."

"How much before?" she asked suspiciously.

"Can I finish my story? I made O'Connor a counteroffer. I said that if he wanted to persuade you that he was still interested in collaborating with you, instead of living off his royalties, he might make an overture of friendliness, like loaning us this picture for the time you occupied your old office."

"I see."

He actually smiled at her. "Do you?"

"You thought you'd use Tomaltach's and my friendship to further your negotiations with him."

"I could point out that I've gained nothing so far. You came in not knowing the painting was here."

"Yet Tomaltach was expecting to hear from me."

"You did agree when you took the job to contact all Walrus Ink's writers and illustrators."

"So then, there was no need for bribery. But Tomaltach didn't know that." She leaned slightly toward him to tap the fax sheets. "This fax says he sent the painting in the hope that you'd put in a good word for him with me. That was a cheap despicable trick!"

His face sobered, the momentary good humor eclipsed by the beginnings of irritation. "I got the picture to please you, but you're determined not to believe it, aren't you?"

"No, I'm just determined to see it for what it is—a James Brant specialty."

He sat up, his pretense at relaxation ended. "What does that mean?"

"It means you couldn't keep to the straight and narrow if you were strapped to it." She was waving her arms in an unusual display of emotion, but the pressure building within her was demanding physical release. "Why be open and honest when you can use intrigue and machinations? I don't know what I ever saw in you."

He stood. "Don't you?"

The warning signs were flying in his eyes, but she couldn't stop. The morning had held too many surprises, most of them unpleasant jolts. To top it off, he had dared to kiss her. And she had let him! She wasn't about to let him best her again, even if it killed her. She crossed her arms to keep them still. "Aside from a raging hormonal rush, no, I don't know why I let you in my life."

"Then you weren't paying attention." He rounded the desk in slow, deliberate strides. "What we had together was no adolescent flush of sexual curiosity. A child wouldn't have known what to do with what erupted between us." He moved in straight toward her as Meryl found herself backing slowly away. "What we created together was a carnal hunger that ate us both up from the inside out."

She could see emotion trying to break through the surface of his expression. A vein pulsed in his jaw. One corner of his mouth twitched. His hands were fists. "Just the thought of you was enough to make the heat rise off my skin. I couldn't be in a room with you without being aroused."

His voice, no more than a growl, hammered away at every syllable. "Anytime. Anyplace. Wherever I was, if you were there, I was aroused."

He had backed her into a wall. "I still feel it," he muttered as if she had forced the grudging admittance out of him. "Dammit, I still feel it."

The hand he raised to touch her was astonishingly gentle. His fingers caught her hair, lifted a dark shiny handful free of her neck and then let it filter slowly through his fingers. Her chin barely trembled when those same gentle fingers curled under the fragile bones beneath her petal-soft skin.

"But I've learned my lesson. I can't just take what I want. I can't just have what I want."

"No," Meryl murmured a little desperately, her hands splayed out, palms flat, along the wall on either side of her.

"That's too bad," he muttered as he bent toward her, his lips brushing the curved edge of her ear. "Because when you move in close, Meryl, a little bit means so much."

Irrationally she leaned in to kiss him first. Only to end the suspense, she told her outraged mind. She was taking the initiative, but just so far.

She felt him stiffen in momentary surprise and then he scooped her body in against his. He shivered, hot and hungry, and deepened the kiss, his tongue demanding entrance and finding a reception. It was different from the kiss they'd shared in the copy room. This time his kiss reached deep into her, into the place she had never known existed until she'd first kissed James Brant in carnal need. The deep core of her softened and ripened as his kiss heated every cell of her skin. She was crushed in his arms, unable to move, barely able to breath. But it didn't matter. His hot, heavy body was moving against hers, proving that his words were no lie. His arousal nudged the V of her thighs.

Suddenly she was free of a burden of two years. She understood!

In the midst of the incandescence that was James's kiss, she knew why she'd acted as she had two years before. It was for this, this overpowering hunger, this dark dizzy madness that made her want to turn herself inside out so that he could kiss and lick and touch every part of her with his heat. For this she had stopped thinking, stopped considering the consequences, stopped being wary or reluctant or careful. It made sense. Who could resist this deep-down melting, the honey-flowing that begged release? Between them, they had generated enough heat to melt glaciers, to push the seas to the boiling point, to force volcanic eruptions. This is what he had done to her. He had made her feel as she did now, that nothing mattered but the demanding need for the touch of his hands and his mouth, his body pumping on hers.

They didn't know how long the delirium lasted. They didn't care. They came of that fiery dance of need like two anguished souls denied entrance to heaven.

For one wild moment the only thing in Meryl's world was a pair of silver eyes tarnished by the smoke of desire. Then she saw his mouth, bruised and glistening wet from their kisses, forming words. "I'm sorry, Meryl. I'm sorry."

With wild eyes she looked across the chasm of the few inches that separated him from her. What was he saying? Did he regret the kiss or only that it had ended?

He let her go slowly, groaning softly as if it pained him. She leaned back against the wall and shut her eyes, afraid she would otherwise fall when he let her go. Then she felt the rush of cool air on her skin as he separated himself inch by inch from her. Her eyes opened in confusion. When had he unbuttoned her blouse, pushed aside her bra, shoved up her shirt? Was she responsible for his shirt hanging open, his unbuckled belt, his hair standing wild on his head? It had only been a single kiss, hadn't it?

She straightened up and pulled the edges of her blouse together. She felt as if she'd been in a car wreck and yet every cell in her body was pounding with hard and healthy life. How had they gotten so far on only one kiss?

Oh, she understood, she understood!

He moved a little away and turned his back to rearrange his clothing. Meryl knew she should do the same, but for a moment she simply stared at him. Even with his back turned she could feel the heat coursing through him, sense the faint sharp insinuation of his shaving cream in the air, read the grip of need in the set of his shoulders. Once he had been the most intimate friend she'd ever had. No, she reminded herself, they had never been friends. There had never been quiet times to bind them together. Out of bed, he was a stranger.

She turned her back, suddenly embarrassed as she began to reorder her clothing. She had made several mistakes in the past few days. Letting James talk her into coming to work here was the first. Allowing him to so thoroughly occupy her thoughts that she could think of little else was the next. The final and biggest mistake had been in provoking him to show her why she'd first been attracted to him.

Okay, so now she knew. The final piece of the puzzle was in place. There was nothing for her to do but get out before she ruined what was left of the rest of her life.

"I've decided to take the sergeant's advice. I'm going back to New York tonight."

Meryl turned warily to face him, her clothes reassembled. He had retreated behind his desk, at least that's how it seemed to her, though she had never actually known James to withdraw from any arena, business or personal. "Why would the police advise you to leave?"

He looked at her, his gaze shuttered, all emotion contained behind gunmetal gray. "Don't you think it would be better for everybody? I'm the cause of the trouble. With me out of the way, there's no reason for anyone here to be hurt."

She knew he was talking about her as much as Walrus Ink.

"You'll be safer in Manhattan, too."

"Yeah. Safer." His voice sounded bleak, resigned, much as it had that final night of their affair.

She had known even then that he was as leery as she of the searing emotional furnace into which they had plunged themselves that first time. Yet she had thought he would grow accustomed to it, as she had been trying to do. It had not occurred to her until this moment that maybe he had run from it, didn't want any part of anything that required an act of submission.

Meryl's heart contracted in compassionate understanding. That explained so much! For two miserable years she had wandered in her own dismal dungeon of self-recrimination and guilt-driven rage, unable to make sense of anything that had occurred between them. Only now, since he had kissed her for the second time that day, had she begun to think rationally again.

He didn't like, any more than she did, the ungovernable desire that ran like lava through their lives when they were together. It threatened to overwhelm even the magnificent

James Brant. And he wasn't the kind of man who would give up control to anything or anyone. Maybe she hadn't walked out so much as been shoved. At last, she had the answer.

All the answers.

And now he was leaving.

"I was going to suggest when I came in today that I make a few calls and plan to visit a few writers to add that personal touch, if that fits into your budget."

He waved a hand, weary of the effort at conversation. "Whatever you want, Meryl. You name it, it's yours."

"A Porsche?"

He frowned. "What?"

Meryl backed down from her attempt at humor. Poor man, he really did seem out of it. If he needed room, where did that leave her? "How about a ticket to Ireland? After I've visited your American authors, I'll have some time. If you really think a new book for the Ash Can series will bring Walrus Ink into the black, then are you willing to pay for me to work alongside Tomaltach, at least until we've roughed out the story line?"

He nodded. "I hear Ireland's lovely in the fall. Yes, do what you think best."

He lifted his gaze from the middle distance to look at her. He seemed about to say something more, perhaps a great deal more. She felt herself swimming in the tide of those hot melted-silver eyes. He was going to say what she'd been thinking, make real the last minutes. His lids flickered. The silver darted away from her. She nearly groaned in disappointment. "Take care of yourself, Meryl."

She didn't mean to go near him again. He had made it plain he thought they had crossed the line. She knew she had. Maybe that's why she didn't feel quite so afraid of him at this moment. Things had gone as far as they were likely to, for now.

She touched the top of his desk with sensitive fingers because she didn't dare touch him. "James, the police could be right. The demonstrations may only be a puff of smoke that will disappear as quickly as they arose. But you need to be careful until you know. Maybe hiring a bodyguard isn't such a bad idea. Ned knows several retired policemen who specialize in personal protection. Would you like me to call him?''

His angry bark of laughter startled her. Then he shook his head once, a tight sideways jerk in the negative. He looked straight at her, animosity striking silver sparks in his light eyes. "I don't need your help. I don't need anybody. I never did."

Meryl sucked in her breath, her hand jerking back from the desk as if it had suddenly developed teeth. "Right."

She turned toward her desk and picked up her purse and briefcase. It was only 11:32 a.m., according to the clock on her desk, but her workday was over in this office. She didn't offer an explanation. It didn't seem necessary. One more minute in this room with this man and she would shatter. She would make her calls from Jacqui's phone. If she were very careful she wouldn't need to see James again for a long time.

"Meryl, don't collect any more memories."

His voice caught her as she opened the door and drew her reluctant gaze his way. "Let them go, Meryl. All of them. Just let go."

He was seated behind a desk worth as much as the average family car. He was a millionaire many times over. He was handsome, vital, capable of attracting anything and anyone he wanted. Yet, as she lingered in the doorway, confusion framing her gaze, it seemed possible that he might just be the loneliest man in the world. How did a man get that lonely?

Who, really, was James Eliott Brant?

She closed the door very softly.

She didn't know.

"The same."

James sat on the same stool he had occupied for nearly

two hours. The leather made squeaky sounds and the wood creaked as he shifted his weight. The half-eaten slice of pizza dripping over the edge of his paper plate had begun to congeal into a sludge of rubbery cheese and stiff sauce on the countertop.

He turned his head to nod a smile at the two gray-haired women who had entered and then gave Phil the high sign. After several daily visits, James knew what their orders would be. One blackberry cordial and one Irish coffee. They stayed exactly half an hour and then left with whichever off-duty officer was willing to cut short his pool game to escort them home.

Now that he had studied it more closely, James had discovered that Charlie's wasn't so much a bar as the blue-collar equivalent of a country club. Police occupied the top rung on this social ladder. The warm expectation that greeted an off-duty officer would have made TV's Norm envious. The clientele was rounded out by dockworkers and neighborhood folk: mostly older, mostly clerks and domestics and retirees on a strict budget. Everyone knew everyone else. The menu ran to pizza, hot wings and anything that could be disguised in batter and fried to cardiac-arrest perfection. The ambience ebbed and flowed according to attendance. Slow nights, like tonight, when there were no pro sports games to lure the attendance of the patrons, the jukebox played country-western tunes about lost love, cheating mates and unfulfilled dreams.

Perhaps that's why Phil had kept his beers coming in an attentive, unending procession. After nearly two weeks patronage, Phil must have decided that, for the moment, the stranger in the suit was a regular.

James's movements carried just a hint of deliberation as he reached for the foaming mug of beer. No one present would guess he was a fair way to being drunk—unless Phil was keeping count. He didn't usually make a meal of a six-pack, but the past two weeks had been full of surprises—all of them bad. He hadn't left Hartford because he couldn't.

The shipment of paper he had negotiated for the press last spring hadn't been delivered as promised. When queried, the paper company had played coy about the lost paperwork, suggesting that in order to expedite matters he might want to simply reorder, at the appreciably higher rate. It was nothing less than a shakedown. He never knuckled under to pressure. Before it was over, he had bought shares in a paper mill. Paper wasn't going to be a problem again.

But the buy-out had effectively tied up the last of his liquid assets. He was going to have to make a decision, and soon, about how to raise capital. That meant he had to think about selling Walrus Ink. And that meant he had to think about Meryl.

She had been on the road since the day after the demonstration. A few demonstrators had returned the following day but, as luck would have it, it had rained, one of those heavy relentless New England autumn rains from slate gray skies. The crowd had dispersed within minutes. A stalled low front off the tip of Long Island had effectively shut them down for the rest of the week. The letters, however, kept coming.

The weather was another of the reasons he had stayed in town. Leaks at Walrus Ink had flooded part of a basement storage area, damaging inventory and causing consternation. The staff raised eyebrows but no objections as he worked alongside them, shifting crates of books and taking his turn at the sump pumps.

He had rallied morale after that first difficult day by offering to buy a round at Charlie's. The next night he had found himself headed here after work because it reminded him of the only social hour he'd spent with Meryl. Every weeknight since, he'd come by to sit and watch and think.

He shouldn't have kissed her. But then he might as well have ordered his heart to stop beating. When the kiss had ended, her eyes had contained golden sunbursts in the green.

It had made things so much worse.

First he'd wanted in, all the way inside her, so deep and far that he would never have to hear the door to freedom closing shut. Then the fear had returned, slamming into him, reminding him that need equaled vulnerability and that it could be fatal. Suddenly he'd wanted out, as far and as fast as he could run.

Hot chills. Cold sweats. The abrupt about-face had left him with emotional whiplash and one hell of a psychological headache.

Everything inside him went still as the bar door opened and a slim young woman with dark hair entered, head down against the wind. A smile tugged at his mouth. His heart did a back flip. He was halfway off his stool when she looked up, her face pleasant but unfamiliar. Not Meryl.

His head buzzed and his stomach growled in flat-out disappointment as he turned back to the bar and pulled out his wallet to settle his tab.

He didn't really expect her to walk in the door. She was in St. Louis tonight, or maybe it was St. Petersburg. Her faxes were curt and to the point. She was doing her job, shoring up loyalty for his publishing company, earning her wages and breaking his heart by her absence. When she came back she would only be here long enough to pack for Ireland.

A few minutes later he was headed up the block on foot. He turned up the collar of his trench coat against the knife edge of the wind. He would walk back to work, let the cold clear his head. Maybe then he could get some work done before he took a cab back to his hotel room.

By the time he reached the after-hours dockside entrance, his fingers were stiff with cold and his cheeks ached from windburn. His stomach had gone sour and he knew he was going to have a bruiser of a headache by morning.

He lifted a hand in salute to the guard station before he realized there was no one there. Probably in the john, he decided. It didn't matter. He had his pass. He stuck it in the security slot. The door buzzed and he pushed it open.

The elevator's chime echoed forlornly at the top floor. The lights were dimmed to conserve energy, and the heat had dropped back to nighttime levels, again to conserve energy. The editorial floor was silent but for the low-level hum of machinery he had to concentrate to hear. He made his way to his office in even unhurried strides, wondering if he had antacid tablets in his desk drawer. No, of course not. He never needed them. But someone on the floor was always complaining of stomach upsets, thought even catsup was spicy. Who was it? Jacqui? No. Carrine? Hell. He couldn't remember. His stomach growled again and he absently rubbed it, wondering if he dared check a few drawers.

Some whisper of sound halted him at the doorway of an associate editor's office. The small room jumped to life when he pushed the light switch. In one corner stood a tall palm tree made of gingham cloth. The palm's fronds were stuffed like pillows and stitched for details. Two toy monkeys swung by the arm from the top of the window ledge. A stuffed elephant the size of a chow dog stood next to the desk. Grass matting covered the floor. Jungle prints and posters of waterfalls, rain forests, and brilliantly feathered tropical birds overlapped one another in a frenzy of color on one wall. A well-used pair of hiking boots stood on the coffee table. Postcards from around the world hung by thumbtacks from the edges of every bookshelf on the opposite wall. Photos on the desk of a grinning young man in khakis and a backpack looked familiar, but James had to duck back into the hall to read the doorplate to identify him. Lance Payton. The newest member of the staff. Meryl would have known who he was from day one. She would have known of his passion for the jungle and found a way to capitalize on it. That was her style. His was to read the nameplate.

He switched off the light. If he couldn't remember names, he had no right to borrow even a paper clip without permission.

The ache had become a gnaw deep in his stomach by the time he reached for the door to his office. He didn't think much of the fact that his computer was sitting open, the screen a pale blue blur in the darkness. He must have left it on, he thought sourly as he began to shrug out of his coat. Not that he needed to worry. The laptop had an automatic shutoff to protect the screen. When he'd first gotten it the device had driven him nuts because he liked to muse while he worked and after only five minutes without use, it switched off. After... five... minutes...

James swung around. The screen snapped off as if he'd frightened it. He stood for a moment, eclipsed by darkness. Something was wrong. The room seemed to be holding its breath.

Then he heard them, padded footsteps moving rapidly away from him. The elevator chimed.

He'd drunk too much to be perfectly coordinated, but anger was a sobering influence. He slung his coat aside and hurried out into the hallway. At the far end he saw the elevator doors closing on a figure. Male? Female? Male. The contours of the body were wrong for any but the most muscle-bound woman. He shouted and ran toward the elevator, but knew it was hopeless.

It began to descend as he reached the last cubicle in the hall. He paused and reached for the phone inside and pushed the security button. It rang once. Then again. And again. It kept ringing until he punched the plunger and began dialing 911.

Something gripped him by the ankle. He lost count of the digits he'd dialed.

He glanced down, the receiver gripped to do damage.

Meryl Wallis's green gold eyes were regarding him from beneath the edge of the desk top with amazingly lucid candor.

She put a finger to her lips, then quickly motioned him to the floor beside her.

James crouched down. He didn't have to ask why she was hiding. Her skin was icy cold where he touched her cheek. She was terrified.

But her voice was amazingly succinct as she said, "Someone else was here. You nearly tripped over both of us, you jerk!"

Before he could reply the fire alarm went off.

Chapter 8

"Jesus! You cost me a few of my best remaining years!" James dragged Meryl to her feet beside him.

"You can spare them," Meryl retorted, but she was smiling at him as if he were Batman, the Lone Ranger and Tonto all in one.

He was surprised when she turned into his arms and hugged him tight. "I'm so glad you came," she whispered against his shirtfront. "I was so scared. I called the guard, but he hasn't responded."

James didn't tell her what he'd begun to suspect, that either the guard had been put out of commission or he was in on this, whatever *this* was.

She released him before he could organize a good bluff. "Come on!" She tugged at him even as he tried again to dial 911.

James gripped the sleeve of her sweater to hold her in place. "Where do you think you're going?"

"The stairs. That man may try to wreck the presses."

The look he leveled at her was one of exasperated disbelief. "We're going to stay put. Hear that alarm? There's a fire somewhere in the building, Meryl."

Meryl swept the dark hair from her eyes with an impatient hand. He'd never seen her so pale. "How do you know? Maybe it's just a ruse to cover his escape."

James shook his head in the negative. "Yes," he barked in answer to the voice that came on the phone line. "I want to report a fire and break-in at Walrus Ink Press." As he gave the address he felt Meryl twist free of his reach.

"Meryl! Come ba—! Yes, operator. James Brant, the owner." After curtly giving the operator the building's address, he slammed down the phone and caught up with Meryl as she hurried through the fire door into the stairwell.

The lights were off. The sudden darkness brought her up short and he steadied her from behind. "This isn't smart, Meryl. I've called the professionals. Let's just wait here on the top floor."

She squirmed against him, brushing his groin with her backside. "Let me go. You smell like a brewery."

"And you smell of rank fear." He clasped her in a bear hug from behind. "Now can we hold off on the juvenile name-calling until later?"

"Chicken!"

The taunt wouldn't have affected him if he'd been sober. He told himself that again and again, after the fact.

"All right, Ms. Wallis. Let's go play cops and robbers."

She moved fearlessly away from him down the first of the stairs.

After a few moments his eyes began to adjust to the darkness. There was light, just not much of it. It came through the window panel in the door on each floor. They moved slowly, not wanting to announce their presence by pounding down the metal stairs. Which was just as well, considering that his stomach and head were vying for his attention by simultaneously rioting. At the third and then second floor landings they paused to peek through the window to determine if they could see any signs of fire or other kinds of damage. They saw and heard nothing.

Finally they reached the first floor. Meryl pushed open the door a few inches and stood listening, an expression of rapt attention on her face.

"There's nobody here," she said after several seconds. "But something's wrong." She glanced up at the ceiling. "If there's a fire in the building, why isn't the sprinkler system working?"

"Maybe it requires more heat," James answered and wondered why the heck he didn't know the real answer. He didn't see anything out of the ordinary on the printing room floor, yet he, too, felt an unnaturalness in the quiet. The machinery stood silent, bathed in the same eerie half-light as the offices above.

In the distance sirens blurred the night with sound. The police were coming and the firemen with them.

"Maybe the fire's in the storeroom." Meryl pushed the door wider and entered the room. James followed, determined that she wouldn't get herself killed if he could help it.

They smelled smoke at the same instant. They were halfway across the main floor when the aroma of burning wood met their senses. Burning wood pulp. Burning paper!

"My books!"

James didn't know if Meryl actually realized what she had cried out, but he did. *My books.* This place still meant a lot to her, enough that she was willing to risk her life for it.

Before she could get away, he grabbed her from behind and held on for dear life. "Hear the sirens, Meryl?" he whispered against her ear. "The fire department's coming. Within seconds they'll be here."

She moved so quickly he didn't expect it. She stepped sideways, flexed her knees and drove her elbow back and up, catching him in the belly just under the diaphragm. His grip slackened even as she spun away, and he dropped to his knees like a dead weight. He heard her whisper, "Sorry,"

and wished he'd had breath to answer with a good old An-
glo-Saxon expletive.

He hunched over, all but senseless from nausea for several seconds. Then he heard voices. The ignominious insult
to injury was that his stomach chose that moment to revolt,
just as the firemen's axes bit into the heavy metal door of the
printing room.

Meryl, too, heard the noises of rescue, but she had already opened the door to the warehouse and found her
worst nightmare beyond. The huge storage facility was filling with smoke, and the sprinkler system she'd personally
had overhauled three years ago wasn't working. She hesitated only a second. She knew from years of playing in this
very room as a child where the fire extinguishers hung.

The acrid sting of burning materials grabbed at the back
of her throat as she plunged into the gray-white fog.

Don't breathe, she commanded herself. There were air-
filtering hoods beside the fire extinguishers. She could hold
her breath the few yards it took to reach them. The actual
fire seemed to be at the other end of the building, near the
back, but the smoke was billowing out in all directions so
she couldn't be certain.

She found a hood and was in the process of sliding it over
her head when someone grabbed her from behind. She'd
heard no sound, no approach, but the grip which locked
around her didn't yield to the tactics she'd used to good effect on James. These huge muscular arms simply tightened
about her until she groaned in pain and gritted her teeth in
expectation of a snapping rib. But it didn't come to that.
Not being able to take a deep breath was enough to hamper
her struggle.

The mask covering her head was crooked, shielding her
eyes from the room and muffling her ability to breathe. He
simply held on to her, keeping her from taking a deep breath
as the pain built with amazing speed. As she thrashed about,
her lungs began to ache, her diaphragm spasming in case her
brain didn't understand the extremity of its SOS. But her

brain was having troubles of its own. Her head began
throbbing with oxygen starvation. Thinking was becoming
impossible. Her body lost its coordination. She was limp
and falling, falling, falling.

Meryl found that gazing into faces of strangers bent up-
side down over her didn't improve anything about consciousness. In fact, she closed her eyes, then tried again.
Something must have happened because when she opened
her eyes again the unfamiliar faces were gone. In their place
James was leaning over her. The improvement was mar-
ginal. He looked awful, as if someone had stepped on his
features. His eyes were bloodshot and his complexion was
mottled. Then she remembered that she might be responsible in part for the way he looked. In rapid succession she
remembered everything. Alarmed, she half levered up from
her back. "The books!"

None too gently, James pressed her prone. "Stay still, the
medics aren't finished with you."

"But the—"

"The firemen have everything under control," he said
tersely. "Dammit, Meryl! Don't you have any sense? You
could have been killed."

She didn't mean to laugh. *Oooh!* It hurt her head too
much to laugh, but he sounded so like an outraged parent
whose child had stepped off the curb in front of a bus.
That's what it felt like; she'd been tossed free of the pavement by a bus.

"You think it's funny?" James demanded, trying to calm
his own case of the shakes. He doubted he'd ever get over
the image of her being carried out of that smoke-filled
warehouse in the arms of a fully geared fireman. She'd been
limp, lifelessly limp. "Ten minutes more in that smoke and
you'd now be under a damned shroud!"

Sobered by his comment, she glared at him. She knew
she'd come closer to death than she ever wanted to think
about. She had no nice memories of the experience. No

white light or warm fuzzy feelings had appeared to guide her homeward. There'd been pain and terror that had made her mind numb. Wanting to get even when she felt so vulnerable, she said the first thing that came to mind. "You look awful."

James raked both hands through his hair, further disarraying it. "I don't feel even that good. Where the hell did you learn that move you used on me?"

"Tae kwon do." A weak smile edged into her expression. "Did you really think I was all porcelain and lace?"

"Steel wrapped in velvet," James answered before he could think better of it. The full-watt smile she offered him almost made up for what she'd done to him. But not quite.

"I need water," she murmured and tried a second time to rise.

"Stay put," James demanded. "I'll get it."

Meryl glanced around as he left her side. She had been laid out on an ambulance stretcher in the parking lot across from the warehouse. She gripped the metal sides and pulled herself into a sitting position. It wasn't an especially good idea, she decided as the congo drums in her ears shifted position to the front of her brain.

"Feeling better, Ms. Wallis?"

Meryl knew that dry, interrogatory voice. "Sergeant Rock," she said as she turned her head very slowly toward the man. "Someone broke in here and tried to burn the place down."

"That's how it would appear."

She narrowed her eyes to gain better focus. He was dressed in a raincoat so battered that it would have made Columbo blush. "Are you up to telling me what you know about it?"

Meryl hung on doggedly to the metal railings. Sitting wasn't helping anything that hurt and everything above her belly button ached. "I was attacked."

"By whom?"

"One of the men who started the fire," she answered and then wondered why he was asking such silly questions. "Did you catch him, the one with arms about the size of hams?"

"The only one we found in the warehouse was you, Ms. Wallis."

"Damn. He must have gotten away."

"How did he do that?"

"I don't know. I think he was setting fire to the warehouse when I went in. He came upon me as I was trying to put on one of the air filter masks. The sprinklers weren't working so I was going to use an extinguisher until the fire department arrived."

"The firemen say the sprinkler system had been disarmed."

Meryl accepted the piece of information with a nod.

"You aren't surprised."

"I'd guessed as much," she volunteered.

"Sergeant Rock, were you looking for me?" James had only to glance at the detective's face to know his intrusion wasn't welcome. That was precisely why he interrupted. He crossed the short distance to hand Meryl the paper cup of water he carried. "I was just chatting with the medics. They say the guard, Anderson, is going to be all right, though he seems to have a mild concussion," he offered as conversation to the detective.

"Then you know how lucky you are, Mr. Brant. The damage could have been worse."

James shrugged and positioned himself within arm's reach of Meryl. "The fire chief said his men are fairly certain the fire wasn't set to do major damage. It was confined to the stock paper, away from the main storage of our book inventory. I'd say this was meant as more of a warning than a genuine attempt to burn us out."

Without comment, Sergeant Rock turned his attention back to Meryl. "What do you think of that theory, Ms. Wallis?"

"She thinks it's reprehensible, as do I," James answered before Meryl could, aware as she did not seem to be, of the direction in which the detective's questions were taking him.

"I'm certain you want to be helpful, Mr. Brant. It would help if you'd let Ms. Wallis answer."

"I want to answer. I think there must have been two people, the man who came up to the editorial floor is the same one who attacked me. The other person must have been setting the fire."

"Why two?" The detective cocked his head to one side like a dog listening to a faraway sound only he could hear.

"Because the fire alarm went off only seconds after the man with Virginia hams for biceps stepped on the elevator." She glanced at James. "Mr. Brant chased him, but the elevator left before he could reach it." Her smile warmed as she continued to look at James. "I was never so glad to see anybody in my life."

"Then why did you attack him?"

Meryl started, spilled a little of her water. "I didn't—"

"It wasn't her fault. She didn't mean to hurt me," James cut in, feeling his macho points were dropping with every recounting of his less-than-spectacular showing. "It was a lucky punch."

Sergeant Rock smiled at him, a tight little smile of amusement at James's expense. "Yet you did say she struck you with enough force to render you, er, ineffective."

"I was only trying to help," Meryl said in annoyance as she smoothed the spilled water droplets from her pant leg.

Sergeant Rock refocused his attention on her. "You have a strange way of showing your loyalty to your new boss."

Meryl flushed. "James wouldn't free me even though I thought I could save the books. He didn't want me to take the risk, but I knew where the fire extinguishers were."

"Why didn't you tell this to James?" The sergeant's pause was wickedly telling and Meryl realized in embarrassment that she had slipped in calling James by his first name. "I meant Mr. Brant. Why didn't you tell Mr. Brant what you intended to do instead of attacking him?"

"I didn't attack— Oh, all right." She glanced sideways at James, wishing she could spare him the ego bashing. "I didn't want his help. He'd had a few beers."

The news struck the sergeant as another source of humor. "Is that right?"

James nodded grimly. "I'd been at Charlie's, the bar down the block. Coming back here was an afterthought."

"Every second counted," Meryl continued, going back over the moment in her mind. "A warehouse full of books is like a gigantic fireplace full of seasoned lumber. It could have gone up in minutes without the sprinkler system in operation. Everything. Months of potential sales. Gone."

"That's quite a picture you paint." The sergeant flipped through the pages of his notebook until he seemed to find what he was looking for. "You were the only one upstairs when Mr. Brant arrived, is that right?"

"No. I said there was someone else, the same man who later tried to choke me to death in the warehouse."

"The guy built like the Terminator?"

"That's right," Meryl answered resentfully.

"Did you try your tae kwon do moves on him?"

Meryl ducked her head, not wanting to meet James's gaze this time as she answered. "He was too strong."

The policeman standing nearby snickered. Meryl fumed. "He was trying to stop me from putting out the fire. He would have done anything to stop me. Mr. Brant is a gentleman."

Nice try, James thought, but not enough to repair the damage she'd inflicted on his image as a take-charge kind of guy.

"You were the only one in the room when the firemen entered. Why is that?" Sergeant Rock prompted.

"As I said, he got away." Exasperation laced her speech.

"How?"

"I don't know," Meryl snapped. "I had passed out."

"The medics say your pupil and pulse signs were consistent with those of a person who'd been suffocated, or choked on smoke."

"The life was nearly squeezed out of me," Meryl said in offense and wrapped one arm protectively around her middle. Her entire rib cage ached with each breath.

"What were you doing at Walrus Ink after hours?"

"Working."

"Did Mr. Brant know you were here?"

Trust the sergeant to ask the hard questions, Meryl thought glumly. She had wanted to do that part of her explaining exclusively to James, but only after she'd had a good night's sleep and could get her story straight in her own mind. "No."

"How did you get in?"

Stonewall, common sense urged. Make him go the distance for every answer. "I beg your pardon?"

"Do you have a pass key?"

"No." Meryl's eyes dipped toward the pavement. The sergeant knew how to use a battering ram. "I borrowed my sister's."

"Why?"

"Because I don't have one."

"Why not?"

"I think I can answer that," James broke in, wanting to spare Meryl this ordeal. "I haven't had time to authorize a pass key for her."

"But she got in, anyway." Sergeant Rock's expression softened a bit, as if he was beginning to feel sorry for her. Why, because he thought she was a lousy sneak? Meryl wondered. Apprehension tickled the back of her already raw throat and she began to cough, which made her moan in pain from her mistreated ribs. James steadied the cup of water she held as she took a few sips.

"I appreciate your diligence, Sergeant Rock," James said as Meryl struggled to recover her breath. "But Ms. Wallis has been through a lot tonight. Won't it satisfy your needs if she agrees to come in and make a formal statement in the morning?''

"I'd rather not waste time, if Ms. Wallis is agreeable,'' the sergeant replied, the voice of authority coming into play at last.

Meryl glanced between the two men. The scent of bull males was in the air. James was embarrassed enough to want to exert a little male dominance while Sergeant Rock looked like a very tired man at the very end of a weak tether. She didn't want to spend the rest of the night arranging for James's bail. "Please. Ask your questions, Sergeant.''

Sergeant Rock's stare deflected to her. "Thanks. Would you mind telling me again why you came to work for Mr. Brant?''

This was not a question she expected. "We went over this last week, the day of the demonstration.''

"Humor a tired cop, Ms. Wallis.''

"I once owned Walrus Ink. Because of that, Mr. Brant thought that I would be the best person to offer creative advice to his editorial staff.''

His eyebrows rose, wrinkling his brow. "And this idea didn't give you problems?''

"No insurmountable ones,'' Meryl replied shortly.

"Didn't you once say you hoped someone would ruin James Brant the way he ruined you?''

Meryl blinked. "I don't think so. Why?''

The sergeant again flipped through his pad. This time he read aloud. "'He'—i.e., James Brant—'deserves to have someone ruin him the way he ruined me.''' He looked up with a brightened expression. "According to this newspaper article, that was an exact quote.''

"Oh, but that quote's two years old.''

"Yes.'' He looked down as if to verify her words with his notes. "Then it is a true quote?''

Letting her annoyance show through her expression once more, Meryl conceded the point. "I was angry. I'd just lost my company in a bitter corporate battle. People say all sorts of things when they're emotional.''

"That's true, Ms. Wallis. Some of them even try to make the bad things they say come true." He flipped his pad shut. "Tell me again why you attacked—excuse me—disarmed Mr. Brant."

"I—" Meryl glanced again at James's rigid expression. His eyes were telling her to shut up. So much for gratitude. She suspected that if she clammed up now it would only make her seem guiltier. "He wouldn't let me go because he thought the alarm was fake. I suspected there was a fire in the warehouse."

"So you've said. Why did you think that?"

"Because it's where any person would start a fire if they wanted to ruin a publisher."

"Exactly."

Meryl felt something icy slide down her spine. "You think I did it. Am I a suspect?"

"I must consider everyone a suspect," the sergeant replied without any emotional inflection. "That's my job."

Meryl scooted off the stretcher, ignoring the roaring in her head. "But I love this place. Ask Mr. Brant. I was the one trying to find out what was going on. I was the one who insisted on coming down here instead of waiting for the firemen and police. I was the one who found the fire."

"All right, that's all for now." Sergeant Rock pocketed his pad and then offered her the first human reaction of their brief association. Pity. "I will expect you to come into the precinct in the morning to make a full statement."

Meryl's jaw dropped. Utter disbelief became her shield against the reality of what he was implying. He couldn't possibly be serious. He must have forgotten that *she* was a victim. She nearly followed him as he walked away.

She turned, searching the night until she noticed James standing just a few feet from her. She smiled, needing to share with him her disbelieving amusement at the absurdity. "Can you believe that man? He thinks I might have started the fire. Me!" She threw her arms wide for emphasis and then groaned as pain sideswiped her thoughts and collided with her skull just above her eyebrows.

James shot forward and caught her as her knees buckled. "Easy, Meryl!"

His hands hurt the bruises on her arms as he lowered her back onto the stretcher, but she didn't care. The change of pain location made her head feel momentarily better. She sat limply as one of his hands reached up to support her throbbing head. A callused palm moved with impossible care over her hair to push the shiny dark curtain from her face. Clever hands. A carpenter's hands. They knew how to strip and smooth and polish rough, worn surfaces, creating beauty from damage. How did the wood look when he finished with it, she wondered absently. What shading did the oils of these hands give each piece? His touch had certainly left its indelible mark on her. Ten days on the road hadn't altered her perspective on him, only given her long uninterrupted hours to think about what his kisses had done to her plans, her dreams and her peace of mind.

"Meryl?"

Close. He was so very close she could see the kohl-dark rim around his silver irises. Her headache retreated as she dove headfirst into that tarnished gaze.

Hard eyes. She had once thought he had the harshest gaze in the world. That was before she'd learned what passion could do to the gray. When heated by passion, a dip in his gaze had always left her vermeiled with his desire. He had made her feel deeply desirable in that glorious way only he could inspire. The look in those eyes made her feel brave and beautiful, made her want to dance naked before him with only a veil of silk as cover. A fundamentally sexy man, he had roused her sensual nature, shown her the possibility of abandoned joy. And then he had hurt her as no one ever had.

Yet, as he looked at her with those hard-tender eyes, she wondered if she wouldn't have forgiven him, if he had ever asked for forgiveness. Anguish tugged at a corner of her mouth. Hadn't they both deserved a second chance? Why hadn't he given it to them?

He sensed her question. She felt the connection made in the tension of his hands still resting lightly on her shoulder and hair. A wary frustration entered his gaze, as if he wanted but didn't know how to answer. Then his expression altered and she knew he'd suddenly realized that he'd left his feelings unguarded too long. Retreat. For the second time in their acquaintance, he had retreated from her.

"You okay?" How impartial his voice sounded.

No! she wanted to shout. *I don't know how to get over how you make me feel. Tell me!*

His rumpled appearance reminded her how very unkind she'd been to him. "About before. I'm sorry, James."

"It's okay, Meryl." He stroked her sleek hair, his expression now as carefully controlled as a bishop's wife in the company of the devil. "You've been through a lot tonight. Too much."

"You can't think I had anything to do with this?" She regarded him with eyes that stung from unshed tears of frustration that had nothing to do with Sergeant Rock's interrogation. "I wouldn't do that. You believe me, don't you?"

"Shh," James crooned as he stroked her hair, damp and tangled from her ordeal. "Don't think about it now, Meryl. Let's just get out of here."

"Yes, I want—" She paused to catch her breath as a funny little tremor of sound escaped. Her lower lip began to quiver as reaction at last set in. The sensations came in quick waves of trembling that began deep in her bones and quickly worked their way to the surface. All at once she was shivering and sobbing, unable to stop.

James folded her against him, grateful that she came willingly into his embrace and that he had found, finally, some way of comforting her. Raked by a guilty conscience, he held her as she cried, trying to shield her from curious eyes while absorbing with his own body a little of her pain. He had been totally ineffectual when she had needed him most. Instead, he'd made a first-class ass of himself and left her to the mercy of an attacker.

Even so, the practical part of his nature wouldn't allow him to ignore the implications of the sergeant's incisive questions. To be honest, he had been second-guessing parts of her story. For instance, why had she come back to Hartford without letting him know? What was she doing in Walrus Ink after hours without a borrowed pass? Had she surprised the intruder looking into his computer files? Or had she been using his laptop when the intruder surprised her? He wished now he could remember what had been on the screen those seconds before the monitor shut off. Sophisticated pass codes would have kept anyone from easily looking into his personal files, but he might at least have learned what the person had been attempting to locate.

He had considered excusing himself to run upstairs and check. He scratched that plan as she murmured something into his shirtfront about feeling queasy. The practical question he wanted pragmatic answers to could wait until morning.

"It'll pass, Meryl. Just take a few breaths." He cradled her more gently. She was a warm and willing weight against him. He shut his eyes and set his jaw on the emotion stirred by her touch. The specter of her had followed him into the empty expanse of his bed every night since she had left town. He had been thinking about holding her, about how she had felt when he had kissed her in the copy room, of the tiny things like the raspy feel of her sightly chipped front tooth as his tongue passed over it. Did she know she always gave up a short catch of a sigh when their lips met?

He'd never heard that unconscious hiccup of surrender in any other woman. He had felt it, though, in the pit of his stomach, that quiver and summons to surrender that she so willingly obeyed. She did that to him, made him ache to surrender, every time, every way, all the way. His aversion to that complete surrender had torn them apart. In many ways she was braver than he.

"She doing okay?"

James nodded to the medic who suddenly appeared beside them. "We'll be packing up, then. Unless she wants to take a ride to the hospital. The guard's already left by ambulance to get an X ray of his concussion."

Meryl lifted her head. "No, I want to go home." She angled her head up from James's chest to whisper. "Take me home, please."

"Anything you want, Meryl."

They both needed a shower, a change of clothing and a little peace. Whatever the reasons behind her appearance here tonight, she had risked her life to try to save his company. He couldn't think of a thing he possessed he would have been willing to risk his life for.

The thought drifted into his mind that the woman in his arms, whom he didn't possess in any fashion imaginable, was one person he would risk his life for.

James lay awake on his back in bed, staring at the ceiling. Lit by the first light of dawn, small gold star bursts caught and winked back at him from the shadowed ceiling where a few silver moons also rocked and sailed. A Meryl whimsy. Childlike but not childish. The king-size contemporary wrought-iron canopy bed in which he lay was gracefully scrolled. Yard after yard of sheer bleached muslin looped in lazy swags over the canopy rails, then fell to the floor in artful cascades on either side of the headboard. More whimsy. Meryl lived in a world of limitless blue skies. No clouds were allowed to darken her horizons.

That thought disappeared as his gaze followed the slant of sunlight slicing in through the window shutters to light the framed pencil sketch on the wall opposite the bed. It was a simple sketch in an elaborate gold frame, which at first glance seemed much too ornate for the subject. The drawing was of a haggard young woman visibly sagging under

the responsibility of the three children who clung to her
Skillfully but simply rendered, each child bore a different ye
haunting expression: wariness, withdrawal and impoten
resentment.

He might never have guessed the artist if he hadn't been
staring at Tomaltach's painting of Timon for two weeks
One child wore a tattered coat. A knit cap covered the head
of the second. There were gold hoops in the ears of the
third. Those items were the trappings of Timon the Ash Ca
Cat. These were street people, homeless people.

Not many people would have been comfortable with this
reminder of the severity of other lives in the serenity of their
own bedrooms. But Meryl not only had opinions, he realized, she believed that actions should follow words.

All at once, he understood her choice of framing. The
museum quality gave the subject weight and dignity: vali-
dation.

He half rose on one elbow and gazed the long way from
the foot to the head of the bed. Beneath a single lace-edged
muslin sheet Meryl lay quietly, the shape of her body delin-
eated in an unconsciously erotic sprawl. Her delicate profile was tucked into the softness of a lace-edged pillow. Her
dark head, as rich and sleek as sealskin against the iceberg
purity of the bedding, struck him as unspeakably precious.
He had spent the night in her bed. What would she think
about that?

He drew himself up carefully, suddenly certain that he
didn't want her to awake and find him next to her. He hadn't
earned that ease with her.

Yet he drew away reluctantly. When he had gained his
feet, he hung by the foot of the bed and stared at her. He
wanted to lift that sheet and crawl in beside her and just hold
her.

No, scratch that. Who was he kidding? He wanted to push
aside the covering and bring her awake to the rhythm of his
lovemaking. He wanted to make her ache and then smooth
the ache, to make her cry with hunger and then fill that

hunger with his body. He wanted to bury himself in her and make them both forget every bad moment of the past two years. He wanted to pump golden star bursts of desire into the green depths of her eyes. He wanted to make them both flush and damp with desire and then limp and wet with joy. He wanted to clean the slate, erase the past, make it possible for them to begin again.

He felt himself tremble with that wanting, yet he didn't move. He made himself stand there and ache for what he couldn't have. Small punishment, no satisfaction. Stupid thing to do. He wanted so damned much, yet he had forfeited the right. So he stayed and stared and let the hunger eat at him.

Chapter 9

Meryl stirred with reluctance, unready to leave the submission to her dreams. Somewhere just outside consciousness, memory whispered to her. *Someone's here. Someone's watching.*

She jerked unpleasantly awake; her eyes snapped open as she half sat up.

"Hi."

Her heart executed a leap. James was leaning an arm against the upright post at the foot of the bed. Arms folded casually across his chest where dark hair whorled over broad pecs and around tight rosy-brown nipples. Beneath those corded arms the shallows of his bare stomach rose and fell with his even breathing. Much farther down, below the hairy hollow of his belly button, the band of his underwear was visible above suit trousers that hung, zipped but unbuttoned, from the ridge of his hipbones.

Her gaze dipped lower for a betraying second. She knew what lay behind that zipper. His waist remained enviably narrow, but he was no lean-shanked youth. Those hips belonged to a man with the girth and power of maturity.

Her gaze rose with the steam of her thoughts. He had obviously been here all night. His hair was tousled from sleep and his smile was crookedly aslant in a bristle of morning whiskers, as if he were absurdly pleased with something, perhaps himself.

"I like your new bed." The gravel in his voice shifted over the husky words. "Comfortable but cozy."

Meryl considered how many options there might be to her reply as she struggled to a seated position, the sheet pressed to her bosom. *Isn't it roomy? Glad you liked it. Did you sleep well? Did we . . . ?*

"Hungry?" His eyes flashed something hot and sexy, turning the word into a whole vocabulary of foreplay.

Meryl nearly didn't reply. The heat of his gaze was evaporating the sheet, steaming her body, curling her hair.

"Coffee. Please." How polite she sounded, as if she were the guest and he the host.

His crooked smile twitched. "I'll be back. I think after last night, I remember where everything is."

Meryl followed his retreating back with inordinate interest. What had happened last night? "The fire!"

James turned back as he reached the doorway. "I've already been on the phone with the fire department. Preliminary findings concur with their speculations that the fire was meant to frighten, not necessarily cause major damage.

"Then why was the sprinkler system shut off?"

James scowled. Trust her to not miss the obvious. "Maybe the vandals got their wires crossed. Coffee coming up."

He disappeared so quickly Meryl wondered if he was running away. But, of course, that was ridiculous. James Brant didn't have a shy bone in his gorgeous body.

He had been in her bed.

Meryl lifted the sheet and wasn't encouraged by the sight of her naked body. "Hmm." She lowered the sheet. She was fuzzy on the details of events after James brought her home. James admitted he had been in her bed. Where else had he been?

The question left her strangely unembarrassed. It resurrected memories of other nights long ago, detailed memories of his rough voice whispering erotic obscenities into her ear, the thrill of his hands and mouth on her body acting out those words. Those memories made her sweat. So then, that was her answer. She might have been roughed up the night before, but nothing short of brain damage would erase the memory of James Brant's lovemaking. She didn't remember anything because there was nothing to remember.

Meryl forced herself to move. She didn't want to. She was stiff in every limb. The bruises on her arms had turned reddish purple. She suspected that she'd find matching ones on the lower pairs of her ribs. When she stopped to think about it, her head still ached. It had been an awful evening.

She didn't bother to glance at the full-length mirror on the back of the door as she reached into her closet for a robe. She knew she must be a real mess. Why confirm it?

The details of what happened came back as she entered her bathroom and found it in complete disarray. There were damp bath towels and several hand towels in a pile on the floor. The clothes she had worn the night before were draped over her wicker hamper. It struck her as poignantly familiar to see James's shirt and jacket hanging from hooks on the back of the door. She recognized the way his socks had been shucked and left as two puffballs by his shoes. His belt lay curved like a snake near the commode where he had discarded it. It was almost like old times—except that now she wasn't trying to recover from the nearly sleepless night that had left her happier but more tired than when they'd slipped between the sheets together.

Meryl picked up his belt and coiled it around her palm with her other hand. She had been surprised to learn that the scrupulously detailed businessman was a slob. They had always come to her place to spend the night because she hadn't wanted to be seen leaving his hotel room the next morning. Sometimes they'd left a trail of clothing from the front door straight to the bed, or the sofa. Once, after a heated exchange in an empty elevator, they had gotten no farther than her entry hall rug.

Her gaze drifted away from his things. The tub was still full, the surface slicked by bath oil. Now she remembered. James had brought her home and ordered her to soak in that tub. He'd drawn her bath and then gone to make a cup of tea for her while she did. She suspected she'd fallen asleep during her soak and that he had climbed in after her, because she always pulled the plug. Reaching down carefully, she pulled the stopper chain.

She had once teased him because he loved to soak in a hot tub. She said he would have made a good despot. Meryl could well imagine a handmaiden waiting on him, nervously hoping to avoid his lusty eye as she scrubbed his back and other more intimate places. He had pulled her in with him and made her do exactly that. Her hand tightened on the supple leather belt that had encircled his lean waist. The idea hadn't lost its appeal.

Get a grip! She began snatching up towels, telling herself that dredging up old feelings was bound to get her into trouble. She should be grateful she hadn't had to fend him off the night before. What she really wanted scared her. It thrilled her. It made her want to run screaming from the apartment.

Avoiding the tub, she opened the shower stall and turned on the faucets.

Five minutes later she reappeared in her bedroom, her hair washed, her teeth brushed, her body tingling, and aching. She'd gotten a good look at herself in the bathroom mirror as she exited the shower and she knew one thing absolutely. She wasn't going to be wearing anything that required a tight fit for several days. In fact, she avoided a bra and chose warm-ups the color of raspberries.

"I've delayed opening the office until noon in order to give the authorities time enough to complete their investigation and clear out." James hung up the phone and began scribbling on the notepad in front of him. "That way, the staff won't have to think so much about what occurred last night."

"That makes sense." Meryl reached across the table to rearrange the centerpiece, apples piled into a wooden maple syrup bucket. She needed to distract herself from taking too much notice of the fact that he sat shirtless across from her. "I suppose I should call Sergeant Rock and make an appointment."

"I did it," he answered, then drained his coffee cup. "I'll drop you off at the station before going in to work."

"You don't need to do that."

He looked over at her, really looked at her for the first time since they'd sat down to drink his excellent coffee. "I'm going to. And then you can come back here and pack."

"Pack? Why?"

"Because I've booked a seven-thirty flight for you to Shannon airport. You wanted to go to Ireland, right?" The steel glittered in his eyes. "Tomaltach will meet you in the morning."

"I'm not going anywhere, not now at least." She gave up trying to make the final apple stay atop the pile and brought it to stand beside her cup. "Sergeant Rock might need me. In fact, I got the feeling last night I was his number-one suspect."

"We discussed that and you've been removed from his list." James was in his CEO mode, which meant he was issuing orders, not making conversation. Too bad, she wanted to talk.

"What's changed since last night?"

"I made it clear to the sergeant this morning that you were a bystander." As a fighter's cockiness lifted his features, Meryl decided she wished she had overheard that conversation. "I saw as much of the intruder as you did. I can make an ID, if necessary."

"Maybe," Meryl temporized, "but I encountered him three times. You only glimpsed him once."

Though he didn't appear to move a muscle he suddenly looked as outraged as if she had just stabbed him in the back while he was busy defending her against her enemies. "I'm your boss. I pay you to take care of my business. I want you in Ireland, working on the new Timon book. The sooner it's complete, the sooner we can start production."

"Yes, but—"

He cut her short with a look. "I hate sentences that begin with 'yes, but.'"

"No doubt it's because you know an objection is coming," she responded tartly, trying not to stare at his chest. The chilly air had made his nipples as hard as nuggets. Or was it emotion?

She lifted her gaze to his. "I'm not going anywhere while Walrus Ink is being threatened."

His gaze narrowed. "Walrus Ink's troubles are not your problem."

Meryl couldn't argue that she hadn't said those very words to him two weeks earlier. She'd even said them to Jacqui, and believed them then. "Things are different now."

"No, they aren't. Whether you worked for me or not wouldn't have affected what happened last night. Since you did accept my offer, you either do the job I assign you or you're fired."

She nearly choked on her laughter. "You wouldn't dare."

Dangerous currents whirled to life in his unsmiling gray eyes. "You're fired."

Meryl shook her head, trying not to be charmed by his bullying tactics. "This isn't the way to win friends."

"It influences people, though, doesn't it?"

She glared at him, fighting the absurd urge to reach across the table and haul him in by the ears so that she could soften the cruel line of his mouth with a kiss. Who was she kidding? She needed to get as far away from this man as possible. "I'll go to Ireland."

He didn't even bother to gloat. He reached for his pad and tore off the top sheet. "Here's your itinerary. Your ticket will be waiting at the airline counter. Oh, and don't forget your Wellies. Tomaltach says they've been experiencing a 'wee bit o' softness.'"

"You've already talked to Tomaltach?"

"Don't worry, I charged it to my number."

Meryl was impressed by his efficiency despite her resentment of his high-handed tactics. "Galway must be flooding in biblical proportions if Tomaltach even mentioned the weather." She glanced at him, but he was writing again. "I really do need a day or two to prepare for this trip. I'll have to stop the mail, the newspaper, things like that."

"Leave your key with me. I'll take care of it," he said without looking up.

She waited a few seconds before beginning again. "It's been two years since I wrote about Timon. I'll need to find my files on the series, read back through them, see if I had any ideas for more books."

"You've an hour before you're expected down at the precinct. Find them now and you can read them on the flight over."

Meryl stared at the top of his head. "You really want me out of the way, don't you?"

His head lifted. "I want you where I know you'll be safe."

His provoking gray gaze held a message she couldn't afford to accept at face value. If she did she'd have to admit that she affected him as much as he affected her and that it went deeper than mere attraction.

For an eternal moment the possibility of reunion danced before her like a mythical chimera, an absurd creation of her fervent imagination. The first time around they'd created a train wreck. She'd be deliberately risking the possibility of disaster if they got together again. What good could come of it?

"I think you're blowing this out of proportion. After all, the protesters aren't after me."

"No, they're after me."

The words sent chills down her back. "So you want me as far away from you as possible."

"I want you safe."

Safe. That word again. But whose safety was he concerned with? She saw it in his face. He was fighting, resisting, looking for distance. He was as afraid as she of the possibility of them getting back together.

She looked away from that rugged face, suddenly fighting for her own rational distance. He had backed off from her a week ago when she had been so devastated by his kiss that she had practically succumbed on the office rug. They had spent last night together, in the same bed, and he hadn't even touched her. He was the one exerting very uncharacteristic control. There must be a very good reason.

One occurred to her. It was the same one she had run up against the day he'd kissed her and then retreated into icy formality. Regardless of the tug of old ties, he did not want her in his life. He was making that as clear as he could without coming right out and saying so. The least she could do was act like an adult and retire gracefully.

"I'll go to Ireland," she said in a voice that sounded more defeated then resolute. "But you're making a mistake if you think I'll be safer there." She was pleased to see emotion flicker his lids. "You've never ridden with Tomaltach. The man's a fiend behind the wheel."

The smile he sent her was devoid of triumph. Unexpectedly it seemed full of gratitude. That shift of expression revealed his weariness. There were more lines than usual in his face and a tightness that stole the sensuality from his mouth. She knew he hadn't slept as well as she. How could he? Someone out there in the city hated him enough to try to burn down his business. No matter how crazy the motives were, or how mad the perpetrator, the knowledge that he was hated that much would have to have had an impact on him.

The hint of hidden emotion in his eyes made her remember Sergeant Rock quoting her hate-filled words back at her the night before. She cringed. How full of self-righteous indignation she had been two years ago. But she hadn't literally meant him harm—or perhaps she had. Perhaps that was what was wrong now, why she felt so guilty whenever she encountered his gaze across the table. She had meant those words then.

She tested the possibility in her thoughts.

If someone had been trying to burn down another of his businesses two years ago, would she have taken a certain satisfaction in that? No. From a deep place inside her the truth stepped forward without effort. If his life had been in danger even then, she'd have stanched her own wounds and come back to stand beside him—because she had loved him. Her hurt had been personal, a lover's sorrow. She had wanted personal revenge, wanted to see him come crawling to her, begging her forgiveness. How she had needed him to be there to hold her when, a few weeks later, the pain of his desertion was compounded by another loss.

She had never wanted to see him damaged, she realized with a new clarity of her feelings. She hadn't even wanted to see him humbled, only for him to admit that he cared for her more than anything else in the world: making money, his reputation, himself. She had wanted what every woman wanted, to feel loved.

She felt cheated by circumstance. They'd never had a chance, not a real one. Their lives had been on a collision course from the moment they'd met. Two more cautious people wouldn't have jumped in with both feet. They'd have spared themselves the agony that followed such brief ecstasy. But he wouldn't be James if he'd acted any differently. So where did that leave her?

It left her aching to wrap her arms about him, to just hold all that lovely heavy muscle and bone against herself and say that she cared, that despite the past she wanted him to continue in one wonderful piece. She wanted him to know that he wasn't as alone as it must appear to him at this moment.

He was staring at her, his expression changing gradually from gratitude to uncertainty to retreat. Could he guess her thoughts?

Struggling for inner balance she looked around for something to do. She thought she found it when she spied a skillet on the counter by the sink. He must have made himself something to eat after she'd fallen asleep the night before.

She hopped up, but came to a halt halfway out of her chair as she felt a distinct *snap* and incredible pain knifed in under her ribs, stealing her breath.

James looked up to see the color drain from her face as she froze in her rise from the chair, a silent cry of pain distorting her mouth.

"Meryl! What's wrong?" He leapt up, sending his chair skidding backward across the tiles as he reached out to steady her in her half-crouched position, an arm clutched to her right side.

"I think I broke something," she whispered, leaning forward in the hope of steadying herself with her forehead against his chest. Instead she nose-dived into the crisp hair just above his left nipple. With her free hand, she clung to his arm, afraid she would pass out if she tried to adjust her position.

James took her by the shoulders. "Can you sit?"

"No way," he heard her murmur as her lips fluttered against his bare skin.

"Okay." His mind was racing. Pulled ligament or cracked rib. He'd done both before. A bear to heal. She'd need an X ray to verify that, but right now he needed to make her more comfortable. She was trembling beneath his hands.

"Okay, baby, just let me move you two steps so you can lean against the tabletop. It's not far. That's right, slowly. Good girl."

Meryl swallowed her opinion of his word choice. He was trying to be kind and she didn't have breath to waste.

With gentling hands he rested her hips against the edge of the table and moved to lift the bottom edge of her sweat top.

"What—?" Meryl grasped his arm with her free hand.

He looked up at her. "Let me see what's wrong."

"No. I'm okay," she said through gritted teeth.

Hard eyes met her pain-fogged gaze. "You're not okay. You're in pain." He reached for the lower edge of her sweatshirt. "Just let me look—"

"No!"

Irritation peaked his heavy brows. "Don't be childish. So you're not wearing a bra. I've seen you before. Remember?"

She did remember and, dear Lord, that was the whole problem. He'd noticed she wasn't wearing a bra! For entirely selfish reasons she was pleased. "Okay."

She shut her eyes and tried to breathe shallowly as he tucked the hem of her shirt over the rise of her breasts, exposing their lower halves and her rib cage.

"The bastard!"

Her eyes snapped open to see his expression twist painfully and then he went down on a knee between her spread legs. Meryl closed her eyes again. She didn't want to see his face when he saw what she had tried to keep hidden even from herself.

James swallowed his rage as he stared at her slender torso. He had seen the bruises on her upper arms last night, but she hadn't said anything about this. Several long angry red and purple bruises followed the gentle curves of her ribs from under her arms forward under her breasts. Her attacker had literally tried to squeeze the life out of her while he'd been retching uncontrollably in the next room. His fault. If he'd held on to her a little tighter, if he'd not drunk so much, if he'd not gotten her involved in his life again. If! If! If! A sorry word.

He reached out and touched the unblemished skin just above one bruise. The light touch left the impression of his fingertips, a telltale sign of swelling.

"I want to hear Sergeant Rock's theory about how you could have self-inflicted injuries like these!" he growled.

Meryl opened her eyes again just as he leaned into her, his hands framing her hips. Before she could question his last statement she felt with amazement the pleasant sensation of his lips on her bare midriff and then the startling warm, wet stroke of his tongue. She reached out and tangled her hands in his hair. She meant to push his head away, but her fingers curled in the thickness and held him there as pleasure spiraled across her middle, dipped lower down and invaded her.

His hands tightened on her hips, pulling her a little closer as he followed the curvature of her ribs with his tongue. Each lick brought him closer and closer to the under curves of her breasts. Finally his nose nudged the full weight and set one gently swinging. She shivered as his breath cooled the wet tracks of his tongue on her skin.

I must be mad, she thought. *I've probably broken a rib. This man kneeling before me doesn't want me anywhere near him. I'm scared to death of what I'm feeling.* Oh, and what she was feeling!

Rivers of desire were running through her stomach to pool in her womb. He hadn't even kissed her and she was rising out of herself, losing touch even with her pain as she concentrated on the feel of his hard hands kneading her hips through her clothes. When his lips closed over a nipple, she gasped.

The pain won.

The violent spasm of her hands in his hair told him he'd gone to far. Too far? Hell! He'd been taking advantage, was little better than the bastard who'd so abused her.

James climbed to his feet, breathing like a man who'd run a mile, and carefully lowered her shirt before looking into her face. Words of apology were already lining up on his tongue when their gazes met. They evaporated.

She reached up. She cupped his head in her left hand and then she pulled his head down and she kissed him.

He felt the top of his head lift off. He leaned in hungrily to her kiss, the crotch of his trousers pressing against the inner angle of her right thigh. He welcomed the pressure to balance the hard, hot throbbing behind his zipper. He didn't touch her. He didn't know what touch wouldn't hurt her. He just hung on to her kiss, trying to hold all of her within the embrace of his lips.

Her fingers were climbing down over his shoulder and then his chest. They stroked his nipple and he groaned. He lifted his arms in the universal sign of surrender as her arm snaked around his waist and then her hand moved up over the contours of his back. He ached to push her back into the table and make love to her. The urge had him trembling. He didn't move.

He stood under the rhythmic stroke of her hand up and down his spine, ignoring the heavy tremors the passage of those gentle fingers cost him. Sweat broke out on his skin as he let her nibble his mouth and then he devoured hers. He had never before felt quite like this, victim to a pure raw need that had him transfixed like a perpetrator waiting for the next order from the police.

Finally she was pulling back. He dipped his head, catching her mouth in a succession of quick, hungry kisses even as she drew away. He lowered his hands onto her shoulders and pulled her face in against his sweaty chest. She was trembling as much as he was. They were like a pair of runners who'd raced for the finish line only to find it moved beyond their view.

He lifted a hand to her hair, still damp from her shower, and cradled her head with a tenderness poles away from his desire. "I want this. But I can't risk what you do to me. Do you understand?"

Meryl did because she felt exactly the same. "Let me go, James."

Hunger and heat and regret fought a quick and ugly battle in his conscience. "Are you sure, baby?"

She lifted her head, gazing up at him in mute misery.

He let her go.

"Find my fisherman's sweater?" Meryl called from the next room.

"Right on top!" Jacqui put the final sweater in her sister's suitcase and flipped the lid closed. "I don't see why you have to leave today. You should be in bed."

"Piffle." A smiling Meryl appeared in the doorway to the bathroom, a cosmetic bag in her left hand. Her right arm was strapped to her side to keep it immobile while her ribs had a chance to heal. One cracked rib and several deeply bruised ones confirmed, two prescriptions and a pleasant fuzzy numbness to take the edge off the toothache quality of the pain in her midsection: that's what a trip to the doctor had earned her.

"I can't believe you're still on your feet." Jacqui shook her head. "Anything with codeine in it knocks me flat on my fanny for twelve hours."

"Sum uf us arr made uf stunner stoof," Meryl replied and then ran her tongue over her teeth because it seemed as if they had suddenly softened.

Jacqui eyed her with a jaundiced gaze. "See what I mean? You can't get on a plane. You could wind up in Tibet."

"Tee-bet? I'd like Tee-bet."

"Oh, I just bet you would!" Jacqui finished zipping the case and lifted it off the bed. "I'm just relieved that the police have agreed to step up their interest in the case. I had a bad feeling about those protesters. Bad vibes, you know? What I can't believe is that you didn't call me last night and tell me what had happened to you. How did you manage?"

Meryl shrugged. She didn't want to explain that James had spent the night with her. That would require a cleverness she simply wasn't up to at the moment. "You're here now."

"Yes, thanks to Mr. Brant." Jacqui chuckled in memory. "He sounded really annoyed when he called me from the clinic to pick you up. I suppose he resented the fact that he had to take you there on his way into work." She turned to watch her sister's response closely. "By the way, how did he happen to be the one to take you?"

Meryl sighed and rubbed the tip of her nose with the corner of her cosmetic bag. There had to be an explanation rattling around in her brain. "He had come by to take me to the police. To give a sta-sta-staplement."

"Statement," Jacqui corrected and again shook her head. "This trip is a mistake. A definite mistake. Let me call Mr. Brant. I'm certain I can convince him of the necessity of you waiting a day or two to fly."

Meryl's attention turned toward the living room as her doorbell chimed the first notes of Beethoven's *Fifth Symphony*. "Company!"

"Definitely dopey," Jacqui murmured as her sister drifted toward the front door.

Meryl opened her door to James. He was shaved, showered and dressed to impress in a double-breasted pin-striped suit. He was big, bold and beautiful. Puzzlement replaced expectation. "What are you doing here?"

Hot, hungry eyes devoured her. "What does it look like? I'm going with you."

"To the airport?" She smiled at his thoughtfulness.

"To Ireland."

Somehow that was a little too thoughtful. Her smile dissolved. "You arr-arr—can't be serious."

"With one arm in a sling you won't be able to manage your purse, never mind your bags."

Her chin went up. "I'll hire a redcap."

His chin tucked in. "You'll deal with me."

Meryl's brow furrowed. "I don't want to deal with you."

"Too bad."

"Hello, there!" Jacqui waved from the bedroom door at the two people who sounded as if they were children playing, "Am not, Are so!" "Mr. Brant? This is a surprise."

James hauled in his private thoughts. "Hello, Ms. MacPherson. I've decided to fly to Europe with Meryl because I need to do business there that I'd been putting off." Geez, he sounded as rattled as a teenager trying to explain to his girlfriend's mother what he'd been doing in her bedroom. "Besides, your sister seems to need an escort."

"You're absolutely right," Jacqui concurred, "if not a keeper. She's already flying without the plane."

James gazed into the plum-fat pupils of Meryl's eyes. "Are you certain you're up to this?"

"'Course I am." Meryl smiled a soft, mocking little smile. "Wouldn't want to disappoint."

"You never disappoint me," he said under his breath. "You just make me a little crazy."

He moved quickly past her, but her perfume followed, casting tendrils at his retreating back. "I've got a car waiting downstairs," he said to Jacqui. His brows lifted at the sight of the one bag she held. "Is that all she's taking?"

Jacqui shifted the bag from her hand to his. "Not quite. There's a hanging bag, briefcase, computer and cosmetic case inside."

"That sounds more like it," James said smugly. Women and baggage.

"What about Sergeant Rock?" Meryl asked, feeling that she was being ignored because she had hung back by the door. She rectified that situation by approaching James. If Jacqui weren't here she knew she would have kissed him just to watch the cold steel in his eyes melt.

"I called him and he checked with the clinic," James said shortly. "He agrees now you were attacked. Though I don't see why it's necessary, he wants you to come by the precinct and look at some photos. Then you're free to leave the country."

Meryl's wandering attention focused at the mention of photos. "Did you look at photos?"

He shook his head, looking like a bad storm rising. "I only saw the jerk who attacked you from the back. But Anderson, the guard, has picked out a suspect from mug shots. Unfortunately, Sergeant Rock doubts he's the perpetrator."

"Why?" Meryl leaned her head to one side because it seemed very heavy. All of a sudden she wished she could lean against James. Such a hard face, such a hard mouth, such hard hands. Everything about him was hard but his touch. She needed that touch right now to steady her gently spinning world.

"The guy Anderson picked out is a professional bone cruncher," James said, observing with guarded interest that Meryl was staring at him as if he was a gigantic Fudgsicle on the hottest day in July. "No job too small or too nasty, if the money's right."

"You mean our ethical protesters hired muscle?" Meryl giggled; she couldn't help it.

James and Jacqui exchanged worried glances.

"If Anderson is right," James continued, "our protesters are into heavy-duty threats backed up by thugs. That means things could get even nastier." He glanced again at Jacqui and noticed she'd paled considerably. "But let's not get ahead of ourselves. The police have to find the guy first. In the meantime, you can earn that exorbitant fee I'm paying you by working in Ireland."

Meryl frowned, trying hard to keep up with the conversation. "What if they need me to make an ID?"

Considering how doped up she was, James doubted she could identify Jacqui from a photo. That wasn't his concern; getting her out of town and harm's way was. "If you pick out the same man, Anderson can ID him in a lineup. The police only need one witness ID to hold him."

Meryl had seen enough TV police shows to wonder about all of this, but James was watching her with the determined attention of a shepherd guarding his flock. She smiled and patted his perfectly aligned tie. "Whatever you say, James."

James shot an uncomfortable glance at Jacqui as her sister's curved fingers slid very suggestively down the length of his tie. "We better get going."

A few minutes later Jacqui stood on the sidewalk waving goodbye as the limo pulled away from the curb. Even now she was wondering about the wisdom of entrusting Meryl to James Brant's care. Meryl hadn't said anything about matters between them, but it didn't take a genius to figure out who owned the man's handkerchief she'd found in Meryl's bathroom as she was packing. "I hope you know what you're doing, Sis."

James looked over in concern as Meryl shifted uncomfortably in her seat. They were an hour out of Kennedy and between first-class courses. "Are you all right? Do you need something?"

She offered him a sad little smile. "Another painkiller?"

Just looking at her made him hunger to touch. He glanced at his watch. "It's too soon." That's why he kept them in his pocket, so she wouldn't accidently overmedicate herself.

Her expression softened. "That's all right. I like your way of killing pain better."

He dove again into the golden currents in her sea green eyes. "What way would that be, baby?"

She crooked a finger at him and, when he leaned in close, she closed her eyes and lifted her mouth.

James was proud of his restraint in the face of temptation. One thing about painkillers, he thought uneasily, they removed inhibitions in some people as well, if not better, than booze. He reached up and pressed a finger into the lush softness of her lips. "Not now."

She looked hurt, but then her eyes widened with a new idea. "Can I sit in your lap?"

"Meryl," he said dampeningly for she was already unhooking her seat belt and then she was climbing across the first-class console and into his arms.

"You're going to hurt yourself," he murmured in amusement and exasperation as she settled herself in his lap, her head toward the window and her right arm turned away from him.

"No. You're going to take very good and careful care of me, aren't you?" She looked up at him with the clear gaze of trust in her eyes. Too bad she was doped up. Don't screw this up, his conscience warned him.

"I'm going to take very good care of you," he whispered into her ear and wondered how he was going to stand the exquisite torture of her backside jammed against his crotch. But she did feel good, perfectly right, in fact. And she smelled of peach blossoms.

To distract himself from every temptation of his senses he turned his thoughts to Sergeant Rock. Though both of them had doubted her ability to function, Meryl had picked out the man Anderson had chosen from mug shots with amazing ease and confidence. Zip Hearst. Street muscle: ugly, crude, but effective. If Meryl had seen him, then it was an even better bet Zip had gotten a good look at her. She'd be safe in Ireland until the police picked up the thug. All the same, he wished he could hide her on the dark side of the moon.

"I'm cold," she said in a petulant voice after a few moments and squirmed against him.

Metal teeth dug into the sudden swelling behind his zipper. James reached for the blanket that had been covering her in her seat and arranged it over them. "Better?"

"Better." She settled her head with a smile of contentment on his right shoulder. "You're so good to me. I wish I could make you feel better, too."

Incredibly he felt her left hand sliding down his stomach and into his lap. He reminded himself that she wasn't responsible for her actions, that he couldn't take anything she did at face value, that he had to protect her from herself. But he wasn't good enough or strong enough to halt the sweet stroke of her hand.

Damn! He deserved to go straight to hell.

"Broken rib. Painkillers," he offered in terse explanation to the flight attendant who paused with a questioning look at them a moment later.

The woman noted the straps of Meryl's sling peeking out above the edge of the blanket and nodded sympathetically. "She'll have to go back to her own seat if we hit turbulence," she cautioned and then moved on.

James tried not to laugh. *If* they hit turbulence? She had no idea of what was going on under that blanket. It was going to be a long, *long* trans-Atlantic flight.

Chapter 10

"Still a women's libber, are you, then, Meryl?" Tomaltach O'Connor asked provokingly. His face wore a permanent scowl that defied an easy calculation of his age or gauging of his real feelings. They were an hour out of Shannon Airport, headed north along a "shortcut" only he knew.

"Absolutely, yes," Meryl responded. She tried not to wince as the Irishman made a wide right turn and then sent his car barreling down the country lane fully astride the dividing stripe. They drive on the left here, she reminded herself. The fact that a steady drizzle obscured all but two half-moons of windshield that the wipers sluggishly scraped clear didn't mean that they were in any real danger.

"Ah, well, tell me, Mr. Brant," Tomaltach said gruffly as he glanced in the rearview mirror at the big man who was wedged tightly in the back seat of his small car. "Would you not rather be known as an able-bodied seaman than an able-boobied seaperson?"

James set his jaw as the car bounced in a rut. From the

moment he'd set eyes on Tomaltach O'Connor at the airport and the Irishman had greeted him with, "So this is the grand man himself, is it?" he hadn't liked him or his surly attitude. His Neanderthal views on women didn't improve James's opinion. What could Meryl possibly see in the man? Clearly she saw something, for she'd rushed up to hug the tall thin man in black leather as if he were a long-lost love.

"You're a devil, Tomaltach, and you'll never change," Meryl said with a halfhearted attempt at disapproval.

"Sure and you did not expect it? I'm an Irishman, lass. You can always tell an Irishman, but you can't tell him much!"

Meryl cast a rueful glance back over her shoulder at James. That way she didn't have to watch the car that had suddenly appeared like a dark lump out of the mists on the road ahead. It didn't help. James's eyes were widening with the concern she was trying to avoid.

"It's better to concentrate on something else," she advised him in a stage whisper, but she couldn't stand the suspense.

Every muscle in her body zinged taut when she turned back to look out the front window. The oncoming car was weaving back and forth across the median while Tomaltach kept his own vehicle steadily in midpath. Hedgerows hemmed them in on either side. There was no room for error.

"Pull right!" she whispered under her breath.

"No, left!" James barked.

"Ooh!"

Tomaltach swerved the car left at the last second. The other veered right. Both cars brushed the foliage, tires bumping over stone-strewn ground.

"Damned drunkards!" Tomaltach dropped the window and stuck his fist out as the car full of young men shrieked past, offering them a crude salute. That incited a few pithy Gaelic oaths from them. No translations were needed.

"Took the pledge not to drink at the age of twelve, I did," Tomaltach went on almost cheerfully after a moment when he'd shut the window. "Take it again every New Year's Day, just to keep in practice."

"Does it keep you sober?" James inquired doubtfully as he wiped from his face the rain blown in through the window.

"Ah, well, no. But it keeps me in practice."

Meryl shot James a look that said, *Don't encourage him,* and then resettled her arm in its sling.

Instantly alert to every nuance of her mood, James touched her gently, his fingers framing her neck from behind. "Are you in much pain?"

"I'm fine, Mr. Brant."

James removed his hand. There was no doubting that tone of voice. The medication-induced tipsy of the provocative woman from the flight had worn off. Too bad. As much trouble as she had been, he'd liked her.

He tried to shift his knees, which were tucked practically under his chin because the front seat was only twelve inches deep. After a moment he gave up and instead distracted himself by concentrating on the back of Meryl's head.

Her mahogany hair spilled over the edge of the front seat, the satin-smooth waterfall just inches from his fingers. For hours during the night he had leaned his cheek against that sleek mane and breathed in the scent of the woman in his arms. It was not until dawn crept into the dim interior of the plane that she had awakened, startled to find herself in his arms.

He smiled in memory. She had seemed outraged by the idea that she had actually crawled into his lap. She'd resumed her seat and a dignified attitude for the rest of the flight, but it had done no good and both of them knew it. Another side of her had been revealed by the potent painkillers. That side had left him suffering from the sweet frustration of unmet desire. Hunger for the ripe weight of her body, the bright wonder of her lips, the dark drag of her fingers on his rigid flesh, consumed him still.

He resented Tomaltach's intrusion, however transitory, in their lives. He couldn't stay long in Ireland, but there was no way he was going back until he and Meryl had settled, once and for all, the reason for the tangible tension between them. It wasn't simply lust that had exploded between them again. He knew it. She knew it. It was time they both admitted it and then dealt with it.

He'd hustled her out of Hartford to protect her. She hadn't wanted to leave, but even Sergeant Rock had had the grace to suggest to him that Meryl might be in danger if the perpetrator suspected that she could identify him. As much as he was going to hate leaving her here, she was better off until the police had caught Walrus Ink's would-be saboteurs.

He expected her to give him a fight. Loyalty, that trait he had taught himself to think of as a weakness, was one she possessed in spades. No one else had ever put that kind of premium on his friendship.

Which stirred up other bitter memories.

In the months after she had left him, he'd come right to the edge of destruction. With the indictment of his business partners he, the king of the hill, had fallen from grace. To his surprise there'd been no one to break his fall. His "friends" were suddenly busy, absent, otherwise engaged. His enemies, and their number was far greater, stood by and watched like carrion birds patiently waiting for the twitching to stop.

James set his mind against his memory tracking back any farther.

"You'll be wanting to stop for provisions," Tomaltach announced suddenly and made a left turn into the hedgerow without bothering to brake.

Miraculously there was a gap in the hedges at that point.

Just beyond it loomed a whitewashed thatched-roof building with a bright red door and a huge painted sign that read Guinness—For Sure!

A yelp of alarm escaped Meryl an instant before Tomaltach trod on the brake and brought them to a halt inches from the piled-stone fence that bordered the shop.

"Dammit, man!" James roared from the back seat as he reached forward to steady Meryl who had winced as the car jerked to a halt. "Do you want to break another of Ms. Wallis's ribs?"

Tomaltach glanced around nonchalantly. "If she were ailing, why didn't she say so before?" He frowned at Meryl, his eyes like chips of blue glass in his pale angry face. "Have you no tongue to speak for yourself, woman?"

"Yes, I do." Meryl stuck out her chin, her own eyes bright with indignation and pain. "You drive like a madman and have no more regard for life than you do manners!"

"And," James added, clamping the younger man's shoulder in a viselike grip, "if you so much as hit another rut, I'll shove you out and drive myself!"

Tomaltach smiled suddenly, his mobile face rearranging itself almost by magic into the features of a rather attractive young man of twenty-six. "That's more like it! 'Twas the devil's own work to get a rise out of the pair of you till now."

James held his temper, but only just barely. Tomaltach might think he was being funny, but if he made Meryl so much as tense again he would happily break the young man's neck!

Once inside the small shop that was equal parts grocery, butcher and hardware store, Tomaltach helped himself in adding freely to Meryl's purchases. Though she demurred, he ordered thick-sliced bacon and two kinds of sausages from the butcher.

"Pork and liver pâté, the very best," he said with a nod. Then he added eggs, currant bread, soda bread, loose-leaf tea, milk and sugar to her modest selections of coffee, orange juice and scones. "Now you can make your boss a proper Irish breakfast."

"I don't know what you're expecting, but I'm not going to cook for you," Meryl said dampeningly, fed up with Tomaltach's less than charming Irish cockiness.

"*Wirra.* It's not me you're stopping with." Tomaltach cocked a black brow at James. "Mr. Brant has that honor."

Then she swung around on James.

"The company rented a house for you," James said tersely, not wanting to discuss this in front of the audience of curious locals who were openly watching them.

Maybe it was only a reaction to the medication she had been taking, but Meryl felt a heightened sense of anticipation as she gazed into James's hard face. It banked the suspicion prompted by Tomaltach's snort of derision. "Just what and where is this house?"

"Cloughan Castle?" Tomaltach inquired as if she had spoken to him. "Sure and it's just the sort of place a darling girl would think herself at home in, being she's that sort of a girl."

Meryl ignored him because James's expression had taken on combat readiness. She might want to throttle Tomaltach from time to time, but she wouldn't put it past James to actually attempt it. She had tried to warn him about the tall, rake-thin man with the thatch of unkept black hair and a misanthropic disposition. Tomaltach was a brilliant artist, but as a person he was definitely an acquired taste. Occasionally even she choked.

The question of accommodations was settled an hour later as Tomaltach slowed his car and pulled off onto the shoulder of the road near a hilly hay meadow. Rising majestically in the foreground, surrounded by a lush green field of milk cows, was a weathered crenellated Norman tower.

"Be it ever so humble," Tomaltach intoned with a cheeky smirk.

Meryl stared in fascination at the medieval fortress, which, highlighted by a welcome break in the clouds as the mists drifted and parted like theatrical illusion, appeared like something out of a fairy tale. "It's lovely. It's magical. What place is this?"

James leaned forward, watching her expression. "You like it? Good. It's your home for the next few weeks."

Her head snapped toward him so quickly her hair brushed his face, a few strands caught in the rasp of his morning beard as it trailed across his lips. "You're kidding?"

He met her doubtful gold green gaze with tender promises he hoped he could keep. His throat went dry. He wanted to get it right—for her. "I think you've earned a little magic, don't you?"

"Well!" Tomaltach said scornfully, "If the blarney's done with, I'll be popping over to open the gate."

Five minutes later Meryl was standing on the gravel lane that ran from the road up to the castle. Her head ached. Her ribs ached. All the sleep she'd had on the flight seemed to have evaporated during the car trip. She needed luxury and comfort, room service and a wide soft bed with clean sheets. Most of all she wanted to curl up in James's embrace and stay there until all the pain and weariness were gone.

She lifted her head back to look the long way up to the top of the tower. Grand as it was, it appeared to be a place that required an open mind and a good deal of tolerance and stamina. She was fresh out of two of the three.

"The booking agent said something about it being built in the 1500s," James said as he came up the driveway behind her.

Meryl's gaze swooped down on him. He had been to fetch the key, as per travel instructions, from the farmhouse nearby. How big and solid he looked next to the painfully lean Tomaltach. She longed to lean into his strength, needed his touch to restore her wavering energy. Her beleaguered mind produced wild fantasies and then wilder needs as he closed the distance to her. He did make her want to fuel the hunger that burnished the silver in his gaze.

Then again, was she ready to resume a relationship with a man who had already proven how badly he could hurt her? Her smile wobbled. Her side throbbed. She felt like crying.

As he met that silent plea for help the impact of her weariness hit James in the solar plexus. She looked ready to drop. Or had she suddenly realized what she had gotten herself into by coming with him? He wanted to reassure her, to take her in his arms, but he knew how she felt about public displays of affection. Not that he meant any touch between them to remain public for long. That damned smirking Tomaltach was all that kept him from sweeping her up in his arms and carrying her into the castle and up the stone stairs until they found a room with a bed. He did the next best thing. "The keys to your castle, milady," he said, handing her the key ring.

As Meryl, using her left hand, fumbled with the massive key in the lock, she heard James and Tomaltach exchanging a succession of quick, low words. They didn't sound particularly friendly, but she supposed it wasn't her business to interfere. After all, Tomaltach nominally worked for James.

By the time she had gotten the key to turn in the lock, the car engine had roared to life. She glanced over her shoulder to see James coming toward her, his arms full of luggage and groceries. Beyond him, Tomaltach was backing his car up the lane toward the road at breakneck speed. His tires spit gravel in all directions, startling the milk cows grazing nearby.

"Where's he going?" she asked in amazement.

"I told O'Connor you needed rest."

Meryl frowned at his dismissive tone. "He drove us all the way from the airport. We could at least have offered him a cup of tea."

"You could have," James said carefully, drawing her full attention. "I would have punched his face in if he'd accepted."

Meryl saw the truth of his statement in the silver flash that flickered in his gaze. She had always known when to back off with James. This was one of those times. She turned to the door and very carefully applied force to it with her left shoulder.

It might not have been the original portal, but it was plenty heavy and creaked with enough conviction to make her believe it was the genuine article. The door was three and a half inches thick with huge metal hinges and shellacked to a mirrored surface. But she forgot all about the door as it swung open on a room straight from Camelot.

The interior was dark and cool, the walls the pale gray granite of ancient times. A tapestry, faded and fraying at the edges, hung in welcome before her. To the left a narrow stone staircase curved up and away toward an ethereal light that seemed to be radiating from the stones above. To the right she spied a heavy plank table in the room beyond and a collection of mismatched carved wooden chairs with padded seats lining the far wall.

"You go up. I'm going to put the kettle on," James said behind her.

"What about the luggage? Isn't there anyone to greet us?"

James smiled at her. "We're it, Meryl. The place is ours, kind of like renting a seaside cottage."

Meryl blinked at him. "You mean there's no staff?"

He leaned forward and kissed her quickly before she could guess his intent. "We're it, baby. Now go on up." He paused, his eyes searching her face for signs of distress. "Unless you need help getting up the stairs."

Meryl shook her head, all too aware of the import of his previous words. *We're it, baby.* They were alone. Together. Again.

"Then I'll bring you breakfast, in bed if you like."

As he turned away, Meryl gave his back a last, lingering look, then turned to climb the stairs. James had rented a castle. Just for the two of them.

She scaled the first few steps slowly, keeping her left palm flat against the uneven surface of the weathered stone walls. A few more steps brought her level with the first of the narrow wedge-shaped windows.

She recognized what it was from having read about them. As a teenager, fantasy novels had held equal sway in her imagination with softball and rock and roll. It was an arrow slit, angled to give an archer defending the castle maximum range and direction while the narrowest point at the outer edge of the wall offered the smallest opening for return fire. This opening had been paned in by glass, to keep out the cold, she suspected. The wall's thickness was longer than the stretch of her arm.

She discovered as she climbed that the winding stair formed the spine of the tower and that the rooms were reached by stepping off the staircase. The first contained a bright brass bed, lace curtains and an armoire at least two hundred years old. It was a pretty room with wool carpets whose colors had been muted by age. The wooden floor was stained dark like the woodwork that framed the windows.

The next landing contained a room with a pair of twin beds and a small corner fireplace. Peat bricks had been laid for a fire. The bathroom was tiny but contained a toilet, sink and shower.

The third bedroom became hers on sight. It was the largest with a king-size canopied bed and full stone hearth. The counterpane was a rose-and-cream floral tapestry banded in green velvet. Matching panels hung in the corners of the four posts. The overcanopy was rose and buttoned in the center so that when she crawled carefully onto the bed and stretched out on her back to look up, it formed a pleated tent. To her surprise the bed was warm beneath her.

She closed her eyes for just a moment. That's all she needed, a moment's peace. Then she would get on with the business of being an author and James Brant's employee.

She awakened slowly, her eyes refusing to open even as consciousness returned. She had been having a deliciously erotic dream. It was too good to release just yet. She was wrapped in James's long, hard, unyielding warmth. Warmth from his torso invaded her shoulders and heated the curve of her spine as she lay on her left side. His groin scooped in tight to hug hard under her derriere. His muscular hairy legs scorched the backs of her thighs and cushioned the backs of her calves.

Slowly a hand reached around in front of her and cupped a breast beneath her sweater. The hand closed, thumb and forefinger stroking the nipple it gently pinched to life.

Her eyes opened to the umber haze of an extinguished sunset. Nothing about this reality was familiar except the touch of the hand at her breast.

"James?"

"Hush, baby." His voice came close by the back of her right ear, his warm breath feathering across her neck. "Just let me hold you. Just let me touch you. That's all."

No dream. She softened against him, moving her hips against his groin in the subtle movement of surrender. She wanted him. Wanted his hands on her, his voice in her hair, his heat easing and comforting her conscience. She was tired of fighting it, tired of fighting him, and oh so tired of fighting herself.

His hand slipped under the edge of her bra, found the full weight of her. She sighed as he patiently and expertly rubbed fireworks into her skin, ignited sparkles of need from her breast and showered her nerves with delight. His lips brushed the back of her neck. He licked at the fine hair of her nape. His teeth traced the cords of her throat as she arched her head back.

Then his hand moved lower. His fingertips drew circles on her abdomen that set off Roman candles lower down in her womb. She gasped at the intensity of sensations brought by so little effort.

He turned her carefully onto her back and then he bent over her. In the half-light of near darkness, his bright silver eyes were the only illumination in the room. They gleamed and hinted at his smile all but hidden in shadow. "Feeling better?" His rough voice stroked her like fine sandpaper, leaving its mark on the grain of her soul.

"Hmm," she replied, not knowing what was the right answer. She felt rested but not refreshed. His clever fingers had banished all hope of relaxation.

"More?"

She smiled back at him, bargaining with the devil. "Um-hmm."

He kissed her, kissed her so softly that she could barely feel it and then so thoroughly she was filled with the taste and textures of his mouth and tongue and teeth. She lifted her hand and touched his hard face. Her fingers curled into the rasp of his five-o'clock shadow, seeking out the bones beneath the warm skin, making as real as possible the dark shadow bending over her. This was James Brant, the demon lover and difficult man she couldn't forget. He hadn't forgotten her, either. The hunger was too strong in him. He tasted of desire and wonder. And she knew she was the cause.

His hand found her again, moved aside clothing and opened fastenings until his fingers were on her naked stomach. They slipped below her waistband, inside her panties and dipped into the core of her.

"Open just a little—yes, that's better. Oh, you are so soft and warm—so wet!"

She kissed him, hard, wanting him to feel what she felt. The wildness shivered on her skin, spread across to him, and his shoulders shuddered under her hands. She tasted his tongue and then sucked on it, trying to match the rhythm to

the insistent movements of his hand, but his rhythm was
stronger than hers. She abandoned the contest for the longing, searching, aching need he was creating with his hand
and lips.

He rubbed and stroked and whispered to her until she was
squirming against him, her fingers balled into fists on the
tapestry. Her hips surged into his hand.

"Yes, yes, you love it," he whispered, half laughing and
half groaning against his own desire.

She closed her thighs, trapping him there. He altered the
pressure, finding the places and the pace she seemed to seek.

"That's right. Let yourself enjoy it. It's good, isn't it?"
A soft, inarticulate moan answered him. "Sweet, sweet,
Meryl. You're all I think about. All I can think about!"

How urgent he sounded, how desperate, how needy. The
rhythm of his hand changed as did the pressure and method
of his kisses. He ravished her mouth, finding ways of making her gasp and whimper and sigh and shudder. She rose
quickly to the brink, hung suspended at the edge between
unbearable desire and exquisite release.

She clutched his shoulders and tried to pull him onto her.
He resisted. Bewildered, she opened her eyes. "James?"

"I can't, Meryl, not without hurting your ribs and—believe me—I've been considering all the options."

"But you—?"

"You'll owe me, okay?" His chuckle was short and dry,
as if something was caught too deep to be dislodged by his
mirth. "I'll just think about how I'm going to collect."

"Won't that make things worse?" she asked in a small
voice.

"No doubt...no doubt."

She felt him moving down her, the mattress buckling under his weight. And then he was gently spreading her legs
and moving between them. The delicious shock of his
mouth on her made her stiffen and sent pain digging into her
right side.

His head lifted. "Too much?"

"No!" she whispered, trying not to squirm in anticipation. "Please, don't stop."

He chuckled. "That's my girl!"

James cupped her hips in his rough hands and kissed her again, tasting and savoring her, loving her and learning her again, as if for the first time. And maybe, in some ways, it was the first time, he decided. Before, he had always been intent on his performance, making certain she was satisfied but always with an eye toward his own fulfillment. This time, he had no such expectations. He just wanted to make her happy, to feel her reactions, to find ways of pleasing her, to make her wild with desire, to give and expect nothing in return but her gratification. It astonished him to learn how much joy that giving gave him in return.

"Oh, James! James!"

"Yeah, baby!" he answered, the sound of her ecstasy-ravished voice calling his name was almost his undoing.

James watched her finish her meal with narrowed eyes, outraged male ego in full strut.

It's just good sex.

She'd said those words to him just moments ago.

He hadn't known what to say. He still didn't. In all honesty he felt like running for the nearest exit. This incredible attraction, this need to touch and possess her, was driving him up the wall. Because directly alongside that need was this powerful urge to push her away.

From the moment he set eyes on her she'd had that effect on him, the ability to make him think unthinkable things, like the future, permanence, a realization of a need that once met could create its own hunger. He knew now he'd never get enough. He would always need her. That awareness of the possibility of an endless need left him feeling slightly off-balance, and a little afraid of himself. Fight or flight, those were the only alternatives left him.

Any other alternative was unthinkable. Wasn't it?

Meryl watched him from beneath her lashes as she finished the plate of scrambled eggs and toast he had made for her. She had offered him his freedom. She hadn't meant to.

They had lain a long time in each other's arms, half-dressed and only one of them satisfied. She had tried to reach out to help, but he had refused to allow her to touch him. She didn't know why and wanted to.

When he had finally left her to pull on his clothes and make something for her to eat, she had meant to face him down and ask him exactly what his intentions were toward her. But she couldn't ask him once she saw his face.

He'd been in the kitchen when she'd walked in. He'd turned at the sound of her voice, looking like a man caught in the grip of his conscience. He couldn't have appeared more acutely uncomfortable if she'd just found him in bed with another woman.

Desire hadn't entirely left him. It escaped his gaze in hard little flashes like lightning. But the rest of his face had been set in harsh lines of self-recrimination. She'd recognized it in part because she had been dealing upstairs with much the same.

What should she expect now, having allowed him to love her—to pleasure her—with a familiarity that didn't exist between them? Upstairs in the darkness, in the heat of the moment, they had been perfectly compatible, if not evenly matched. He'd been right. Her ribs couldn't withstand his brand of lovemaking. He was like a locomotive: hard and swift and powerful. But why the generosity? Was it simply the spontaneity of the moment? Was that all?

Or was it a reminder of how easily they had gotten into trouble so long ago, causing a kind of pain neither of them wanted to repeat? The sex was great—no, amazing. It was the rest of being together they had never found a way to manage.

She had smiled at him and he'd withdrawn even more so she'd said the only thing that came to mind. "Thanks."

Disbelief had moved in his face and it had been like watching a mountain move. "For what?"

She'd braved the gale of his gray eyes. "For the sex."

"Is that all?"

She'd shrugged, backing off the challenge in his eyes. "It was sex and it was good. It's just good sex."

Meryl stared at the gray speckled pottery plate with a smear of yellow from her eggs and wondered how she could have used the words *just, good,* and *sex* in the same dull sentence. Anytime sex and James were connected the results deserved words like *brilliant, magical, superb, wondrous, memorable.* Every glorious time was memorable. Because she loved him.

Dear God, it was only a short leap from that thought to total insanity. She could sign the commitment papers herself. James didn't commit. James didn't love, at least not in ways she could live with. She couldn't be in love. Lust must have addled her mind, short-circuiting her emotional register. She'd felt this way before and it had nearly ruined her life.

"More cocoa?"

Meryl lifted her head, startled to realize how far her thoughts had drifted. "No, but thanks for the food. I hadn't realized how hungry I was."

"I knew." His voice made her jump again despite the fact she was looking at him. He knew. Of course he knew. He knew all about her hungers.

She met his gaze guiltily. "Are you okay?"

He shook his head. "You don't want to know."

No, she didn't, because then she'd begin to think again of ways she might remedy the situation that he'd made no effort to hide from her. Short of draping a dish towel over his lap, there was no way of disguising the fact that he was still aroused. Her gaze skittered sideways.

"Meryl, we need to talk," he said after another long silence. She glanced up to see that he was frowning, his thumb patting a rhythm against his cup. "This strain between us has got to end. What do you say we spend the next few days going over the various accusations and counteraccusations between us, one by one?''

Meryl held her coffee very carefully between her palms. letting the heat radiate through the mug into her bones. ''Okay.''

''Good.'' There was satisfaction in his voice. He was the CEO conducting a meeting, a mode he was familiar with. ''Shall we begin now?''

Meryl hid her disappointment in her cocoa cup. They were going to have a business meeting to discuss their sex life. Wonderful. ''If you'd like.''

He nodded. ''Tell me what you want from me?''

She stared at him, every nerve in her body zingingly alert. Was he joking? She wanted from him what every woman wanted from her lover, to feel loved. But did he really think she was going to share that heartfelt confidence with him just like that? Amazingly she could see it in his face. That's exactly that he expected. He was sprawled in his chair, legs extended, his hands laced flat across his belly, watching her with the concentration of a laser.

''This maybe your—*our* only chance.'' His deep voice gave the words a sharp, urgent edge.

She knew he was right. If they couldn't solve things here, together, away from everything and anyone who could possibility come between them, they never would. But she wasn't going to do an emotional striptease until she had gauged what he wanted.

''All right.'' She leaned forward with a smile. ''I want what every woman wants.''

''Good sex?'' he suggested hopefully.

She laughed and the knot in her chest eased a bit. ''A date.''

''What?''

''It's the one thing we never had,'' she went on reasonably. ''A date, a real date.''

His face cleared of every emotion but surprise. "You're joking?"

She smiled smugly. "Never mind. You asked me, but I can see you already had a different answer in mind."

He sat up, his lazy recline abandoned. "No, no. Back up. A date." He said the word as if it were an unfamiliar term. "I'm giving it some consideration." Silver eddies of interest warmed the currents of his gaze. "You say we never had a date. What about all those expensive dinners we've shared?"

She shook her head, shifting dark hair over her shoulders. "Those were business dinners. Half the time we worked right through to dessert."

He grinned wickedly. "You were dessert." He saw her brows lift in warning. "Never mind. Let me think. Ha! What about the time we took in a movie?"

"That was a de facto date. We ducked into that theater to get away from a reporter who was following you. I just happened to be in tow."

"Okay. What do *you* call a date?"

She had him. "A prearranged meeting to do something mutually enjoyable."

His voice lowered. "I can think of several mutually enjoyable things we've done together."

"Out in public," she added.

"I'm game, but it could get us arrested."

"Dinner," she persisted, struggling against the tidal drag of longing his voice always produced. "Or better yet, a walk on the beach. A drive. A picnic. A visit to a museum. A night spent eating popcorn and watching TV."

James chuckled. "You've never seen Irish TV."

"A boat ride." Meryl glanced up and out of the window at the far end of the long table. The hill behind the castle was a black hump, the sky a velvet carpet of midnight blue. The colors of night, the night that stretched before them, here, alone, together. "And I want flowers and poetry."

"Poetry?"

His disgruntled tone made her smile. "Poetry."

"I don't do poetry."

She looked across at him. "Fine."

"Okay, poetry." He muttered something unintelligible under his breath. "But I don't have to write it, agreed?"

She shrugged. "I think when you want to impress someone you should be willing to go a little out of your way, take a risk, maybe make a fool of yourself."

He took a breath and dove headfirst over the edge of the Empire State Building. "Why not?"

"Good. Now it's my turn to ask a question. Tell me about yourself."

"What?" He leaned back in his chair, unconsciously tucking a hand inside the waistband of his jeans. Was that to relieve the too-snug fit in the groin, she wondered. "You know everything."

"I know nothing." She dragged her gaze away from things better left uncontemplated in her injured condition. Her bright gaze caressed his face. "Not even your mother's name. Do you have brothers and sisters? Is your father very proud of you?"

"I have two sisters. Married. Two nephews, two nieces. Mom lives in Albuquerque."

"Your father?"

"My father's dead!"

The snarl surprised her so much her cup rattled in its saucer. Just that quickly something shut down in him. His eyes were impenetrable as lead, but he couldn't control the emotion breaking over his face. She knew without asking that the pain she saw there wasn't the usual kind. It was too deep, cut too close to the bone, to be an ordinary loss. Something wrong was connected to that death. "Tell me about your father."

James shot up out of his chair. "No." It was a small word said quietly, but it might have been a bullet for all the force it carried.

"That's it, then."

He swung his head toward her, not understanding the meaning of her words. "That's what?"

"You asked me what I want. I want to know you."

He shifted impatiently. "You know me."

"No, I know only what you want me to know."

"That should be enough."

"It isn't."

For just a second he glared at her and she remembered why others feared him. But strangely, this time she didn't quake except with sympathy for a man who held so much— too much—back.

"Don't dig there, Meryl. You won't like what comes up."

"Maybe not, but it's my right to know the man I'm getting involved with, if I'm going to get involved."

"*If* you're going to get involved?" Something equally dangerous to violence snaked through those silver depths. "Is there a remote possibility we aren't involved?"

"You tell me. How does the idea feel to you in here?" She pointed to her heart.

He smiled a don't-you-wish smile. "That's a second question. You're getting ahead of yourself. It's my turn, again."

Something in the predatory way he said it alerted her to danger a fractional second before he leaned forward and placed both hands on the tabletop so that his face was only inches from hers. She hoped he would kiss her. Instead, his words smacked her between the eyes.

"I want to know where you were and what you did those first three months after you left me."

Chapter 11

"That's damned silly! I won't do it!"

"You're being entirely unreasonable," Meryl replied calmly and snatched the menu from the hands of the man sitting across from her. "You're not listening to me."

Tomaltach's angry face darkened in embarrassment as the other patrons in the pub turned openly amused smiles in their direction.

"Now you see what you've done," he groused as his ears reddened, "inviting the neighbors to our private party."

Meryl shook her head. "You're shameless, Tommytock, and you know it."

"Aye, lass, I am," he agreed with a quick grin and a pat of her hand, though she'd used her pet name for him in public. "Else I'd be after finding myself a quiet corner instead of a noisy pub in which to make mad passionate love to you."

Meryl chuckled and darted a glance toward the man who sat at the other end of the small room drinking a pint of Guinness.

James had been inordinately patient with the pair of them. She wondered just how much longer that patience would last.

James could have told her. Jealousy was a new emotion for him, but he was very nearly convinced that he was going to behave very badly any minute now. Tomaltach's touch of her hand had stripped a few more threads from the shredding rope of his control.

For two days now, he had been watching them argue like children over the new project. The one time he had tried to step in to smooth things over they had both jumped on him. One thing was certain, all that heat and fire and clashing egos wasn't just the result of artistic differences. Some of it was sexual, if only on Tomaltach's side.

James surveyed his competition for Meryl's attention with an adversarial eye. The tall, thin Irishman wasn't bad looking, once a person got past the initial impression of punk-band reject. He had that arresting Irish combination of black hair and deep blue eyes, a fine wit that he too often perverted with anger and a insolent insouciance that was bound to intrigue a woman. But most disturbing of all, he shared a passion with Meryl for books and literature and art.

James sipped the thick concoction the Irish called beer, but he found as filling as a meal. For days he had sat and listened to them discussing books and artists he'd heard of but never read or studied. It had made him feel left out, unnecessary and somehow diminished in Meryl's eyes. Tomaltach's smirking understanding made him want to put a fist in his face.

Right now he'd been relegated to chaperon, out of direct sight but as vigilant as a bird dog in the field. He loved to watch her, like now. Her hair was loose and cascading over the shoulders of the thick wool fisherman's sweater she wore. Her feet were tucked under the hem of a long flowing skirt with its field of tiny flowers. She was thirty-two, but she might have been nineteen. He wished suddenly that he

had known her all those years in between. When she glanced
his way again he saw her smile. It was all the invitation he
needed.

"We're just going to order lunch," Meryl said in greeting as he brought his beer to their table. "Would you like to
join us?"

"Sure." James plunked his beer down and took the chair
next to Meryl on the opposite side from Tomaltach. "You
kids getting any work done?"

"Not much," Meryl admitted uneasily. "We've been
away from the project a long time. It's taking a while to
reestablish a sense of shared vision."

"Were you to call off your guard dog we might well get
something done," Tomaltach offered as he leaned back in
his chair until it rocked on two legs.

James met his smirky challenge with a flat gray stare.
"I'm not going anywhere."

"James," Meryl said persuasively and laid a hand on his
arm. "Can we talk over there?"

Damn! She was going to try to get rid of him.

James stood when she did because not to would have
made him seem like the jealous irrational lover he was.
Make that would-be lover.

He hadn't touched Meryl sexually since that first night.
It was stupid of him to let a little thing stand in their way,
but she had made such a big deal out of it that he'd not been
able to simply brush it aside. She'd flatly refused to give him
even a clue about where she'd gone or what she'd done after she'd left him two years ago. She wouldn't even give him
a hint. He knew one thing about Meryl, she wasn't petty.
Something serious had occurred during those three months
and she didn't want him to know. If he had secrets, so did
she. The impasse had left them both wary and protective,
circling each other with suspicion.

Tomaltach had used their estrangement to his advantage,
coming early and staying until Meryl was practically asleep
in her chair. Why didn't she throw the guy out? Why did she

indulge his ego and his bad manners? What was going on between them?

With that last thought nagging his steps, James followed her to the door where beyond its glass panes the misty afternoon was working up to a rain.

When she turned to face him he remembered that, unlike with Tomaltach, she felt no compunction in calling him on the carpet for his manners. Her first words confirmed it. "What are trying to do, James, ruin everything?"

All attempts at friendliness vanished. "You and Tomaltach, what's your history?"

She opened her mouth on silent laughter. "I don't know what you mean."

"Yes, you do." He closed the considerable gap she'd left between then, stopping just inches short of brushing her breasts with his chest. "Don't play with me, Meryl. I'm not in the mood. You look me in the eye and tell me if you've been lovers."

She lifted her head to look up into his face, her gaze eager and insolent and just for him. "What difference could that make to you?"

He basked in the glow of her indignation. "The difference between whether I'm going out that door or sticking so close you won't be able to draw breath without smelling me."

Her gaze dropped and then rose in a bright declaration of carnal invitation. "Is that a promise?"

The heat rose with feverish intensity to his skin. "Meryl!" he growled in warning.

She relented, having teased him enough. "We've never been lovers, not really lovers. A few kisses. That's all."

"What kind of kisses?" He felt like an adult dealing with an oversexed teenager.

She arched a brow. "Would you like a demonstration?"

"Possibly."

"Well, you're not going to get it!" She laughed at his indignant expression. "I was thirty when you and I met,

James. I've been an adult for a long time. I'm not asking for names and dates from you."

"You want them, you'll get them."

She shook her head. "It would only confirm my worst suspicions."

She was right. "Okay. Compromise. I want a day of your time. For a date. Tomorrow."

"Oh, but we were going to drive to Dublin. Tomaltach has an exhibit—"

"I'm leaving the day after."

He hadn't meant to use the fact as a threat. Oh, hell, yes, he did. He'd been waiting to tell her he'd made the arrangements this morning, but the moment hadn't seemed right until now. Now it made an impact.

"Tomorrow?" It was worth the wait. Her smiling expression recomposed into lines of distress. "So soon?"

He swallowed back the inclination to relent. Her lovely face filled with disappointment was doing a lot to rebuild his battered ego. "You knew I couldn't stay long. As it is, I'll have missed nearly a full workweek. I do have several other businesses to run."

"Okay. We'll have our day tomorrow." She glanced back at the scowling Tomaltach. "We can do Dublin another time."

He touched her shoulder. "How are your ribs?"

She blushed deep rose. "Much better." He wasn't so much concerned about her ribs as what effect they'd have on their day tomorrow and they both knew it.

The morning dawned gray and misty but dry by Irish standards. By 9:00 a.m. a pale yellow sun was struggling to top the hay field behind the castle. It was as good as the unreliable weather got this time of year.

James packed a lunch from the things he had bought while in town the afternoon before. He'd been as good as his word, leaving Meryl and Tomaltach alone while he'd sampled the fare of a few of the thirty or so pubs in the town of

Loughrea, population three thousand. No one went thirsty for lack of opportunity in Loughrea.

They started out by driving to Galway in Tomaltach's begrudgingly loaned car. There they walked the streets of the centuries-old city and then moved to the beach. It was windy and cold and Meryl clung to his arm, laughing when the wind snatched her scarf and sent it kiting out over the bay.

In one of the narrow street markets James bought her a tweed hat to replace it. The masculine lines with its short turned-back brim accentuated the feminine lines of her jaw and cheekbones and earned him a kiss. She hung on to his lips with hers, touching only the expanse of his mouth, but making him feel that she held him completely.

Then they headed south. Along the way they stopped to watch men digging turf in a bog with instruments older than memory. They paused to pet shaggy burros, took pictures of roof thatchers at work and the vistas of Galway Bay from the high hills. Farther south they made the spectacular climb to the Cliffs of Moher. By then the sun had broken through the ever-present mists and reflected back green and gold scales from the slithering silver-backed sea. There in the wind, with the taste of the sea salting her lips he kissed her as he had wanted to for three excruciatingly lonely days.

One long, deep, heart-swelling kiss followed another until another of the cliff visitors shouted cheerfully, "I hope you have the ring on your finger, darling. You certainly have the bull by his horn!"

They ate smoked salmon on brown bread, with tomato and onion slices, warmed themselves with Irish coffee in a pub and simply stared at each other as if it were the first time they had ever been together.

Meryl couldn't put her finger on the mood developing between them. James had tried to pack a week's worth of sight-seeing into the space of a day. Did he, too, feel that their time to sort out their past was running out? She didn't know how to ask that question, because she didn't know if she wanted to hear the answer.

It was late when they started back, but James was not yet done with this adventure. "There's one more place I want to take you," he said as he turned off the road just a few miles short of their castle residence.

They wound through some of the roughest county she had seen until finally she spied a Norman tower through some tree branches. It was bigger than the place where they were staying. She recognized it from pictures, though she had never before been there.

"Thoor Ballylee!" she said in delight. "William Butler Yeats's summer residence."

"The very place," James answered as he swung the car onto the low stone bridge that spanned the stream running past the tower.

There wasn't another soul in sight and Meryl understood why when she exited the car and read the sign. "Open May to September. Rats!" She turned back to James, disappointment showing though her smile. "It was a nice idea, thanks. But it's closed for the season."

"When have I ever accepted no as an answer?" James replied as he came toward her. "Come on, there's got to be a way in."

Meryl allowed him to shepherd her with an arm about her waist to the gate, but when he began shaking it she laughed and clutched at his wrists. "Are you crazy? You can't get in like that."

He arched a brow at her. "Are you certain?"

"Come on. If someone sees us, we'll be arrested."

"If this won't work I'll just have to try something else."

She cocked her head to one side, enjoying the rare laughter in his eyes as much as his antics. "What, for instance?"

"How about this?" He produced a key from his pocket. "Shall I, or would you like the honors?"

Her look was disbelieving. "You've got a key? How?"

"Magic," he answered, more pleased than he would have thought possible. Her smile lit up a place in him he didn't even know was languishing in darkness. And then she hugged him, quick and tight. "You're a genius!"

The muscles of his vocal cords tightened. Something shattered inside. Those barriers he had spent so many years erecting were in shambles. New feelings rushed into the breach of his once impenetrable ego. He felt awkward and delighted and just a little scared that he was making a very big fool of himself.

"You wanted poetry," he said almost harshly. "Contrary to your hopes I've enough self-respect to know I'm no poet. Instead, I'm prepared to offer you a tour of the inspiration of one of Ireland's greatest poets." He held the heat of her smile inside him and it made his voice rough with desire. "Thoor Ballylee is the most poetic place I know."

Her eyes widened. "You've been here before?"

He nodded. "Years ago. I took a year off from college to backpack across Europe."

She regarded him with gold green eyes as wide and curious as an owl's. "There's so much I don't know about you."

His smile dimmed momentarily. "Likewise. Come on."

"But how did you manage—?"

"Hurry, woman," he countermanded. "Soon it'll be too dark to see anything."

The key opened the side gate that took them through the souvenir shop and then into the courtyard of what had once been a working mill long before Yeats's day. The massive door to the main floor of the tower opened with the same key and then Meryl was standing in the main hall. It was large and spacious, with proportions to match its antiquity. The furnishings were sparse but well chosen so as not to take away from the wonder of the place itself. Across the room were tall lead-glass windows beyond which the mill stream sluiced past with its bounty of autumn leaves.

Meryl moved across the room, unlocked and pushed those windows wide, then leaned out to catch the last rays of the afternoon sun, fast disappearing in the west. The sounds of the clear gurgling stream and the hushed rustle of the wind shifting through dry leaves entered the room. After a moment she sat on the stone ledge and drew her feet up under her long skirt as she leaned her back against the frame.

"I should have brought you here sooner," James said from behind her. "I knew you would like it."

"Yes." Meryl said the word quietly, listening to the peace and solitude of the stone edifice where genius had once labored.

"There's just one more thing I brought you." He pulled from under his sweater a slim leather volume. "It's not exactly a rose, but it will have to do."

Meryl reached for it and smiled when she read the title. "Yeats's poetry?"

"From the best," he answered, feeling uneasy with his gallantry. She was right. He didn't know much about dating or courtship. He had been too busy as a young man to do more than pick up women as they came along, for an afternoon, an evening, never for long. After he made his fortune, women sought him out. He'd never had to strategize because no matter how beautiful, how sexy, how interested, they never lasted long. Now Meryl was looking at him with joy and gratitude and desire and he felt his heart swell with emotions he had never before known. He wanted to hold on to this moment forever, the moment that said, for now, he was all she needed.

She opened the book at random and began reading.

"Although you hide in the ebb and flow
Of the pale tide when the moon has set,
The people of coming days will know
About the casting out of my net,
And how you have leaped times out of mind
Over the little silver cords,
And think that you were hard and unkind,
And blame you with many bitter words."

She looked up at him, her eyes full of the realization of those words. "We haven't talked of growing up."

His heart twisted painfully. "Your Irish friend, to give him credit, is a handy man to know. It was his notoriety and the fact that I'm his American publisher that got me the key today."

Meryl glanced back at the gurgling stream. "Tomaltach was one of them, an Ash Can kid." She bit her lip, her face averted from James. "You must never tell him I told you. He ran away from home at nine. He said he'd had enough of his father's beatings. He lived on the streets of Dublin on and off and, to hear him talk of it, it wasn't any kinder than his home. He was in and out of reformatories and foster care for a time. One foster mother was an artist and it was she who first noted his talent as a painter. But he has a vicious mouth and no family would keep him for long. Finally, he began painting for a living and he became one of the lucky few to get noticed at a starving artist sale."

She turned back to him, her eyes stricken with an inner pain. "I didn't know any of this when I chose his work for the book. But later when he told me what I've just told you, I understood why he could capture the character of Timon so well."

"Many people have tough lives, Meryl," James said reasonably. "He seems to have landed on his feet. He's talented, respected, making money. I don't see any reason to cut him slack in the juvenile delinquent behavior department. It's too self-serving."

"Maybe it's because he's scared," she whispered. He could see she was struggling with something, another confidence? "He's been through drug detox twice since I've known him." She shrugged. "He says this time he thinks he's going to make it."

James opened his hands, uncertain about what to say next.

Meryl was a crusader of lost—no, tough causes. Tomaltach was one of them. "I think I understand what he means to you now."

"I know you do." She nodded and smiled. "You've been remarkably good. Most people would have tossed him out by now. You let him hang around, even eat with us."

"You did those things, Meryl. I tolerated him."

She laughed. "That's what I mean. You tolerated him. He's very much in awe of you and that makes him uneasy, and so he makes you the butt of his jokes. You haven't cut him down. Even about me." She lowered her gaze almost shyly. "He is jealous."

"He's not alone in that feeling."

She looked up and then held her hand out to him. "You really are a better man than you'd like people to think."

He came to her slowly, wanting to savor the moment, to remember that this time she had held her hand out first. He hadn't had to push her, hadn't had to dominate or provoke a reaction, hadn't had to make her face what there was between them. She thought he was a better man than he was. For once he wished it were true.

Her hand was curiously cool in his. His fingers wrapped over her palm, enclosing her hand in his. She pulled him down beside her. He moved in close, his free hand going to support himself on the window frame above her head as he bent to kiss her.

Meryl tasted the storm within him and answered with calm reassurance. After a long lingering while she put a hand to his chest and pushed him gently away. She wasn't yet ready to ride the rough seas of his lovemaking, not until she was certain she wouldn't drown.

His eyes were dark as the sky when his face receded to within focus range. "I love the way you taste. I want to taste all of you, Meryl, lick every lovely inch of you. Tell me you want it, too."

Meryl stroked his cheek, but her gaze wandered away from him toward the stream just beyond the window. "I don't sleep with men on the first date."

He caught her chin and turned her face back to his. "You're playing games. This is not our first date."

She dropped her hand from his cheek. "It is as far as I'm concerned."

His banked his quick frustration with dogged determination. He'd come too close to lose this time. "First dates are for people who are strangers. We hardly qualify as that." He placed his hand on her left breast and lightly massaged her. "I know things about your body that your own mother doesn't. Like, for instance, how you blush from head to toe after you've reached—"

She stopped his words with fingers pressed to his mouth. "This isn't going to win you any points."

He gently pried two fingers back in order to say, "You just want me to work harder before you give in."

She laughed. "You just want to have sex to prove a point."

He licked her finger and smiled. If she could laugh with him, there was a chance she would capitulate. "Now what point would that be?"

"That I—that you can move me."

He licked her again. "Can't I?"

"So what?" She looked away, trying to sound unmoved by the repeated application of his tongue to the sensitive pads of her fingers. "Mel Gibson moves me and I've never even met him. I can concede the attraction without submitting to the urge."

He lifted her hand so that he could apply the sinewy length of his tongue to her palm. "The more you talk, the more it sounds like you're sandbagging."

Meryl smiled ruefully. Perhaps, she was. He had always been so much more confident of her feelings than she had ever been of his. She needed the assurance that this wasn't just a lovers' game that his competitive nature wouldn't allow him to lose. "Name three reasons why you want to sleep with me."

He gave her a shark grin as he moved a hand to lift the hem of her sweater. "Okay. I've had the pleasure before and liked it."

"Next."

His hand moved up under her sweater until he found and squeezed one full, sensitive mound. "I like the way you respond."

Meryl's breath caught in her throat. He played the game better than he knew. "That sounds like a variation on number one."

"Then let me elaborate." His hand pushed the strap of her bra off her shoulder. "I like the way you hang back at first, like now, as though it requires a conscious decision on your part each time to submit to me." He peeled back the lacy edge of her bra. His fingers delved inside and found the stiffened nipple. "I like feeling that I've overcome even your token resistance. It turns me on."

"I suppose that qualifies as a distinction," Meryl breathed unsteadily and wondered what resistance he could possibly be talking about. She was already half out to sea. "Number three?"

"I have never found your limit." His other hand dove under her sweater as he leaned in to kiss her deeply. For a moment their tongues tangled and then he was licking at the corner of her mouth. "How deep does that need in you go? I can touch you places no one has ever been and still I can't find the bottom of your desire."

Meryl shut her eyes on the impossible pleasure of his touch. "How do you know?"

"I know."

"So?"

"I want to know why."

She leaned in against his hands, her nipples stabbing his palms in painful need. "Are you certain you'd like the answer?"

He gave the question serious consideration as he kissed her again. There were so many facets to her. There was the businesslike and very capable publisher he had met two years ago. There was the quite astonishing sexually liberated woman she became in his arms, and the gifted children's book author and quiet crusader who considered anonymity part of doing good deeds. The courageous soul who had risked her life to protect a legacy that was no longer hers and who nurtured tortured souls like Tomaltach O'Connor was as complex a human being as he had ever known.

Each time he was with her he saw himself more and more as he must appear to the world around him. Once he hadn't given a damn for the opinions of others. Now he could think of little else but how Meryl viewed him. What he saw didn't make him want to dance a jig.

That last thought finally drew him back from drowning in the sensation of her response. He leaned away, but his hands refused to break contact with the lovely flesh he had exposed. He watched her for a moment, wanting to capture the scene forever. What he saw took his breath away.

She sat in the rapidly gathering twilight, her dark head rolled back against the stark white of the window frame, her body arched to offer her breasts to his hands. Her eyes were closed, the lashes casting sooty shadows on her upper cheeks. Swollen and damp from his kiss, her parted lips trembled with her every breath. His heart contracted with desire. Surrender had never looked so tenderly poignant to him. She abandoned everything to her desire. He did not know if he had that kind of courage.

He was a practical man, a man given to dealing with hard issues, to making tough decisions, and living with the results, win or lose. But this act of blind faith, gambling on things he could not touch, own or direct, required skills he had never valued until he met this bright positive woman. Had his past life bankrupted his character as well as his bank account?

"I don't know if I can do this, Meryl, but I'm not afraid of hard truths."

She opened her eyes, looking at him with the heavy-lidded gaze of sexual desire. "Aren't you? Then tell me about yourself."

There it was again, the unanswered question. The question about his father.

His slipped his hands free of her sweater and leaned back against the opposite frame of the large window. He could feel his heart pounding, but it wasn't all the motion of desire. He was a little afraid. Would she understand the combination of admiration and groveling shame he felt whenever his father crossed his mind? Would she sympathize with how he could both love and revile the man who had given him life? He didn't know how to tell her that alongside his love was an abiding hatred and bitterness and rage he didn't know how to lay aside.

"My father committed suicide when I was seventeen."

He saw her shut her eyes briefly and then she was regarding him again with golden green eyes to fight for, to live for. "Tell me."

He did. Slowly at first, haltingly. It was harder than he had feared. Several times his throat closed with rage or unshed tears. He had to go back, as things came to him. He told the story badly, out of order, out of character for a man who made his living being sharp and insightful, terse and to the point.

He learned things in the telling. He had been the one to find his father, but he had forgotten it was because he had been playing hooky with a girl who was eager to join him in an illicit afternoon in his bedroom. He remembered that he'd had to call his mother at work and tell her to come home, but had forgotten until now that he'd had to head off his sisters when they returned from school to find their driveway full of police and emergency vehicles and curious neighbors. Most times when he was forced to recall that day, he experienced again his irrational anger that his father had spoiled his afternoon—and the shameful thought, painful as a scorpion's sting, that his father was a coward.

"Relatives and friends said he killed himself because his heart was broken over losing his business, which had destroyed him financially," James said after another long pause. "He had gotten shafted in a raid."

"A hostile corporate takeover?" Meryl asked, breaking his monologue for the first time.

He smiled at her, but there was no humor in it. "Right. My specialty. There's no irony in that. I decided early on that I wasn't going to be my father. He went down because he let friendships and loyalties determine his choices. He was vulnerable. I have no vulnerabilities." *Except you.* Why couldn't he force those words out?

He wiped a weary hand down his face. "A few days before he died he told me he'd been offered a golden parachute, but he'd refused it because he owed it to his employees to protect their jobs. Want to hear the irony of that?" Bitterness corroded his voice to a rasp. "The winners kept his employees on. Only my father was bankrupt."

Meryl heard the blood rushing through her body, so silent had the evening become. Even the stream seemed to have been hushed to stillness under the spell of his litany of pain.

"I took over the family—there was my mother and my sisters to look after. I left school, went to work in an uncle's business. We had to eat. Eventually I found a way to fit college into my schedule. Mom found a job, and we made it work. But it was hard and it was humiliating; and it was his fault." The last two words ricocheted off the stone walls, a bitter virulent epithet for his father.

Meryl didn't say anything for a long time. She knew he must have heard or read every possible psychological theory going about suicide, and then some.

"He didn't think of that."

He lifted his head to her and she saw the slick, unmistakable track of a tear on his lean, hard cheek. "I don't need your sympathy, Meryl."

She didn't dare look away from him, but she wondered all the same where her temerity came from to try, after all this time, to explain to him what could never be fully explained. "The urge to end his life took advantage of the moment, a weak moment. He didn't think of leaving you behind," she said so quietly she wasn't at all certain he would hear her.

"You said your father didn't leave a note. He didn't stop to think about it. He couldn't remember his family in the anguish of that dark place where his thoughts had taken him and it killed him."

"If I'd come home—!" He bit off the plaintive conditional "if" of all regrets.

"Oh, no!" She lunged forward and threw her arms about him.

"You mustn't ever think that, never that." She pressed her face to his hot, damp cheek. "Depression is an illness. He needed more than for you to walk in the door that day." She tried to gather him against her, but he held stiff in resistance until her efforts hurt her. She relented, but she didn't release him. She palmed his cheek in her hand and rocked her brow on his. "His depression must have come on so quickly no one had time to notice. The overwhelming sadness of it caught him in a bad moment. That's a tragedy, but it's no one's fault."

James gave up and held on to her because he had nowhere else to go, nowhere else he wanted to be. He tried twice before his voice caught and held sound. "You're too generous with me, Meryl."

"Possibly," she said by his ear.

Hard truths. He could face hard truths even if it cost him this. He pushed her back from his embrace. Anger erupted at the tenderness he saw on her lovely face. He didn't deserve it and he was going to make certain she understood that.

"You want to know the truth. I became everything my father hated just so I wouldn't be like him. I never let myself think much about that. But it's true. I'm ruthless and immoral. I don't let anything get in the way of what I want. When it does, I destroy it. I tried to destroy you." *Because you were getting in too close.* Why couldn't he finish the confession? Why couldn't he tell her the truth? Perhaps because he knew her well enough to know it would let him off the hook with her and he didn't want to be let off even by the truth. Even so, he saw the generosity remain in her eyes and on her mouth.

Meryl weathered the flash of fury in his eyes. "I think you were running on automatic for years and I just happened to be in the way. You were known to be trouble. I should have looked both ways before I stepped in front of you."

Doubt hovered at the edges of his eyes. "When did you come to that overly generous conclusion?"

"Sometime in the past few days," she admitted. "Maybe just today." Two weeks ago she had been ready to launch an attack to wrest back Walrus Ink from him. What had changed? Only her heart.

"We'd better go. It's dark." She rose to her feet and pulled him to his beside her. "Let's go home, James."

James weighed his options. He hadn't made her a single promise, hadn't offered her a single reason to walk out that door with him and back into his life. "Why?"

Meryl closed her eyes against the question she couldn't answer yet. "Later."

"How much later?"

"After we've made love."

They drove home in silence shot through by the hum of desire.

Chapter 12

Meryl lay quietly as James's hands passed over her glistening body. Only the occasional sharp catch of her breath in her throat broke the silence of the room. The mood was peaceful, the brunt of the first storm of passion already spent.

The first time had been fast and furious. James wasn't a brute or inconsiderate, but he was a man whose passion made heavy demands on his body and those needs demanded quick and explosive release. They hadn't made it past the first bedroom door. He'd slipped off her sweater and skirt in the stairwell, pressing her flushed body to the cool stones as his hands and mouth roamed freely, rousing and soothing and seeking responses she was all too ready to give. She had thought he would take her there, against the stone, but, though drugged by desire, he remembered her still-sore ribs and had carried her the rest of the way to a bed.

"Beautiful," he murmured now as his fingers circled her

breasts, lifting and tugging, making them ache with need. He thumbed her nipples as his lips covered hers.

Meryl closed her eyes and concentrated on his languorous, almost playful touch. Making love with him the first time had been like riding the sea in squally weather, the powerful lifts and plunges exhilarating and a little frightening. His hunger too intense, his needs too long denied, he could not control them once inside her. His rough, quick thrusts left no room for doubt or hesitancy. There was nowhere for her to go and nothing to do but hold on and ride it out, astonished and amazed, anchored securely to his body by the force of his nature.

Yet the surrender was its own reward. Her body left behind its puny soreness for the glory of his invasion, welcoming the rhythm and steel and heat of him. It had been two long, lonely years since he—since any man—had touched her this way and her body was as hungry as his in its own way. When he hoarsely cried out her name she was there with him, soaring out over the edge of the world.

Now he was rewarding her, taking her slowly back to where they had skyrocketed before. She felt the need to please in his hands, the generosity he thought he didn't possess in the curvature of his mouth on her skin, the kindness and tenderness this hard man hadn't wanted to get in his way. But they did get in his way and they had gotten in hers when she had tried to hate him.

As his hands folded over and under her hips and he pressed his face into her abdomen, the weight of him made her remember why she had hidden from him after she had left him. She was going to have to tell him why she had been afraid to come back, why she knew that if she'd seen him again too soon she'd have begged him to take her back. But not just yet, not until he had convinced her and she had proved to him that this is how they belonged, together again and for always.

She let herself sink into the hunger as he opened her again to his intimate kiss. She caught her breath and lifted her hips and offered him everything he demanded through the pressure of his hands and his quick whispers and low groans of approval. She became one with the exquisite pleasure of his mouth on her, let him feed the hunger and her need for him. And then she let go even further and cried out his name and sighed and wept over it as though it was the only word in her vocabulary of love.

When he came into her this time, their bodies clung and fused in the moist heat of lovemaking. His thrusts were hard and slow and deep, each time making her vividly aware of his filling, stretching invasion. "For you," he whispered again and again in her ear as she writhed and whimpered and smiled in the darkness. "Only for you."

She understood. He, too, was caught and seduced by the rough magic they produced together. Together they were more than partners, they were complete and inviolate, if only for these precious moments away from the world. Yet it was a place they could, if they chose, go again and again for the rest of their lives.

They tasted, touched, murmured and moaned, dissolving even reality in the shimmering heat of ecstasy.

The room was silent for a long time. She would have thought he slept if the tension in his hand on her waist hadn't betrayed his alertness. He was thinking over the past two hours, as was she, wondering exactly where it left them now that they had come full circle.

"I was pregnant."

She whispered the words, but it was enough. His hand on her waist tightened so painfully she gasped.

"I didn't know when I left you."

She could feel him thinking. His whole body seemed to hum with activity. "Why didn't you tell me?"

"I didn't know how. We had had a pretty ugly fight over your threat to sell Walrus Ink. We'd made no commitments. I wasn't prepared."

"My fault." He sounded furious. "That first night I didn't think, wouldn't let you think, didn't use protection."

Meryl found she could actually smile. "We didn't use anything tonight, either."

She heard the curses echoing in his head. "What happened?" The pause was electric. "You took care of things."

"Oh, no!" She levered up on one elbow. Though it was much too dark to actually see his face she looked him straight in the eye. "I wouldn't, couldn't, have. I lost the child a few weeks later. The doctor said it sometimes happens. No reason. I pretty much fell apart. It seemed so unfair to lose so much so quickly. But a child . . ."

"After what I'd done you'd have kept my child?" He sounded stunned.

"It was mine, too."

That seemed to silence him for good.

Finally she reached up to touch his face. He flinched. "I would have told you about the child if I hadn't lost it. But things happened so fast and I was so sick about it all. After I got myself back together I didn't contact you because I didn't want you to think that I thought I had any hold over you."

"You would have." His voice was so tight he seemed to be strangling.

"No, that wouldn't have been right. I did hear everything you said to me, James. I heard no commitment, no strings, no future. I knew you weren't ready. While I—well, let's just say the lines of communication between my head and my heart weren't the best."

"You were in love with me."

Meryl decided they both deserved the complete truth. "Yes."

"You wrote it down," he went on as if she hadn't spoken, "in the leather diary you once carried." How far away he sounded, as if they were talking long-distance from very remote parts of the world instead of within each other's arms. "I found it just a couple of months ago. It had gotten wedged in the back of your desk. The last entry was my name with a heart and the words *The One* beside it."

Despite all that had transpired between them in this bed during the past two hours, Meryl felt herself blush in the dark.

"Are you sorry?"

Meryl shook her head. "Yes, no. Maybe both."

"Were you all alone?"

She didn't answer.

"I can't imagine any reason why you ever let me any where near you again."

"Can't you?"

Again another long silence that stretched the limits of her ability to hold her breath.

"Meryl, my life's in shambles. My reputation is shot. Somebody's trying to ruin me. I don't know quite how much danger there is, but you've already been hurt. I can't let you risk anything else by being with me."

"So this is it, one perfect night, and I should be grateful?"

He didn't hear the exasperated humor in her voice. "No, I should be grateful. And I am." He sounded as if he wanted five minutes alone with himself and the use of a rubber hose.

She touched his face, hidden in the darkness, again. There was new moisture on his cheek and it made her want to weep. "Regardless of how sophisticated we're all supposed to be about sex, we didn't start out right. We began at the end, in bed, and there didn't seem a way to get back to a beginning after that, until we came here. But I know you now, know you better than you think I do. I like what I see, James Brant. I don't know how you feel."

James knew how he felt, like he wanted to slink away and die. He had hurt her in every way a man could possibly hurt a woman and yet, miraculously, she was here in bed with him. But it wasn't because she was stupid or weak, or a fool

She was here because she thought she knew him better than he knew himself, saw things in him, possibilities he hadn't even wanted to consider three weeks ago.

The trouble was, he didn't know if he could live up to her expectations even if he wanted to. And, God, how he wanted to!

"You think about it," she said softly, bending down so her lips moved against his ear. She smoothed her palm across his sweat-soaked brow. "You think about it here." Her hand drifted down to the broad expanse of his chest, her fingers pressing hard over his left nipple. "And then you think about it here." Her fingers grazed his belly, making it jump and his stomach flutter and then she gathered him, stirring in her hand, and wrapped her fingers firmly over him. "And you think about me here."

His chuckle sounded forced. "It's all I've been thinking with where you're concerned."

She smiled in the dark. "You do some of your best thinking about me here."

He surged up off the bed, catching her shoulders and pushing her back onto the bedding so that he leaned over her. "I don't want to hurt you."

"Too late." She said it lightly because she was afraid she might cry if she gave in to even a tiny fraction of the feelings near bursting for release. Regret was beginning to creep in at the corners of her happiness. Perhaps she should have kept her secret a little longer.

"I don't want to hurt you again."

She reached up and traced his mouth in the dark. "Then don't. Be kind to me, James."

"I will, Meryl," he said and bent to kiss her. She tasted so much in him: the pain and sorrow, regret, self-recrimination, remorse, sadness, guilt—a whole litany of should-haves and if-onlys. And she went with him into that dark morass of feelings because it was where she had dwelt for such a long time that it was nice, this time, to have his company. And when the kisses became more intense and the pain could no longer hold them, she went with him up to the top of the highest peak and sailed off with him into the sunrise.

"That man's mad bad in love with you." Tomaltach was slouching in a chair in the main terminal of Shannon Airport, waiting with Meryl for her flight to be called.

"That man" had become's Tomaltach's way of referring to James in the ten days since he'd left Ireland. It was "that man" this and "that man" that. This time "that man" had left a message for her at the courtesy desk at the airport telling her he'd be at Kennedy to pick her up and had made arrangements for her overnight stay in the city.

"Mr. Brant is just being considerate," Meryl maintained as she resumed her seat. "Hartford is a two-hour drive from the airport, not an appealing prospect after a trans-Atlantic flight."

"Stuff him!"

Tomaltach's permanent scowl rode shotgun on a meaner than usual mood. She knew that if he hated anything more than meeting people, it was saying goodbye to the few friends he had. She hadn't expected or asked him to come. He's just shown up as she was getting into a cab. After he offered to bash in the face of the driver who resented losing his fare, she'd sent the taxi away with a huge tip.

"That man lives in Manhattan, doesn't he?"

Meryl smiled because Tomaltach's accent gave Manhattan an exotic inflection no New Yorker could ever manage. "Yes, Mr. Brant does."

"You seen his place before?"

"No," Meryl replied primly.

"You will this time, I'm thinking." His smirk was in full spread.

"You're presuming a great deal."

"Oh, I know you never told me how you're that man' lover—and I want you to know I appreciate it."

Despite two weeks in his company, Tomaltach's audacity still had the ability to leave Meryl breathless. She changed the subject. "We've done remarkably good work. The sketches I'm taking back are certain to be approved. I think you should go ahead with the final paintings. If things go as we've planned, you'll be coming to the States for the publication party in the spring."

"Will you still be at Walrus Ink then?"

"I don't know," Meryl admitted honestly. "My contract was for two weeks and I've already been on the payroll for three. Mr. Brant will have to decide if I should continue." The sudden anger in his expression made her hurry on. "My working arrangement at Walrus Ink won't affect our book project. We have a contract. I don't have to work directly for Mr. Brant to work with you."

He leaned forward suddenly, his eyes blazing. "I told that man the morning he left that if he hurts you I'm gonna come to New York and tear his head off his neck and stick it—"

"Tommytock!"

He actually blushed. "Well, I will!"

Meryl smiled and leaned into him and quickly kissed his cheek. "I love you, too. So you will take care of yourself this time, won't you?"

"Aah, what's it to you?" He flung himself back in his seat, as if insulted by her sign of affection.

"I care." She studied his vivid blue eyes where loneliness and wariness and old woundings had cut so many tiny scars. "Find yourself a girl, Tommytock. Life can be beautiful."

He rolled his eyes and made a terrible face. "Women! You're all the same, thinking no man's happy who can call his soul his own." She smiled at him again because, in spite of his scowl, his eyes had softened for her. "Fall in love very soon. It will be the making of you."

Her flight number came over the loudspeaker and she rose to her feet. He came instantly to his, insisting on carrying her things all the way to the customs line. When she had to leave him, he flung his arms about her suddenly, holding her a long time to his hard, thin body. And then he bent his head and kissed her full on the mouth. It lasted only a second and his expression looked as if he'd kissed a pig, but Meryl saw the tenderness in those blue eyes and she touched his face briefly. "Stay safe for me, Tommytock!"

A muscle jumped in his lean, flushed cheek. "For you lass."

"They're quite good. I like them." James nodded as he bent over the sketches spread over his dining room table. He removed his reading glasses. "Whatever you can say about his lack of polish as a human being, that man's got talent. What's so funny?"

Meryl's chuckles subsided slowly as her gaze slid over the contours of his torso outlined in a formfitted dark blue shirt. The collar was open at the neck, exposing a few red-brown hairs she wanted to tweak with her fingers. "That man has a name—it's Tomaltach."

He grunted. "He's in love with you."

"You've said that before."

James lifted his head just enough to glance across the width of the table at her. "Did he try to make love to you after I left?"

"Of course." Meryl grinned at the deepening frown on his face. He now looked like that famous picture of Rocky Graziano, who glared at the camera from beneath lowered brows. All that was missing was a pair of boxing gloves. "What did you expect me to answer to so leading a question?"

He made a sound just short of a snort. "He threatened to come after me if I hurt you. Did he tell you that?"

"Oh, yes, though his version was much more...colorful."

James muttered a deprecation. "So should I consider him a serious rival?"

Meryl ran her hand lovingly over a corner of the satin-smooth surface of the tabletop. His hands had smoothed this wood. She understood why it glowed. His hands on her body produced the same results. "Are you looking for an easy way to get rid of me?"

He straightened up. "What?"

"Well, you've been curiously remote since I stepped off the plane." Her fingers drifted over the top of the sideboard as she moved toward the end of the table. "Other than a welcoming kiss, you haven't so much as touched me." She paused to glance back at him. "If you don't count helping me off with my coat."

James rammed his hands into his trouser pockets. "I didn't want to rush you." His gray gaze was as guarded and watchful as an owl with a field mouse in sight. "I know how you feel about public displays of affection."

"I see." She sat down on one of his upholstered dining room chairs and crossed her legs, letting her long skirt fall open where it was unbuttoned halfway up her thighs. "And what about private displays, Mr. Brant?"

She watched the heat edge up the silver mercury in his eyes. "You must be tired after so long a trip," he murmured.

"Exhausted," she replied. She stretched her arms up over her head and arched her back to give emphasis to her words. "Absolutely bone weary." His gaze fastened on the thrust of her breasts and held. "I really should go right to bed."

"Yes." He said the word on a gust of desire. "Straight to bed."

They made it as far as his living room sofa. Pushing, shoving, scattering clothing in all directions, they fell into the down pillows of his overstuffed sofa with sighs and groans of urgent desire. Minutes later they were laughing and trying to check their runaway breaths as they pushed the hair from each other's eyes.

"You're a wild woman, Meryl Wallis."

"And you, Mr. Brant, are quite satisfactory."

"Only satisfactory?" He thrust his hips into hers.

"I don't want to swell your head," she replied tartly.

"You can swell any part of me that pleases you," he answered and kissed her hard. "How have I lived without you?"

"Less well than now, I hope."

His gaze caught her unprepared. "I can't think about what you do to me or I'd never get anything done."

That was quite an admission for a man who had spent his adult life thinking he didn't need anything or anyone to survive. She hugged it to her heart, but she pushed him away.

"Now that that's settled," she said as he lifted up off her, "I really do need to go to bed. And then, over dinner, you can catch me up on things at Walrus Ink."

James reached for his shirt before he spoke. "There's nothing much to tell. The police still haven't located Zip Hearst and we've closed shop for a few days."

Meryl sat up and smoothed the hair from her face. "Has something else happened, James?"

The look he gave her was as carefully devoid of expression as a doll's face. "Nothing has happened."

"Yet," she finished for him and reached out to grip his arm. "Don't lie to me. My sister works there, in case you've forgotten."

He blinded her with the warmth of his smile. "I haven't forgotten." He stood and pushed his arms through his rumpled shirt. "We got a supposed tip and the police were called in." He half turned to look down at her. "They found a crude homemade bomb in the mailroom."

"My Lord!"

"Exactly. We aren't equipped to deal with that kind of threat. Until we are, I thought the team deserved a short vacation." How confident and unconcerned he sounded, yet she saw a hint of worry in his frown. "I'm having a whole new security system put in."

He smiled again, eclipsing the concern. "Your friend Ned the cop turned out to have friends who could help me."

She smiled back, feeling a little easier that he'd gone to Ned. "I'm glad he could help you."

A wry, indulgent look came into his face. "You have a lot of male friends."

"I know. It's embarrassing." But she was really secretly pleased that he was keeping count. "I'm everybody's big sister."

The fire that leapt in his gaze belied that he'd ever seen her as anything other than a carnally arousing woman. "Just so they stay little brothers. There's just one more thing. You're fired."

Meryl heaved an elaborate sigh. "Sorry, I don't fire and I don't resign—you're stuck with me."

He reached out and snatched her blouse out from under her hand as she bent over to pick it up from the carpet. That got her attention. She looked the long way up the bare front of him to his face. "Listen to me, Meryl. This is not something that can be negotiated. I don't want you anywhere near Walrus Ink until we catch these lunatics."

"You have several dozen other employees," Meryl reminded him reasonably, but the angle of her view was distracting her concentration. "Are they all getting pink slips?"

He lunged for her, dragging her to her feet so that every bare inch of her front was pressed to every bare inch of his. "Don't make this hard for me, Meryl. Please."

The last word was wrung from him. Pain etched harsh lines in his rough-sculpted face. He looked like a man being tortured. That torment was for her, she realized with a rush of love. He really did care for her, though he had yet to say the words.

"I'm a grown-up, James. I'm willing to take my chances right alongside everyone else, including you."

It didn't help. His expression stiffened. She could see the instinctive withdrawal in his eyes, the old struggle not to be drawn in by his emotions or let them direct his actions. He lifted his hands from her arms, but she could tell that he couldn't bring himself to step away from their bodies' contact.

"I don't know how to be a gallant swain or whatever the hell kind of white knight you want me to be!" he snarled. "I do know I can't concentrate on anything if I have to wonder where you are and how you are and if you're safe."

This time he did step back and turn away, leaving her breasts lost without the heat of his chest to warm them. "The police tell me they've beefed up surveillance. The security people assure me that only the most sophisticated kind of incursion could get past the new precautions."

She supposed that when he felt safety had been reached he turned back to her, his unbuttoned shirt his only covering. "I'm betting my future on that protection, but I'm not willing to bet your life. Hear me?"

Fascinated by his resilient body, Meryl didn't even answer. She just smiled and picked up his cotton shorts and held them out to him hooked over one finger. "Want to try that again, without the distraction of the heavy equipment?"

He choked on sudden laughter and then he was coming toward her again. He walked right up and framed her face with his hands and kissed her, hard, several times. Finally he leaned his forehead against hers. "Meryl, Meryl, what am I going to do with you?"

She wrapped her arms about his neck and basked in his smile. "Tuck me in your bed?"

His hands moved to her hips and pulled her in tight. "With pleasure!"

"Meryl! How was Ireland?"

"Kent?" Meryl said into the phone, glancing guiltily around James's apartment even though she knew he'd gone downstairs to the limo with their luggage. "This is a surprise."

"I heard you were in the city and I didn't want you to get away without me seeing you."

Embarrassment was making the hair stand on the back of her neck. She thought she was being so circumspect. Someone must have spotted her in James's company and told Kent. Had he been savvy enough to put two and two together? "Who told you I was in the city?"

"Jacqui. I called her when I got back from the Far East and she told me you were in Ireland, due back two days ago. I tried your Hartford apartment last night and then again this morning before I called Jacqui back. She gave me this number."

"Oh, that's nice." Meryl could have strangled her sister at the moment. She had let Jacqui know where she was staying, but that didn't mean she meant for her sister to give out the number. What had Jacqui thought she was doing? What if James had answered the phone?

"You sound strange, Meryl. Are you all right?"

"Absolutely. It must be jet lag." Or James lag. The man was insatiable!

"Don't I know! The flight from Tokyo to New York left me disoriented for two days. So were you successful? Is O'Connor ready to join your team?"

"He's agreed to do another book for Walrus Ink, if that's what you mean." Her gaze swung toward the front door as she strained for the sound of footsteps in the corridor.

"Excellent, because we're ready to move, Meryl, whenever you give the word."

"What do you mean by move?" Was that a key in the lock?

"I've been busy since I got back. Made a few discreet inquiries, found you some additional investors, set up a dummy company that Brant won't be able to trace back to you until it's too late. It's a go, Meryl. You're going to get controlling interest of Walrus Ink after the buy-out, but you'll have to go public with additional shares to make up for the lack of capital on your part. I'll hold the mortgage, so to speak, but you'll have room to maneuver, expand, replace old equipment, whatever you deem needed as majority stockholder and CEO." He paused. "Why don't I hear cheering, Meryl?"

"I—I wish you had talked things over with me before you went so far out on a limb for me."

"I thought it's what you wanted from me, capital backing?"

"I did. But things are changing, have changed. I can't discuss it right now. I'm on my way out the door for Hartford, but we need to talk. Will you be in this afternoon?"

"I can be, if you'd like for me to be. Or, better yet, how about I join you on the ride to Hartford?"

"Sounds like fun," Meryl said, trying to sound enthusiastic instead of desperate, "but the limo is already waiting. Why don't I call you at, say, 2:00 p.m. and we can discuss whether you should come out."

"Sure, Meryl, if you prefer." The temperature in his voice had dropped appreciably. "Is there something going on I should know about?"

"No." Definitely nothing he should know about! "Well, maybe. Have you heard about the demonstrations going on at Walrus Ink?"

"You bet. It couldn't have worked out better for our purposes." He chuckled. "I've even thought about contributing to the campaign."

She tamped down her annoyance. He must not know everything. "Two weeks ago someone tried to burn the building down with me in it."

"What?" He sounded appalled. "I heard there was a fire, Meryl, but the papers said nothing about people being present or that it was suspected arson."

"James was able to keep it out of the papers. He thought it would only encourage the sickos involved."

"That's it, Meryl! It's time you got out of there until the negotiations for the buy-out are complete. As I've said, my people are ready to go. We can be in Brant's office first thing Monday morning. Even Brant will have to see the sense in selling now. It's a lose-lose situation for him. He won't have to know your part in it until after he's signed on the dotted line.''

"We'll talk this afternoon, okay?" That was definitely the sound of a key in the lock. A second later, James walked through his front door. "I'll call about two o'clock. Bye now."

Dressed in a black cashmere overcoat that accented his broad shoulders and draped him like a king's royal raiment, he seemed worth every penny of the millions he was purported to possess. And he was smiling at her. "Who called?"

"It was for me. Business." Meryl turned away from him on the pretense of picking up her purse. "James, there's something I have to tell you. Something about Walrus Ink."

He stepped in behind her and hugged her, cupping her breasts through the fabric of her suit jacket as his hips moved into intimate contact with her derriere. "I don't want to talk business." He brushed her hair aside with his nose and kissed the back of her neck. "I want to sit in the comfortable seclusion of the limo that's waiting for us and hold and kiss you until you can't catch your breath."

Meryl tried to shoulder away from him, but his embrace was too strong and, treacherously, her body was listening to what her ears did not want to hear. "James," she said a little raggedly. "This is important."

"This is more important!" One of his hands moved down strongly over her stomach, molding as it went, until he found her low down through the fabric of her skirt.

She caught and held his roaming hand even as she sagged against him. "I want to buy Walrus Ink from you."

"You can't," he murmured into her neck behind her ear. "I've made other arrangements."

Meryl jerked within his embrace. "You what?"

He turned her in his arms so that she could see his bold smile. "Want to hear what they are?"

"No." Realization that he wasn't joking made her heart slam into her chest. All desire was gone. In its place came galloping frustration. While she thought they were closer than ever before, he had outmaneuvered her yet again. "You should have told me what you were doing."

He didn't bother to disguise the satisfaction in his voice. "Why?"

Meryl stared at his happy, handsome face and wanted to slap him. "Because I have been thinking about this for some time." Every moment since he'd stepped back into her life! "You must have known it would at least cross my mind."

"I might have. So what?" He hugged her in closer even as she leaned way, which kept them joined only at the hips. "You haven't said anything that would have made it necessary for me to tell you my plans until now."

"That's not fair, James." She tried to get on top of bitter disappointment and resentment, but she didn't quite succeed. He was too smug, too amused at her expense, too certain that she wouldn't be able to resist his considerable charm and force of personality. "I suppose it's true what they say about leopards."

The zinger hit home. His expression altered. "They never change their spots?"

Instinct warned her to back off. Her heart cried that she was lobbing bricks at a glass house. Reason told her he had no clear way of knowing what was on her mind. She'd taken great pains to hide it from him. This was just a measure of how well she had succeeded. "James, I didn't expect this."

The recoil in his gaze told her the words had come too late. "But you could have predicted it, if you'd stopped to think about it, right?"

His statement was too close to her thoughts for her to rush into an easy lie. As the silver cooled and hardened in his eyes she felt something cold and metallic settle in her middle. They were losing something. She felt the ground sliding out from under her so fast she didn't think she could keep her footing if he kept staring at her with that hardened I-should-have-known dispassion. She was desperate not to lose entirely.

Acting totally in response to self-preservation, she lay her a hand on his chest, rubbing his left nipple through the fabric of his shirt. "Can I persuade you to at least listen to my proposal?"

He reached up and gripped her hand, squeezing her fingers a little too tightly for comfort. "It's not going to change my mind about how I intend to dispose of Walrus Ink."

"Dispose?" The blood in her veins seemed to cool as a chill swept through her body. "It sounds like you're tossing it away."

His lids lowered to half-mast, deliberately eclipsing the formidable power of his gaze. "I'll ask you again. Do you want to hear my plans?"

Meryl felt as if he'd reached into her chest and squeezed her heart as tightly as he was griping her fingers. "No." She shook her head as if she could dislodge the thought. "I don't think I do."

He let her go without a struggle. She had seen the pain flicker in the depths of his eyes the moment before he released her. She wanted to cry. She wanted to slug him. She wanted to shout at him for ruining what had been so perfect.

She didn't do any of those things, but her hands shook as she picked up her coat, and her throat ached with the raw bile of disillusionment as she hugged it to her chest. He had been changing, she was certain of it. No, she had been certain she could change him. That was the cardinal mistake of every woman who'd ever gotten herself into a bad relationship, an overconfident belief in the power of love.

Meryl turned without even a goodbye and headed for the door.

She was amazed when he beat her to it. She didn't look at him, couldn't bear to see his face when it might be for the last time.

"Where are you going?" he demanded when she reached for the knob.

She kept her head down, feeling as belligerent as he sounded. "Home, where I belong."

He didn't touch her, but he leaned into her range of sight. "You're making a mistake walking out without hearing my side."

She turned her face away. "I've heard your side before, James. It's always the same. Whatever James Brant wants, James Brant gets."

"I guess that says it all." He snatched open the door. "After you."

They rode the elevator to the first floor in silence. She didn't say thank-you when he helped her slip into her coat. She didn't resist him when he took her elbow to steer her through the sidewalk crowd. She didn't say a word until the limo driver had opened the door for her. She turned, looking no higher than his tie and said, "I guess this is goodbye."

"Like hell!" He made an impatient movement with his arm. "Get in first, Meryl."

That autocratic tone was one push too many. Her gaze snapped up to his face as she forgot, this once, how much he daunted her with that silver-bladed stare. "Where do you think you're going?"

She felt the fire in him, saw the rage simmering just at the brink of his control. "I'm going to Hartford with you."

"But I don't—!"

"Don't even say it, Meryl," he warned, his voice a slow growl. "I'm no longer in the mood to indulge your righteous indignation. Now step inside."

She hesitated only a second. She didn't see any profit in creating a scene on Park Avenue, and she suspected he would give her a scene that certain circles in Manhattan would be gossiping about by lunchtime.

She tucked herself into the far corner of the limo, even pulled her coat in close so he wouldn't accidently touch it as he entered. She saw his jaw tense at her action, but she didn't care. She was as miserable as it was possible for her to be and she wanted him to be miserable, too.

Chapter 13

James sat and heard out the three gentlemen arrayed before his desk in polite indifference. It was a good offer. He'd be making ninety-five cents on every dollar he had invested in Walrus Ink. Considering the fact that his company was under attack and that the fact was public knowledge, he would have expected them to come in with a much less generous offer. That's where they had made their mistake.

He didn't enjoy doing business with men he felt were inferior and incompetent. If they'd wanted to gain his interest, they should have begun by offering him thirty cents on the dollar and then explained in a hard-hitting demonstration of their understanding of his business difficulties why he was lucky to have been offered that much. He would at least have given their offer his full attention. He wouldn't have considered it, but he would have been entertained. This way, he was just allowing them to waste his time until Meryl came in.

He glanced pointedly again at his watch as the attorney

ran down the list of stipulations that he'd have to agree to. They were laughable.

He was beginning to suspect Kent Davis was behind this deal. He was the only man he knew desperate enough to offer so sloppily conceived a deal. Maybe Kent thought he if got his hands on Walrus Ink he could hand it to Meryl as an enticement into her arms. James smirked. Davis could forget it. Meryl was his and was going to remain his, even if, at times, she did make him want to put his fist through a wall.

She had gone so far as to slam her apartment door in his face when they reached Hartford. The limo driver had been forced to leave her luggage on the doorstep. That was three days ago. If her anger hadn't kept her away from Walrus Ink, he would have broken down that door by now. But it was the price he had been willing to pay for trying to keep her safe. Now it seemed no longer necessary to pay that price.

There hadn't been any more trouble since the discovery of the bomb. New security made them as safe as Fort Knox. While the police still hadn't been able to locate Zip, the only suspect in the arson case so far, they were nearly convinced the protesters had had nothing to do with the fire. In fact, the demonstrators had completely disappeared after police inquiries made it plain that they were prime suspects as accessories to a felonious arson and any further trouble would be added to the list of suspicions against them.

James relaxed. Life was looking up for the first time in two years. And it was going to get better. He was expecting Meryl any minute now.

He had called her in on the pretext that he needed her to wrap up her consulting work for him by making a presentation to his editorial staff this afternoon. If things went as he planned, no one would have to worry about setting foot in Walrus Ink ever again. The decision he had come to days ago was now a fact.

He held up a silencing hand, cutting into the tail of the attorney's litany, and reached for his phone as a blinking light indicated a call from his secretary.

"Ms. Wallis is here, Mr. Brant."

Smiling, he hung up and rose to his feet. "Thank you, gentlemen. But my answer is no. Now and forever." He extended his hand to each of them, ignoring their expressions of surprise or outrage. "Thank you for your time and interest, but I have an important meeting to attend." He didn't wait for them to precede him out of the door, but left it standing open saying, "I'm certain you know your way out."

Meryl was waiting outside the boardroom. His gaze devoured her whole. She wore a copper red suit and smoky hose on her long legs. Her hair was swept back from her face on either side and clipped in tortoise-colored barrettes. She looked cool and serene, sophisticated and untouchable. His hands itched to muss that perfect hair, to unbutton that very uptight suit and slip the hose off those impossibly long legs so that she could wrap them around his waist. If she had any idea of what she did to him, she wouldn't be standing there looking so cool or serene. She'd be running out of the door before he reached her.

"Hello, Meryl."

She executed a smooth half turn on her toes, a move he suspected she had learned years ago as a student in dance classes. Her unconscious poise had always stirred him.

"Hello, Mr. Brant."

He didn't miss the deliberate distance in her tone or the reserve in her golden green eyes.

"I hope you have something to show me," he said as he stared boldly at her.

"I have a presentation to make to the entire staff," she answered, her lips moving no more than necessary.

He resisted the smile her manner provoked. She might just walk right out and he had plans for her. "If you'll be good enough to step inside—" he indicated the boardroom "—we should be ready to begin in about fifteen minutes."

She went out of her way not to touch him as she moved past him through the door he opened for her. He suspected she was still furious with him. He didn't blame her. But he did resent the way she was still so ready to believe the worst about him.

After all they had said and done, lost and suffered, he had thought the bond they had been forging in Ireland couldn't be broken or breached. It just went to show how little he knew and understood relationships. Well, he didn't care that he was a lousy relationship-building male. He had to be himself, and if that occasionally struck sparks off the woman he adored, then so be it. As long as she was within range for him to strike those sparks off of she'd also be in range for him to set fire to, as well.

The subtle insinuation of her perfume caught him in its seductive snare and his knees nearly buckled. It took so little, remarkably little, to set him afire. And every time she did she burned his world right down to the ground. He shut the door before the smoke behind his eyes set fire to his mind.

Meryl was grateful that James didn't follow her into the boardroom. She didn't want to deal with him behind closed doors just yet. She put her things down at one end of the long polished table, but her thoughts were all inward.

She had had a very disagreeable few days and they were her own fault. She should never have gotten Kent involved with her misplaced desire for revenge. He hadn't been at all sanguine about her decision to retreat from her original desire to try to wrest Walrus Ink from Brant. He had been disbelieving and then cajoling and finally bitingly satiric. She hadn't given him any personal reasons for her change of heart, and heaven knew most of her reasons were very personal ones, but he had figured it out, anyway. She had fallen a second time for Brant.

Kent had told her it was to be expected. Brant's reputation as a ladies' man was legend. But that she was a fool if she thought her love would make a difference. Men like James didn't change. He might take her in, even make her president again, but when the time came he would sell Walrus Ink right out from under her. That bitter truth might have had more impact if James hadn't already told her he was disposing of Walrus Ink. The only reason she hadn't told Kent as much was because she didn't want to endure his pity at what he would consider her gullibility.

Alone in her apartment for three days she had had to face facts. James hadn't changed. He was the same. The question was, could she live with that?

One look at him just now had seemed to answer that question and yet provoke others.

He looked wonderful, fit and well rested, the belligerence missing from his expression for a change. He seemed like a man who had won the lottery and retired from the arena of life, a man who saw only blue skies and hammocks in his future. Something fundamental had changed in him while she'd remained in Ireland. She had sensed it at the airport. But then she'd gotten so caught up the red-hot passion between them, it hadn't seemed to matter. It mattered now.

She'd gone over and over it in her head, how undisturbed he was by her offer to buy Walrus Ink. He had said no, but he hadn't been angry or suspicious or resentful. Two years ago he would have grilled her, probed and searched, demanded and threatened, until he had gotten every detail of her decision and the reasoning behind it. Yet, this time, he hadn't done that. He'd smiled and kissed her and then moved on as though it didn't matter. He hadn't resorted to anger until she provoked him with taunts about his old bad habits.

That was a mistake. She had figured that out about half the way back to Hartford, but he was such a difficult man to apologize to. And she had plenty of reasons to be angry.

His smug superiority, his swaggering male prerogative, his my-way-or-no-way attitude—they all infuriated her. And yet, when they weren't fighting, being with him was stimulating. He kept her on her toes, sharp and ready to defend her beliefs. Despite her uncertainties about many things, she knew Kent was wrong. James was changing.

"And that is why you're going to apologize," she said aloud.

"To me?"

Meryl turned to find Jacqui standing inside the doorway. "I'm the first, but the others are right behind me," Jacqui said as she approached. "I just came early to wish you good luck." She gave Meryl a squeeze. "I hope you've got a thumping good show. Guess who's just arrived?"

"Beebe Hatcher?"

Jacqui nodded. "You knew?"

Meryl shook her head. "But it makes sense. I hacked her presentation to pieces. I suppose James feels it's only fair she get a shot at me."

Jacqui shuddered. "Aren't you worried?"

Meryl smiled. "I've tangled with the best! Hatchet-Job doesn't scare me."

The door opened again and the two sisters exchanged guilty glances because Beebe Hatcher stepped through the door. If she'd overheard their exchange, however, she didn't show it, perhaps because James was right behind her.

"Show time," Jacqui said after everyone else had taken a seat. She patted her sister's arm. "Break a leg."

Meryl gave her preliminary analysis with calm efficiency.

"So, then, we are left with three choices. One would be to accept an outright sale, preferably to a larger publishing house, one which could absorb Walrus Ink as an imprint. The benefits are self-evident—a larger canvas to work from, better resources, better cash flow, built-in markets, national marketing and sales forces, automatic distribution, et cetera. The downside is equally obvious. We'd lose ourselves in the buy-out. Strict editorial control would be gone.

Walrus Ink, for all intent and purposes, would cease to exist as an entity."

She paused to give James a long, considering look. He didn't so much as twitch a brow.

"Secondly, we can continue to hold the course that has taken Walrus Ink to its present height in the publishing world. We can continue to do children's books, mostly picture books. We're good at it. Ten to fifteen books a year of quality. It seems a prudent path to continue along."

"It is a prudent path!" Sam Carey volunteered.

She smiled at the other more sober faces ringing the table. "I'm not finished if that's what you're wondering. I have a third and, I feel, the best alternative." She opened her portfolio and took out the pictures that Tomaltach had sketched for her. "First, I propose we continue the viable lines. I've contacted five authors who will have projects to show us in the next three weeks."

She avoided Beebe's stare as she said, "I also contacted the author and artist of the Ash Can series. They promise to have a manuscript ready in time for Walrus Ink to produce a new series book for the spring lineup." Applause greeted her announcement. "Please pass these sketches among yourselves. I think you'll agree this is some of Mr. O'Connor's best work yet."

The buzz that greeted the sketches confirmed her words.

"Next, I'm proposing that we begin a young-adult line. A nonfiction line. It's to be entitled Dope: Streetwise and Hassle-free. Dope is, of course, the street word for anything that is good, positive and righteous. The author of the first book I'm proposing for this line is a Hartford policeman by the name of Ned Miller. He and I have been working together on his manuscript for several months and it's just about ready for production." She smiled ruefully. "That is, it's ready for a Walrus Ink editor to look at."

"If you say it's ready, it's ready," Jacqui offered in encouragement with a sidelong glance at their boss. James still hadn't moved a muscle.

"How do you propose that Walrus Ink promote nonfiction to young adults when the company has never before produced nonfiction or young-adult books?" Beebe Hatcher's voice cut clearly across the buzz produced by Tomaltach's work. "Aren't you asking a lot from so small a company?"

"Yes, I am," Meryl answered, smiling. "Therefore I'm proposing that we get the nonfiction line off the ground by hiring Hatcher Associates to produce a media campaign for Walrus Ink based on some of the suggestions you made in this very room a few weeks ago." She turned for the first time to James. "I've asked Ned to come by later today so that you might judge for yourself that he would be a good representative for the new nonfiction line." She turned her attention to the room at large. "Ned is young, good-looking, tough, knows the streets and the kids. We are going to need that kind of credibility if we're going to have an impact in the media market."

"Street kids don't buy books," Beebe countered.

"You're right, but they watch TV and listen to the radio. If we can get Ned booked for that kind of publicity, we'll be getting the message out, regardless of ability to buy. There are plenty of parents who will buy books for kids who ask for it. The message is more important than book sales. The book is only one conduit."

"Sounds like it could be controversial," James observed mildly. "Are you willing to deal with more controversy?"

Meryl nodded. "You haven't seen the text, but it's worth fighting for. And Ms. Hatcher's specialty is handling difficult subjects, isn't that right?"

Beebe smiled tightly, neatly caught between acknowledging the compliment and accepting the dig that went with it.

"Finally, I know most of you are aware that our associate editor, Lance Payton, is quite an accomplished amateur photographer."

Meryl pointed with a smile to the young man at the table with shoulder-length hair dressed in flannel, denim and

hiking boots. "I've talked him into compiling a pictur
book, a photo book, for children. If it works out, we shoul
consider other projects with text."

"That's an expensive project. I assume you're talkin
color photography," Sam Carey responded. "That'll re
quire special papers."

"And a higher retail price," James added.

Meryl nodded. "Yes, color, Sam. And, yes, Mr. Brant
it'll be expensive." She paused, not realizing until this mo
ment how much these projects, though they would not b
hers, meant to her.

She let her fervent gaze trail slowly around the faces at th
table as she said, "As your former owner liked to say, Wal
rus Ink is a tiny boat in a very big ocean. Everything we d
has got to count." Her face took on the seriousness of a
evangelist seeking converts. "Not every project may suc
ceed, but we have to take chances. That's why this press wa
founded, to take the chances the big boys can't or won't. W
may not sell as many books as a New York-based company
but we can stay afloat and that's all we're after."

For a moment there was absolute silence, and then ap
plause greeted her statements.

James watched Meryl accept in faint embarrassment th
praise of her former employees with equal amounts of ad
miration and pride. There wasn't a vain or self-intereste
bone in her body. She believed every word she had spoken
She was rare. She was one of a kind. She had to be his. The
just needed a level playing field. He was going see they go
it.

James rose to his feet when the applause died down an
shook Meryl's hand. "Thank you, Ms. Wallis. I think it'
self-evident that your third proposal is the one that this staf
backs. But before we proceed further, I have a little an
nouncement to make of my own."

Meryl held her breath as she slipped her hand free of hi
proprietary hold.

Thankfully for her peace of mind he turned his attention to his staff. "As you are aware, my presence at Walrus Ink has created its own share of unique problems for the company. I'm not a man who likes to admit defeat. In fact, I don't think I've ever admitted defeat before." He paused with a slight frown, as if the taste of the words were unpleasant. "In any case, I'm going to now." His expression brightened. "As of today, I am no longer the owner of Walrus Ink."

A collective gasp swept the room. Behind it Meryl dropped a little weakly into her chair. She knew it. He'd told her. And yet she didn't quite believe he would sell Walrus Ink out from under her a second time.

As James went on talking, she stared at her hands and tried to test the depth and nature of her feelings. How much was hurt, how much was disappointment and how much was anger? She found only a tiny bit of disappointment in her feelings. She had wanted to help both Ned and Lance bring their projects to fruition. But somewhere along the way, she'd lost her desire to get back the company she'd lost. Because during the past few days she had come to realize what it was that she had really lost two years ago.

What had hurt so much that she couldn't get over it wasn't the loss of Walrus Ink. It was the loss of James Brant.

Threatening to sell the company had been James's method of driving her off. She knew that now, knew why he had done it. The specter of his father's death had driven him down an isolating path that he hadn't known how to escape. He had been even more wary than she of the love that had sprung up so fiercely and suddenly between them. The passion had masked the reality of those deeper feelings for a time. By the time she recognized the love, he had already positioned himself to leave her. She had let herself be run off by circumstances because she had known in her heart of hearts he was going to leave her.

She could be perfectly honest now. The idea of buying Walrus Ink hadn't been born out of a need for revenge, but as an excuse to be near James again. She suspected he had used the tactic of hiring her to work for him as an excuse to lure her back to him, as well. They would have to talk about that, and other things at some other time. But she certainly wasn't going to let the sale of Walrus Ink stand between them after all this time, not when they both knew what they wanted, and it was each other.

She came aware suddenly of the silence in the room.

She glanced up to find all eyes trained speculatively on her.

"Well, aren't you going to say something?" Jacqui prompted, looking like someone had just set off a fire-cracker under her chair.

Bewildered by the avid expressions facing her, Meryl glanced up at James, who was watching her with a tiny frown and narrowed eyes. She felt herself blush. "I beg your pardon. My mind must have wandered. What did I just miss?"

The table exploded in laughter.

"How about the fact that you're the new owner of Walrus Ink!" Sam Carey shouted the length of the table at her.

"What?" She looked from Sam back to James, feeling as if she'd just gone deaf or the language they spoke had become suddenly unintelligible.

James was smiling at her in that old intimate way that made her want to curl her hands into fists or into the hair on his chest. "I've signed the company over to you. Walrus Ink is now yours."

Meryl sat on the floral chintz sofa in the office she had shared with James for so brief a time and stared at him. She had let him lead her dumbly from the boardroom after accepting the well-wishes of everyone but Beebe Hatcher, who had conveniently slipped way. She hadn't complained when James disappeared and came back with a soft drink for her or when he insisted that she drink a good deal of it before she asked him any questions.

The can was half-empty, her hands were slick with condensation, but her sense of reality was still reeling. "I don't understand why you did this."

James smiled at her, hugely enjoying the still-stunned look on her face that made her eyes seem almost too large for her face. "Let me ask you a few questions first. How long did it take you to meet Lance Payton after you came back to work?"

Meryl shrugged. "I met him the first day. I went around and introduced myself to everybody. Why?"

He nodded. "How long did it take you to learn that all those photographs in his office were taken by him?"

"I asked him about them when I saw them that first day."

He nodded again. "Lance has been here eighteen months, yet I wasn't certain of his name when I stepped into his office three weeks ago, the night of break-in. I didn't know those were his photos until you told me in the editorial meeting today. That's why this company should belong to you. You care enough to know everything about everyone. A small company like this needs that kind of caretaker attention."

"That sounds all well and good, James, but to simply hand the company to me—an outright gift." She shook her head in wonder. "I can't accept it."

"Why not?"

"It's too much. No one gives a whole company to someone else."

"I'm not just anyone."

"I know." Oh, did she know that.

Meryl hesitated, not wanting to embarrass him, but felt compelled to bring up the most serious objection because he hadn't, or wouldn't. "James, not a month ago you told me that Walrus Ink was the only profitable company you had afloat. It was more than rumor, you planned to sell it once you'd made it an attractive property. Can you afford to just give it away?''

His gaze shuttered over for a moment and then he was looking at her with riveting attention. ''I stole it from you. That was standing between us.'' He shrugged and, uncharacteristically, looked away. ''I can deal with the consequences.''

Sheer amazement made it difficult at first for Meryl to grasp the enormity of what he'd said. He was willing to risk his financial future, everything, for her? The old James Brant wouldn't even have considered such an action, let alone acted on it.

All the love she was afraid to confess swelled inside her until her chest ached. He had changed, so fundamentally that the knowledge made her suddenly shy. ''Still, how will it look?''

''To whom?''

''Anybody. The IRS, for one.''

''I'm covering the legal cost of transference and all taxes up to the day you take over.''

''Aren't there laws against this?''

''Not a one. Now if you don't have any more objections...''

''But I do.'' She chuckled. ''I just can't think of them right now.''

''Have I silenced the shrewd and clever Ms. Wallis at last? I'm impressed.''

''Actually, I do have another question. Why did you let me think you were going to sell it to someone else?''

He gazed at her a moment, a small, quiet smile on his face. ''If you will recall our conversation, I tried to explain and you wouldn't let me. You made a lot of assumptions and accusations.''

''I'm sorry.''

He leaned forward and cupped his ear. ''Pardon? What did you say?''

''Dratted man! I said I am sorry.''

He leaned back in his chair, his eyes burning silver between lowered lids. "How sorry are you?"

"How sorry would you like me to be?"

"Oh, lady, come here and I'll show you."

But Meryl merely leaned back in the cushions of the sofa and crossed her arms. "This is my office now, is that correct?"

"Correct."

"So, nominally, I should be the one directing whatever transactions take place within these walls, yes?"

Lightning quivered in his gaze. "Power mad, Ms. Wallis?"

"No, just trying to establish the ground rules, Mr. Brant."

He glanced deliberately at her green carpet. "The ground would be just fine, Ms. Wallis."

"You're getting ahead of yourself, Mr. Brant."

"I sometimes like to rush things, as you well know."

Desire shivered along her nerve endings as his voice caressed her with familiar yet impossibly exciting promise. "Yes, well, forbearance has its rewards," she murmured.

"Shall we test your theory?"

"Here?" She glanced meaningfully at the doors. "Why, Mr. Brant, what sort of establishment do you think this is?"

He rose very quietly, and though she tensed, he didn't come toward her. He went to the doors and pushed them tight with the flat of his hand. Then he moved to punch four numbers into the keypad that had been installed on the wall nearby.

"What are you doing?"

He turned his face toward her, his expression positively wicked. "It's a magnetic lock. No one can get in, or out." He came toward her, slipping off his jacket and discarding it on the floor, and then he wrenched loose the knot in his tie. "Now, Ms. Wallis, you can issue all the orders you want and nobody can come and rescue me until you're good and ready to let me go."

Somehow, Meryl thought as he knelt on the carpet before her and pushed her knees apart so that he could lean forward between them, he wasn't the one being held hostage.

He reached forward and began unbuttoning her suit jacket. "I really hate the clothes you wear."

"I thought I looked very nice," she objected, but didn't move to stop him.

"You look like a competent businesswoman, a little uptight and hard-nosed." He pulled her forward into his chest as he peeled the jacket from her shoulders.

"But I like that image," she protested as he nuzzled her neck, and her arms slid free of the jacket.

"And I hate it. I like you much better hot and tousled and naked." He reached for the buttons of her lace blouse. His eyes were heavy with desire, his gaze as possessive as the hands seeking out her body. "Let's try it my way and then you tell me which you like better."

He kissed her then, surging into her. His hands slipped up her thighs under her skirt and then around her hips to grip her panty hose. He stripped them off ruthlessly. They would never be worn again, he noted in satisfaction. And then he reached under her skirt again to pull her hips forward into his groin.

James heard that little catch of passion in the back of her throat as he made intimate contact through their clothing and he smiled deep inside. And then he kissed her with three days' worth of pent-up passion.

Chapter 14

Meryl gathered her coat at the neck, shivering as the sharp late-October wind cut in under the wool. If she hadn't been bare legged she wouldn't have felt quite so cold.

She smiled as she hurried across the security-monitored parking lot toward her apartment. She supposed that losing a pair of hose wasn't a bad trade for being loved by James. He had been so aggressive, so overwhelming, so hungry, that she had never caught her breath from beginning to end the first time. If he hadn't been smiling through it all, she might have been just the tiniest bit afraid of him. Yet she knew him and trusted him.

Often the first round of lovemaking with James was just a warm-up, so to speak. He had never yet let her get away before he had loved her so well she could scarcely think and barely walk. Talking came with a great effort of will. Each time was like the first time and the last time and the best time all rolled into one. James never did things by half.

After he had collected himself enough to leave, he had walked out with the smiling promise that they would celebrate "properly" that evening.

Happy and daunted, she had called her secretary with instructions that she was not to be bothered the rest of the afternoon. She was too embarrassed to face anybody who might suspect even a little of what had taken place behind those closed doors. She had planned to work. What she had done was fall asleep at her desk. By the time she awakened, it was after five and the offices were empty. Her employees believed in keeping punctual hours.

Her employees.

The realization hadn't quite set in. She believed James when he showed her the papers in his briefcase signing over Walrus Ink to her. She believed him when he said that he had made up his mind to give the company to her after they'd been in Ireland. She even understood why he had wanted to keep it a secret even if it cost them a fight. Yet it felt so strange to sit in her old office and realize that tomorrow morning and the day after and every workday after, this is where she would be. As long as she wanted it.

It felt good. It felt right. But she had learned a few valuable lessons in the process. When it stopped feeling right for her, she knew she would give up that day-to-day control without a qualm. There were other things she wanted that being the active editor in chief might interfere with. For instance, she was going to want to be with James in New York from time to time. His life wasn't going to fit within the confines of Hartford, Connecticut. And she wanted to travel with him, vacation with him, just be with him. And she had her dreams.

Marriage.

Children.

"Whoa, lady, you're definitely getting ahead of yourself," she murmured and then smiled as she put her key in her lock. James had come a long way. She trusted that, in time, he would go the rest of the way. But right now she just wanted to live for the next few hours.

"Meryl!"

She glanced around quickly to see a man coming toward her from the street-side entry. "Kent? What are you doing here?"

He was smiling at her, looking quite like the cat who'd been in the cream. "I've got great news for you. The best. By tomorrow morning Walrus Ink will be yours!"

Meryl frowned as she pushed opened her door. She would have preferred not to deal with Kent just now, but she supposed she was just being selfish. She had never liked unpleasantness, but she was going to have to tell him the truth sometimes. "Come on in, I'm freezing."

She flipped on the entry light. "Make yourself at home. I'm going to change and be right back." She hurried down the hall toward her bedroom. One thing she wasn't going to do was face Kent in rumpled clothing that smelled faintly of James Brant.

She hopped in an out of the shower in record time, pulled on leggings and her fisherman's sweater and pinned up her hair in a topknot. She put on lipstick and studied her face a moment. Other than the ridiculously happy smile on her face, there was no trace of evidence to betray to Kent how she'd spent a good part of the afternoon.

She found Kent comfortably seated on her sofa, a drink in hand, listening to Mozart issue from her stereo.

"You look great," he pronounced warmly. "But then you don't know any other way to look. Let me get you a drink."

He rose halfway to his feet before she could say, "No thanks." She perched on the edge of the overstuffed companion chair to the sofa. "Really, I'm fine. After our last conversation I didn't think you'd be coming to Hartford for some time."

He dismissed the idea with a gesture. "The best of friends disagree. I forgive you. But, in fact, our backers were getting nervous and I decided we couldn't wait until you and I had settled our personal differences before we moved ahead, businesswise." He winked at her. "So we did. This morning. Three men representing the dummy company I pulled together put the deal to Brant this morning."

"Did they?" Meryl murmured absently, wondering how to break the bad news. "It was a wasted effort. James—"

"Is a hard-nosed bastard," Kent finished for her without heat. "But, Meryl darling, he has a breaking point. Every man does. He saw the writing on the wall. By morning you will own Walrus Ink."

Meryl opened her mouth to say, "I already do," but realized that she couldn't put it that baldly to him. Kent had, after all, gone to a lot of trouble for her. He had pulled others into his scheme, as well. "Kent, there's something you should know. Brant has made other arrangements, arrangements made without my knowledge, I assure you, otherwise I would have told you at once."

"They don't matter." He sat forward suddenly, looking quite earnest. "Let me assure *you*, Meryl, Brant's not done anything he can't back out of. We have him right where we want him."

"Right where we want him?" Meryl echoed, liking less and less the way he had of appropriating her feelings. "Where might *we* want him, Kent?"

He shrugged and sat back. "I know you're partial to the man. I won't lie and say I'm not jealous as hell. But to each his own." His voice sounded light, but he was no longer looking at her. "The thing is, Brant wins too often. No one can win all the time. It's a lesson he needs to learn."

"I think he has learned it," Meryl said carefully, growing more uneasy at the moment. "In fact, I'm certain he has because he offered me—"

"The editor-in-chief position at Walrus Ink?" Kent's voice dripped with scorn.

"It's a little more than that," Meryl countered, sorry now she'd tried to spare his feelings.

"It's a ploy, Meryl. Brant practically jumped at the offer this morning. He was salivating."

"I think your men overstated—"

"They didn't!" His voice didn't rise in volume, but the words carried the sting of a whip in them.

"How can you be so certain?"

"Because he's a greedy bastard."

Meryl recoiled from the sudden anger in him, but he didn't seem to notice her withdrawal for he went on talking as though she were hanging on every word. "They offered Brant more than any reasonable buyer would at this point. He'll take it. He wants to unload the company while he still can. He's under attack. After the arson and the attempted bombing, he knows it's just a matter of time before something more unfortunate occurs."

Meryl didn't like the way he seemed to be enjoying the possibility of Brant's troubles. "The protesters disappeared over a week ago. The police think it's over."

He shrugged. "Sounds like poor thinking on the department's part. If I were a demonstrator planning something really big, I'd pull back for a while to let people think it was over. Wouldn't you?"

"Sergeant Rock struck me as a very shrewd man."

He chuckled. "Why are we talking about the police? I came to tell you that you can prepare yourself to walk into Walrus Ink tomorrow and claim ownership. I just ask that you let me walk in with you so that I can see Brant's face when you tell him it was you who bought his company."

"You really do hate him, don't you?"

Kent smiled and lifted his glass to her. "I want what you want. Revenge."

"I think I will have a drink, after all. No, fruit juice," she added when he moved toward the whiskey decanter. She popped up and headed for her kitchen. He followed.

As she opened the refrigerator door and leaned in, effectively shutting off her view of Kent who stood in the doorway, she tried to recall the first time they had had a conversation about revenge. Had it had been only a month earlier? Yes, the day he came to offer her a job in New York, if she would agree to lure authors and illustrators from Walrus Ink. Before that, she and Kent had seldom spoken of James except to cast bricks at his character.

She remembered James's barb about her reason for dating Kent—that their mutual dislike of him was all they had in common. James could be cruel, but he was usually insightful in his cruelty.

"What are you expecting from me in exchange for this huge favor, Kent?" Her voice came from the depth of the refrigerator as she stared absently at the carton of orange juice in front of her.

"Why, the loan of Tomaltach O'Connor," he replied without missing a beat. "That man has a mouth I'd like to put my fist in, but he's a superb artist. My imprint will make a star of him."

Meryl squatted down before the open door. The blast of cold air was nothing compared to the chills Kent's voice was giving her. "You've talked to Tomaltach? When?"

"Just yesterday. He seems to think he can't spit without your permission. He also had some really nasty things to say about Brant."

Meryl held her breath during his nail-biting pause. "Why didn't you tell me Brant accompanied you to Ireland?"

Meryl rose slowly to her feet. "Maybe because I didn't think it was any of your business."

For a long moment they simply stared at each other as the motor on the refrigerator hummed in a losing effort to keep the temperature balanced.

"He's going to hurt you again," Kent said finally.

"I don't think so. Not this time."

She saw he was sizing her up, trying to gauge her feelings, trying to find a weak place in her emotional armor. "You shouldn't count on it. Things will change when you get control of Walrus Ink. He doesn't like to lose. No man does."

Meryl heard the echo of his personal feelings for her in his voice. Kent Davis didn't like to lose, either.

"I'm sorry, Kent, but I never lied to you."

"No, you never lied." He seemed to consider that statement. "I'd have felt better if you had. At least it would have meant that you cared enough to try not to hurt me."

Meryl bit her lip. He sounded sincere, but it was too much like a play for sympathy. She shut the door without getting her juice. "What's going on, Kent? You and I both know James won't be stampeded into anything he doesn't want to do."

"Then let's just say I've narrowed his options."

To have been so alien to her nature, the answer came remarkably easily to her mind. "You've hired somebody to force him to take your offer."

James tasted blood with some satisfaction. At least they were past the preliminaries where he was the victim about to be assaulted. They'd backed him into the alley, but he'd broken free momentarily by landing a couple of well-placed punches.

Of course, his opinion of his situation could change, especially since he was facing down a pair of street thugs, one of whom was Zip Hearst. Zip's partner was small, wiry and smelled like a public urinal. Despite appearances, his gut told him that the smaller man might be the more dangerous.

Zip produced a manila envelope from inside his baseball jacket. "We got papers needing your signature. You sign. We're outta here. Nice and neat."

"Certainly." James reached for the envelope as if it were the most natural thing in the world for wise-guy messengers to abduct him and demand his signature.

"Just a minute," said the smaller man, grinning like he'd just sneaked a peek under a girl's dress. "We got a message for you, too."

Even before he saw Zip's hands curl into fists, each of which was the size of his companion's head, James knew that he wasn't going to get away with just signing. Someone had ordered a beating and these guys aimed to please. Service with a smile.

James tossed the envelope into the trash at his feet.

He hadn't been thinking clearly as he'd crossed the street when he left Charlie's. He'd gone there to arrange a celebration party for Meryl. He thought she'd enjoy that more than an elegant bash at one of the finer restaurants in town. He'd been so full of plans and joy and downright blind-eyed happiness that he hadn't paid any attention to the two figures hanging out in the nearby alley as he'd approached his car parked halfway down the dark quiet block. But they had noticed him. He now realized they had been waiting for him. The moment he'd turned to open his car door, they'd grabbed him from behind and hauled him back into the alley so quickly he was certain no one saw them.

"Me first!" Zip stepped up before James, blocking out the last of the light coming up the narrow end of the alley.

James slipped off his overcoat and dropped into a fighter's crouch. He knew he wouldn't have much time. He could take a punch, but if it came to a slugging match he'd go down under Zip's hamlike fists like a nail under a hammer.

Weight and momentum, two factors to use to his advantage. Zip's first swing went wide. James dropped into a deeper crouch and pushed his fist upward into what should have been the soft underbelly of a normal man. The jar of the muscle impact with that washboard expanse ran all the way back up his arm to his shoulder socket. Even as he pivoted away he knew he was in a different level of trouble than he wanted to think about.

The next sequence of events occurred in that distorted place in time when seconds can be divided into lifetimes. He knew he'd never figure out what happened in what order. He did know it involved pain and blows exchanged and more pain and blood and, above it all, a clear, burning rage.

He was so damned mad that he wasn't going to be in any shape to hold and make love to Meryl tonight.

The shouts and running feet seemed to come at the end of a long nightmare from which he was gratefully awakening.

The owner of the hands that turned him over got a vicious kick for the effort.

"Police!" someone shouted above him and then a flashlight was stuck in his face. "Mr. Brant?"

James heard someone chuckle. "It's Ned!" The flashlight swiveled away from James's eyes to reveal the face of Ned the cop lit from beneath like a death mask.

James lay on his back in the gutter and smiled. "Did you get them?"

"We got them," Ned replied and chuckled again. "Only maybe we shouldn't have interfered. You seem to be having a really good time."

"Swell," James muttered and wondered if he'd ever walk again.

"You're lucky," Ned said as he helped James to his feet. "A passerby ducked into Charlie's to say he'd seen a man being dragged back here. By the time we got here you had one of the perps on the ground."

"Which one?" James took a step and then grabbed the policeman's shoulder to keep from stretching himself facedown in the alley.

"Zip Hearst!" The admiration in the policeman's voice almost made up for the fact that James knew he was about to pass out.

A few minutes later, Ned came over to where the paramedics were administering to James's external wounds. "Do you feel up to looking at something for us, Mr. Brant?"

James nodded and Ned handed him the envelope Zip had passed to him in the alley. He opened it and looked at the contracts contained within.

"Do you have any idea what this is about?"

James began to shiver with a new surge of adrenaline. "Yes." He gripped Ned's shoulder. "We've got to get over to Meryl Wallis's home. I think she could be in trouble too."

Meryl dropped into the first chair she reached. Once she'd said the words she couldn't quite get her mind to grasp the thought. "You hired someone to make Brant sign your offer?"

"Let's say persuade him." Kent shrugged off her look of horror. "The demonstrators gave me the idea of using harassment against Brant. Bad press was the one thing he couldn't afford in his tenuous situation."

Meryl's jaw seemed to have come unhinged. It took three tries before she could get it to work properly. "What kind of harassment? Threats?" Her voice rose abruptly. "Arson?"

Kent wagged his head and set his glass aside as he came toward her. "You're upsetting yourself, Meryl. This isn't a B movie. Brant's just going to learn that he's not the only one who won't take no for an answer."

She drew back from the hand he would have settled on her shoulder. "That's—it's disgusting."

He dropped his hand and pulled up a dining room chair before hers. "Try not to think about the method. Just remember I'm doing this for you." He leaned forward, arms on knees. "After all, you asked me to help you."

She gasped. "I never wanted any part of anything like this!"

"That's why I intended to keep it from you." Again he reached out, only to pause when she drew back. "I knew you'd be frightened and distressed, but you needn't be. Brant will never know you had any part in it. He will think the protesters hired those men to frighten him into giving up ownership. He won't come after you. I'll protect you."

She didn't believe him. She didn't believe he didn't want her to be distressed. He was watching her with too much interest, as if she were going through these emotions for his benefit. He knew she and James were lovers. Kent wanted revenge, against her as well as James.

She ruthlessly reined in her emotions, determined to give him as little satisfaction as possible. Think, she told herself. Ask questions. Distract him until...until what?

"How can you protect me if I'm going to get the company? Won't Brant notice a little thing like that?"

Kent sat back in his chair and crossed his legs. "You'll convince him that you had nothing to do with the coercion. You know him better than me. You'll find a way."

"And if I can't?"

Kent shrugged. "There are ways of keeping men like Brant silent. No, not murder. I would never condone murder."

"Oh, boy, that's relief!" How scathing she sounded when inside she was shriveling up with fear. Where was James? How could she warn him?

"You're overreacting. Believe me, you'll feel differently once Walrus Ink is yours."

Meryl glanced at the wall phone a few feet away, but realized that Kent could easily reach her before she could even dial 911. Keep him talking, she thought, and then maybe he'd get tired and go away. "You think I'll keep quiet to protect myself?"

He cocked his head to one side. "Won't you? To protect Walrus Ink? It'll be yours. If you speak up, you'll lose it. Is that what you want?"

She forced a little laugh. "Of course it isn't. What kind of fool do you think I am?"

"I don't think you're a fool. Far from it. I think you're a beautiful, sexy woman whom Brant took advantage of and then threw away like yesterday's news."

"That's true," she replied, hardly able to keep her seat. "But I don't think James will simply accept my duplicity as justice. He's going to come after us."

Kent sneered. "Do you think Brant will go to the police with the complaint that his girlfriend, whom he dumped two

years ago after stealing her company, hired men to beat him
up so she could get her company back? I think he's too
proud to put himself through the humiliation of the public
ity."

Meryl let her anger speak for her. "I think James would
walk barefoot through glass to get back something that be
longs to him."

"Possibly, but he'll have to convince the police that you're
capable of setting fire to your own company in order to se
him up."

She went very still. "Are you responsible for that?"

He shrugged. "Do you think he's really going to send you
to prison?"

"Us, send *us* to prison," Meryl corrected.

He smiled and shook his head. "Oh, Meryl, you don'
think I was foolish enough to attach my name to any of this?
Not a penny of my money is backing you. I merely acted as
conduit, as you asked, to set things up. I have notes from
our every conversation. Then there's Jacqui who heard you
ask me to help you get even with Brant. You said you'd do
it by going behind his back while you were working for him.
I was merely helping a friend in setting up your dummy
company. Where's my motive to burn down Walrus Ink?
don't benefit at all."

"Except by ruining two lives." Meryl said the words,
though she couldn't quite believe that he could be that dia
bolical.

"I'm only interested in ruining Brant." He sighed. "I
you want to martyr yourself for him, you go right ahead."

Meryl stood. "Get out of my house."

"Certainly." He stood immediately and to her amaze
ment he was still smiling. "But I'll be back with the signed
papers. Once they're in your hands you tell me if you're
willing to lose your company a second time. And for what?"

Meryl followed him to her front door, unconvinced that
he was leaving, yet understanding his confidence in his own
nasty brand of logic. Kent had wanted revenge agains

James. He had conceived the idea of using her as the instrument to exact his revenge because she had chosen James over him. He thought she couldn't go to James with the truth without confessing her part in the plot for revenge, and James couldn't go to the police without the risk of sending her to prison. It was devious: it was clever and subtle and might just have worked. Except that Walrus Ink already belonged to her.

Her doorbell rang just as Kent reached the door. He looked back at her, smiling confidently as he reached for the knob. "Shall I?"

He turned and swung it wide and then his face fell.

"Dear God!"

"Not hardly!"

The uppercut to the chin landed with a sickening crunch.

Though the blow aggravated his swollen and torn knuckles, James was smiling as he stepped over Davis's collapsed body and into Meryl's welcoming embrace.

"Part of this is my fault," Meryl said for the tenth time in as many minutes. Sergeant Rock was present in her living room and standing over her with his ever-present pad in hand. "I did go to Kent Davis several weeks ago and ask him to help me outfox Mr. Brant. I was trying to get my company back." She glanced guiltily at the man sitting beside her. "I'm so sorry, James."

"You didn't ask him to hire thugs to burn down Walrus Ink or to have me beat half to death," James interposed. He looped his less sore arm about her shoulders in a reassuring gesture as the sergeant glared at him over the top of his pad.

"Let Ms. Wallis finish her statement."

"Certainly." Grinning, James regarded the detective through the one eye that hadn't completely closed. "But I don't blame her for any of this. In fact, I've probably deserved a good beating at least once during our association."

"Don't make fun of it," Meryl protested, appalled by th condition of his face and his hands. She touched his swol len cheek gingerly. "I've never wanted to hurt you. Never."

The sergeant heaved a sigh that said he knew it was goin to be a long night. "May I just ask if Mr. Davis confesse to you that he had hired men to beat Mr. Brant?"

"Yes, well, indirectly." Meryl shook her head. "He son of intimated and gloated."

"Intimated and gloated." The sergeant wrote down th words and then stared at them. He looked across at Jame and frowned. "Mr. Brant. You need to have a few suture put in that cut above your brow. I think we have enough t hold Mr. Davis for twenty-four hours. With luck, we'll hav finished interrogating Zip and the other perp by then an will have enough to make a connection between them an Mr. Davis."

"Will Kent go to prison?" Meryl asked, still not quit believing she had seen him escorted out of her home i handcuffs.

"That's for a jury to decide, Ms. Wallis. We're just her to make certain all the facts go into the D.A.'s office."

"Then we can make statements tomorrow."

The sergeant smiled for the first time and flipped his boo shut. "I think that's a fine idea. Good night, Ms. Wallis Mr. Brant."

"We've got to get you to a hospital," Meryl said in dee concern as she surveyed his battered face. "I think you nose is broken."

"Again?" James reached up and gingerly felt the lump bridge. "Did I ever tell you about my boxing days in col lege?"

"No," Meryl said, kissing the only unbruised place sh could find on his face, his left temple. "You can tell me a about it in the emergency room."

"I don't think I'll ever be able to conduct business in thi office again." Meryl sighed as she gazed up at the ceilin from the floor of her office at Walrus Ink. Beside her, James lay grinning like a man whose every fantasy had just been fulfilled. He had come in from New York after a week apart to take her out to dinner. But, somehow, they'd never gotten past the door of her office.

They had made love a short while before and neither one of them had yet been able to find a single reason why they should move from the spot where they lay so happily.

"No, I'm almost positive I won't be able to keep my mind on business in here after this."

"Redecorate," James answered as he sprawled in boneless satisfaction on the carpet beside her.

She turned her head to smile at him. "That's all very well for you to say. You don't have to pay for it," she reminded him.

"I'll pay for it."

Meryl rolled over onto her stomach and half over him. "Oh, no, you won't! You need every penny you have invested in your latest venture. Besides, I like being independent again."

She saw him open lazy lids, pouring the heat of still-molten silver into her heart. "Whatever you say. You're the boss."

"I am, aren't I?" She chuckled and bent her head to playfully bite his bare shoulder.

"Hey! Your teeth are sharp."

"So I'm not all bark?"

James reached up and spread a hand through her long dark hair that looked like satin and felt like silk. "Lady, your bite is lethal. I don't think I'm ever going to recover."

Her expression grew solemn as she met his gaze across the short expanse of his shoulder. "Do you want to?"

She felt herself rise as he took a deep, smiling breath. She felt her spirits soar as he said, "No."

The word was so simple. The single near-universal negative utterance that had ruined so much for so many. Yet this time, for her, it was the sweetest, most reassuring word in the world.

"I love you."

She saw it just for a nanosecond, the flash of doubt and instinctive recoil. He was trying, but it was going to take time.

"You don't have to look as if I just took a bite out of a particularly sensitive area," she said with a chuckle. "It's okay for me to love you."

But she wished she hadn't seen that fractional hesitation. She kissed his shoulder and then rolled away from him.

He caught her in a half roll and followed her body with his so that they ended up with him lying halfway over her, one heavy hairy leg forcing an entry between her knees. His eyes were wide open now and they were looking so deeply into her that she felt him touch that place inside her only he had ever been able to find.

"I love you, Meryl."

She tensed, wanting to protest that he didn't have to say that. But that would have been a lie. She wanted, needed, had waited two years, to hear him say those words. So why didn't she think they sounded quite right?

"Is this your first time?"

His eyes widened dramatically, his brows peaking at puzzled angles. "My first time?"

She looked up at him with all the love she had to offer. "Is this the first time you've ever said those words to a woman?"

"You mean, 'I love you'?" He broke into a silly smile. "Yeah!"

"Well, then, that wasn't so bad for a first time." She lightly ran a finger down his newly realigned nose, which was straighter than before it was broken. "But you need practice. Lots of practice."

The corners of his eyes pleated more deeply. "May I practice with you?"

"Anytime, anyplace, Mr. Brant."

He moved over and completely onto her and positioned himself between her soft willing thighs. "Don't you think it's about time you called me something a little more intimate than Mr. Brant?"

"Like what?" she asked suspiciously, then gasped when he found the place he was seeking.

"Oh, I don't know." He rolled his hips, sliding deep within her. "Husband, maybe?"

Meryl went perfectly still. She hadn't expected that, not so easily, so naturally. But as she gazed up into his face she saw the permanent fractures of happiness she had made in the belligerent expression he had once used to keep the world at bay. The doubts of moments before evaporated. Yet, being a woman, she wanted to hear the words. "Are you proposing a merger, Mr. Brant?"

He smiled like a man who'd just clinched the best deal of his life. "Marry me. I love you, Meryl."

She knew then that she'd been wrong about his discomfort with expressing his feelings. This was how "I love you" sounded when James Brant said the words.

She looped her arms about his neck. "Oh, yes, Husband."

* * * * *

COMING NEXT MONTH

MILLION DOLLAR SWEEPSTAKES (III)

No purchase necessary. To enter the sweepstakes and receive the Free Books and Surprise Gift, follow the directions published and complete and mail your "Win A Fortune" Game Card. If not taking advantage of the book and gift offer or if the "Win A Fortune" Game Card is missing, you may enter by hand-printing your name and address on a 3" X 5" card and mailing it (limit: one entry per envelope) via First Class Mail to: Million Dollar Sweepstakes (III) "Win A Fortune" Game, P.O. Box 1867, Buffalo, NY 14269-1867, or Million Dollar Sweepstakes (III) "Win A Fortune" Game, P.O. Box 609, Fort Erie, Ontario L2A 5X3. When your entry is received, you will be assigned sweepstakes numbers. To be eligible entries must be received no later than March 31, 1996. No liability is assumed for printing errors or lost, late or misdirected entries. Odds of winning are determined by the number of eligible entries distributed and received.

Sweepstakes open to residents of the U.S. (except Puerto Rico), Canada, Europe and Taiwan who are 18 years of age or older. All applicable laws and regulations apply. Sweepstakes offer void wherever prohibited by law. Values of all prizes are in U.S. currency. This sweepstakes is presented by Torstar Corp, its subsidiaries and affiliates, in conjunction with book, merchandise and/or product offerings. For a copy of the official rules governing this sweepstakes offer, send a self-addressed, stamped envelope (WA residents need not affix return postage) to: MILLION DOLLAR SWEEPSTAKES (III) Rules, P.O. Box 4573, Blair, NE 68009, USA.

SWP-S1295

Are your lips succulent, impetuous, delicious or racy?

Find out in a very special Valentine's Day promotion—THAT SPECIAL KISS!

Inside four special Harlequin and Silhouette February books are details for THAT SPECIAL KISS! explaining how you can have your lip prints read by a romance expert.

Look for details in the following series books, written by four of Harlequin and Silhouette readers' favorite authors:

Silhouette Intimate Moments #691
Mackenzie's Pleasure by *New York Times* bestselling author Linda Howard

Harlequin Romance #3395
Because of the Baby by Debbie Macomber

Silhouette Desire #979
Megan's Marriage by Annette Broadrick

Harlequin Presents #1793
The One and Only by Carole Mortimer

Fun, romance, four top-selling authors, plus a FREE gift! This is a very special Valentine's Day you won't want to miss! Only from Harlequin and Silhouette.

VAL96

INTRODUCING...  WINNER'S CIRCLE

A collection of award-winning books by award-winning authors! From Harlequin and Silhouette.

Falling Angel
by Anne Stuart

WINNER OF THE RITA AWARD FOR BEST ROMANCE!

Falling Angel by Anne Stuart is a RITA Award winner, voted Best Romance. A truly wonderful story, *Falling Angel* will transport you into a world of hidden identities, second chances and the magic of falling in love.

"Ms. Stuart's talent shines like the brightest of stars, making it very obvious that her ultimate destiny is to be the next romance author at the top of the best-seller charts."
—*Affaire de Coeur*

A heartwarming story for the holidays. You won't want to miss award-winning *Falling Angel,* available this January wherever Harlequin and Silhouette books are sold.

It's our 1000th Special Edition and we're celebrating!

Join us these coming months for some wonderful stories in a special celebration of our 1000th book with some of your favorite authors!

Diana Palmer
Debbie Macomber
Phyllis Halldorson

Nora Roberts
Christine Flynn
Lisa Jackson

Plus miniseries by:

Lindsay McKenna, Marie Ferrarella, Sherryl Woods and Gina Ferris Wilkins.

And many more books by special writers!

And as a special bonus, all Silhouette Special Edition titles published during Celebration 1000! will have **_double_** Pages & Privileges proofs of purchase!

Silhouette Special Edition...heartwarming stories packed with emotion, just for you! You'll fall in love with our next 1000 special stories!

1000BK-R

You're About to Become a

Privileged Woman

Reap the rewards of fabulous free gifts and benefits with proofs-of-purchase from Silhouette and Harlequin books

Pages & Privileges™

It's our way of thanking you for buying our books at your favorite retail stores.

PROOF OF PURCHASE
Offer expires October 31, 1996

SIM-PP86

Harlequin and Silhouette—
the most privileged readers in the world!

For more information about Harlequin and Silhouette's PAGES & PRIVILEGES program call the Pages & Privileges Benefits Desk: 1-503-794-2499

Silhouette®

SIM-PP86